Bl...

"You like jazz?" Drake asked, impressed. He got up and joined her, then checked out her collection.

"I listen to a little of everything. That's one of the great things about your fair city, Mister Mayor."

"What is?"

"The music. It's 24/7, and you can get everything from classical to jazz to classic rock to old school to techno. I've never lived anyplace that jams like Detroit."

"We are Motown. The more music, the better."

Then, just like in his conference room, time seemed to slow and they found themselves caught up in the sight, scents, and nearness of each other. Unable to resist, Drake reached out and slowly traced a finger over the dark satiny skin of her cheek.

Drake whispered, "How about we get this first one out of the way. . . ."

By Beverly Jenkins

Black Lace
The Edge of Dawn
The Edge of Midnight

BEVERLY JENKINS

Black Lace

HarperTorch
An Imprint of HarperCollins*Publishers*

This is a work of fiction. Names, characters, places, and incidents are products of the author's imagination or are used fictitiously and are not to be construed as real. Any resemblance to actual events, locales, organizations, or persons, living or dead, is entirely coincidental.

HARPERTORCH
An Imprint of HarperCollins*Publishers*
10 East 53rd Street
New York, New York 10022-5299

ISBN-13: 978-0-06-081593-6
ISBN-10: 0-06-081593-0

First HarperTorch paperback printing: November 2005

Printed in the United States of America

Visit HarperTorch on the World Wide Web at www.harpercollins.com

10 9 8 7 6 5 4 3 2

Prologue

Detroit City Councilman Reynard Parker hadn't always been rich and powerful. A high school dropout, he'd started out in the trash business like every other Black man who hadn't finished high school—on the street slinging cans in the heat of summer and the balls-freezing days of winter. During those years, he'd gagged while picking up maggot-infested garbage, taken shit from condescending suburban customers, and come home smelling worse than an abandoned Porta-John to a wife who despised him.

Then life changed. In 1986, on his thirty-fifth birthday, he hit the Michigan State Lotto. Twelve million dollars. He had sense enough to return to school for his GED, then go on to college, where he impressed himself and his professors with his grasp of economics. He graduated at the top of his class with a degree in Business Economics.

The degree and his lotto money came in handy

when his old trash employer went belly up in 1994. Reynard purchased the remains for pennies on the dollar. He then painted PARKER ENVIRONMENTAL on the trucks, hired his own people, and proceeded to build an empire that let him rub elbows with crooked politicians, corrupt union officials, and businessmen as shady and as greedy as he.

Now, at age fifty-four, Reynard's hair was gray and his belly soft, but he had lucrative trucking contracts on both sides of the U.S. border for hauling trash, toxic wastes, and other tainted loads. The profits, coupled with the hustles he had on the side, brought in more than enough to pay for his fancy Palmer Park home, suits from Toronto, and shoes from Italy. He ate in the best places, and when he decided to run for City Council, his contacts helped bankroll his campaign. His high profile charity work with felons and his position on the boards of a few local nonprofits further cemented the good guy image he wanted to project. He also had a new young wife; she despised him too, but not his money.

So all in all, life was good for Reynard Parker. He had only one dream left, and that was to become the city's mayor, but there was an obstacle in his path: Drake Randolph.

One

The surprise snowstorm had *re*duced Detroit's early morning freeway traffic to a crawl. Lacy Green peered through her windshield, trying to catch a glimpse of the long line of cars ahead of her, but for all intents and purposes the wipers were useless. The thick blowing snow filled the cleaned glass just as soon as the blades swung back. It was 6:30 A.M., still dark, and the visibility was so bad she could barely make out the cars moving beside her. Last night's meeting in the city of Ypsilanti had run so late she'd opted for a hotel room. Now, she had to get back to her job in downtown Detroit. Lacy was from Atlanta and she'd never seen anything like this weather in her life. For the past week, the temperatures had been warm enough for the tulips in the pots on her balcony to break through the soil, but overnight a major storm had roared in out of nowhere, and this morning it was still blowing and screaming.

Concentrating on her driving, Lacy held the wheel tightly. This was her first Michigan winter, and she was still a bit shaky maneuvering on the snow, but she knew that the middle lanes were the safest places to be, so that's where she and her ancient Escort were. The far left lane, which on regular mornings funneled cars rolling at eighty to ninety-plus miles per hour, wasn't even cleared. The plows were using the lane to pile up the five inches that had fallen overnight. Schools were closed and the airport was reporting a three hour delay on departing flights. Today was the first day of April, and apparently Mother Nature had a wicked sense of humor.

On the radio, the traffic reporter was advising folks to stay home. Lacy clicked off the sound and kept her eyes on the road. The last thing she needed to hear was someone stating the obvious. Lacy, like the thousands of others commuters region wide, *had* to go to work.

The Escort's groaning wipers cleared the windshield just in time for her to see a snow-covered Grand Am merging too fast onto the freeway. The car did a 360 and spun tail first into the snowbank on the right shoulder. The driver was lucky. Had the spinout been in the far left lane, the car most likely would've gone down the embankment and into the mawlike ditch that served as the median on Michigan's main highways. Once in, the only way out was by tow truck.

In reaction to the Grand Am's dilemma, traffic slowed even further and brake lights twinkled like dull red flames in the whirling eddies. "Michigan, my Michigan," Lacy muttered sarcastically, quoting the state's motto.

A glance up at her rearview mirror showed a ghostly stream of headlights strung out behind her like jewels. At the very back of the pack was one set of lights that seemed to be moving back and forth as if the driver was weaving in and out of the traffic. The sight made her shake her head. Conditions were too dangerous to be trying to get anywhere in a hurry, so she prayed the idiot kept his or her distance.

Lacy grimly concentrated on the traffic ahead, but every few seconds glanced up at her mirror to gauge the lane jockey's position. The car appeared to be making progress, but in all of this traffic, they were looking for an accident, and would probably get their wish. She, on the other hand, just wanted to get to work in one piece.

Just as that thought crossed her mind, brake lights flashed ahead. The car in front of her began to slide. All around her other vehicles went on the defensive, angling and attempting to get out of the way of what looked like the beginning of a major pile-up. A tense Lacy downshifted and gently braked, praying she had enough space to stop safely. She did, and let out her held breath, but a quick look at the rearview mirror showed the lane jockey about to plow into her rear end. She opened her mouth to scream "Nooo!" but the solid impact threw her forward. The air bag deployed and the car began spinning like Kristi Yamaguchi in a death spiral.

Panicked, Lacy fought to turn the wheels in the direction of the slide, but the snowbank on the left shoulder was too close. The Escort spun trunk first, hard, through the piled wall of snow and rumbled down the snowy embankment. It hit the bottom nose first, flipped onto its hood, then flipped again and landed hard on its tires. That was the last thing Lacy remembered.

She came to lying flat on her back. For a moment she lay there on the horizontal seat listening to the furious thumping of her heart. As it slowed, she realized she was alive. Very gingerly she wiggled her toes inside of her boots, and the pain in her right ankle responded with a screaming aria. She bit her lip in reaction then did a quick check of her remaining limbs and appendages. Her neck was sore and would probably be worse tomorrow, but everything else seemed intact. Still reeling, though, she slowly fumbled for the seat button beside her. Upright again, she rested her head against the air bag and took in a deep shuddering breath. A look around showed the snow surrounding her and the faint lights of cars above her on the highway. She supposed she should have been wondering whether help was on the way, but right then all she wanted to do was breathe and savor the realization that she was alive.

Mayor Drake Randolph didn't waste time yelling at his driver for causing the accident; there'd be time for that later. Right now his only concern was helping the driver of the Escort. Throwing open the limo's door, he and his two bodyguards got out and headed down the hill.

Other cars had stopped in response to the accident, but they didn't pay them much mind because the going was rough. The wind was screaming. The blowing snow stung the men's faces, making Drake wish he'd stayed in the car, but the oath he'd taken as a doctor took precedence over the oath he'd taken as mayor of the city of Detroit. He made his way down the knee-high snow praying the driver hadn't sustained serious injury.

When the still shook-up Lacy heard the knock on the window, it took her brain a moment to process the meaning of the sound. A man's face appeared on the other side of the snow-covered glass. She assumed she was dreaming. *Why else would Mayor Randolph be outside the car?* She heard him yell, "Can you unlock the door?"

She tried to shake off the cobwebs clouding her thinking.

"Are you hurt?"

Lacy studied his handsome brown face. He appeared to be genuinely concerned. The women of Detroit had dubbed Mayor Randolph *"His Fineness,"* and even Lacy, who had yet to meet a politician she didn't want to burn at the stake, found his good looks almost blinding. The man made Denzel look like Shrek. When her brain asked why she was indulging in such asinine thoughts, she shook herself, then reached down and flipped the lock button.

The door opened. Swirling wind and snow filled

the car making her instantly draw away from the fury.

He asked again, "Are you hurt?"

The cold air hitting her in her face made her brain a bit clearer, but she was still a bit woozy. "Just my ankle. Neck's sore. What are you doing here, Mayor Randolph?"

He gave her that smile, the smile Detroit's female citizens prayed they'd be blessed by at least once in their lives; a smile packing so much charming wattage it seemed to warm her insides. "Came to see about you," he responded.

Even in her groggy state, and with the wind whipping around her, she felt stroked by the soft tone of his voice. She blamed the reaction on the aftershocks of the accident. "Appreciate it," Lacy mumbled. She could feel a hellacious headache starting to form. "Did you get the plate of the idiot who hit me?"

Neither the mayor nor his bodyguards answered. Instead, the mayor said firmly over the wind, "Let's see if we can't get her back up to my car." He looked at Lacy. "What's your name, miss?"

"Lacy Green."

"Ms. Green, you said your ankle's hurt?"

"Yes." She didn't know whether it was the weather or the shock, but she was freezing.

"How's your head?"

"Hurts."

He leaned in closer and gently began examining the bones in her neck, arms, and shoulders. "Any of this hurt?"

"Neck's sore."

He ran his hand over her neck and shoulders again. When he finished, the handsome face studied her with serious eyes. "Do you think you can walk?"

Lacy waved him off. "Yeah."

He stuck out his hand and helped her out. The sharp "Ow!" she yelled settled the matter of whether the ankle would support her weight or not. She leaned against the car until the pain subsided to a dull roar.

The mayor looked up at the highway. "We'll take you back up to my car."

Lacy was all for that. The wind was whipping like a winter hurricane, and she was so cold her teeth were chattering.

Until that moment her main concern had been herself, but now, for the first time she could see the Escort's physical condition. The sight made her eyes widen in dismay. "Look at my car!"

The hood was so mangled, the engine and its innards were exposed.

She cried out again, "Look at my car!" Overwhelmed by the extent of the damage, she thought she might be sick.

One of the men said, "How 'bout we get you up to the mayor's car and you can call a tow truck."

A devastated Lacy realized she was going to need not only a tow, but a couple month's pay to get the Escort back on the road. Her headache worsened.

The mayor asked, "What do you need out of here?"

She forced herself to deal with the now. "My tote. Oh, and my CD case on the visor."

He leaned in and grabbed her stuff. Then came the task of getting her up the steep embankment to where the limo waited. The two big men with the mayor locked arms to form a seat, and she was transported like Cleopatra to the embankment, but because it was physically impossible for them to carry her up the steep slope and maintain their balance, they each grabbed one of her armpits and carried her the last few feet that way. Her toes dragged a bit, increasing the discomfort in her ankle, but they made it. A few moments later she was in the car. She was so relieved to be someplace warm and dry, she leaned back against the limo's black leather seat and let out a breath of relief.

The mayor got in beside her. One of the guards settled in on her other side, while the second man took the passenger seat. The thin-faced older man behind the wheel introduced himself as Burton. He turned and asked Lacy, "You okay, honey?"

"No," she offered truthfully. Between her headache, throbbing ankle, and the damage to her car, she knew it would be a while before she was *okay*. "Thanks for stopping to help, though. Did you see who hit me?"

The silence that followed made her look up into his brown eyes. Under her pointed scrutiny, he dropped his head, then said, "I'm real sorry."

Lacy swung to the mayor. "You hit me?!"

He gave her a chagrined look. "Technically, Burton did. Our apologies. He was trying to get me to a meeting downtown."

"A meeting?" she snapped. "I almost lost my life so you could get to a meeting!"

"My plane from San Antonio got in late from the airport, and—"

"So you ran me off the road?"

Drake's lips thinned.

"Do you see that snow out there?"

Drake nodded. "I do."

She summed it up. "He was driving too damn fast."

The mayor eyed his driver for a moment then nodded. "I agree."

Lacy plopped back against the seat.

"The city will pay for all damages, of course."

"Of course." She snatched off her wet hat and ran a hand through the small twists crowning her head. She was so angry she wanted to smack somebody.

Drake pulled off his gloves and tried to apologize again. "I know you're mad—"

The blazing look she turned on him rendered Drake instantly silent. He supposed she didn't want to hear him state the obvious. "How's your head?" he asked instead.

"Still hurts," Lacy admitted. To her surprise, he placed a finger beneath her chin and raised her face so he could look down into her eyes.

"Want to see if you have signs of concussion."

The warmth of his touch spread up her cold chin and down her shoulders. Once again blaming her reaction to him on the accident, she let him look for a few seconds more, then backed out of his hold. "I have a headache, but that's probably normal after being *run off the road.*"

He winced visibly. "Point taken, but let's take a look at your ankle."

"It's fine." Lacy knew he was a doctor and that it made sense to have a doctor look her over, but she was so outdone by all this drama, she was having trouble thinking straight. It occurred to her then that once she made it to her job, she had no way home. Who knew how long her car would lay in the ditch before a tow truck could get to it? In this weather it could be days. She supposed she could get one of her coworkers to help her out but she hated imposing on people. Her head was pounding.

Drake wanted to make sure the ankle wasn't broken but guessed she'd had enough interaction with him for now, so he didn't press. Burton was wisely staying out of the line of Lacy Green's fire, which Drake thought made sense.

Burton said, "I called the police and made the accident report."

"Good," Drake said. "Do they want us to wait?"

"No, the dispatcher said they were too busy. I guess a semi spun out over on the Lodge Freeway. Radio says the road is a parking lot."

Burton turned around and said to Lacy, "I told them it was my fault. They said they'd send somebody out to interview you about what happened in a few days. I'm getting a ticket, though."

Lacy thought he deserved one.

"I also called Triple A. They'll tow your car just

soon as they can get to it. You have to call them later this afternoon and let them know which body shop to take it to." He sounded and looked genuinely contrite.

Lacy nodded. "Thanks."

Drake told the guard in the front seat, "You should probably drive."

Burton puffed up. "I'm the driver here."

Drake shook his head. "Move over."

Lacy could see that Burton wasn't pleased, but he slid down the long seat to the passenger side. The other man, a dark-skinned giant who'd introduced himself as William "Billy" Cruise, got in behind the wheel and eased the big car out into the slow-moving traffic.

Drake said to him, "Let's run by Henry Ford Hospital so Ms. Green can get herself checked out. Is there someone I can call for you. Husband, family?"

"No, but I should call my job."

She opened the tote that doubled as her purse and fished for her phone. Her neck didn't like the movement but she ignored it as best she could.

Drake asked, "Where do you work?"

"A few floors below you. Environmental Enforcement."

He couldn't hide his surprise. "Are you a secretary?"

"No. Assistant director."

Drake paused. He'd never met her before. "How long have you been in the office?"

"About six months."

Lacy turned her attention to her phone call. There was no answer at her office. She assumed the bad weather had impacted everybody's arrival. She decided to try later.

When she put the phone back into her tote, Drake said, "Sorry we had to meet this way."

"So is my car."

Drake turned his attention to the snow scene out his window and smiled.

On the slow drive into the city, Drake kept taking peeks at her. Her skin was black as a summer night and looked just as soft. He'd always had a thing for dark-skinned women, probably because of his dark-skinned mother, but whatever the reason, Drake liked his berries black. Lacy Green's hair was done in those tiny twists black women had taken to wearing in recent years. He'd never liked the style. In his opinion, most of the women sporting the 'do resembled mops, or contestants in the Westminster dog show, but on Lacy the style flattered the lines of her dark face and added a certain jazz to the onyx eyes and the sensual curves of her lips and mouth. To quote the vernacular, the sister was *hot*. He also noted that she had no ring on the third finger of her left hand. Granted, that didn't mean she didn't have a man, but Drake had an often uncanny sense about that sort of thing, and to him it said Lacy Green was unattached. Unfortunately, for Drake, Burton had driven her off the road, totaling her car, and as a result, he knew that trying to talk to her was going to be harder than finishing med school.

When the mayor's big Lincoln pulled up in front of the large brick building that bore Henry Ford's name,

Lacy looked out of the window at the imposing structure. This would be her first visit to the world famous medical facility known for its cutting-edge techniques.

The mayor opened the door and said to the men, "Keep the car warm." Then to Lacy, "Be right back."

He returned with a wheelchair. She sat in it and he pushed her toward the door.

Inside the hospital, the mayor's presence sent the staff and the citizens into a frenzy. Folks gawked with surprise. Others ran up wanting autographs. Some simply wanted to shake his hand. Drake Randolph was one of the most popular mayors in the city's history. In spite of his battles with the City Council over implementation of some of his more controversial programs, the residents loved him.

After leaving Admitting, he pushed her onto the elevator, and Lacy could see the two nurses already in the car studying her speculatively. The mayor's reputation with the ladies was well known, and Lacy was certain the women were wondering how she and His Fineness were connected. Neither was rude enough to ask, which suited her just fine, because she planned on dumping him and his no-driving chauffeur ASAP.

Although Drake knew next to nothing about the lady he was pushing in the chair, he found himself intrigued by the fact that she didn't act as if he were the Second Coming. She didn't seem impressed by him at all, and the novelty of her reaction was a welcome breath of fresh air. Everywhere he went, women swarmed over him like carrion beetles. Not this one.

She looked like she'd rather sock him, and he respected that even as he wondered if the city was going to have yet another lawsuit on its hands because of the accident.

A short while later Lacy was wheeled into the X-ray department. A few people were seated in the large room, waiting to be seen, and the mayor's entrance made every one wide-eyed. The female attendant looked as if she might faint when she saw him, but quickly pulled herself together.

"Good morning, Mayor—Dr. Randolph," she gushed.

" 'Morning, Denise. This is Lacy Green. She was in a car accident this morning and needs her ankle and neck X-rayed. Is Reg Carson in the building somewhere?"

Denise, a short round woman with breasts so prominent they pressed against her white coat as if trying to escape, gave Lacy a sympathetic smile. "I'll find out. In the meantime, come this way. Which ankle, honey?"

"Right."

Drake rolled Lacy to a small examination room and Denise closed the door. "Dr. Randolph, if you'll take her boot off, I'll page Dr. Carson, get these other patients started, and be right back."

He nodded. "Thanks, Denise."

Denise exited and the mayor knelt in front of Lacy in the chair. Their eyes held. Lacy felt something pass between them that made her pulse jump just enough to be noticeable, but the last time she'd had dealings with a man as prominent and handsome as this, she'd lost everything, and she had no plans on going there again. "Who's Dr. Carson?"

"Friend of mine. He's an orthopedic surgeon on the staff here." Drake didn't let her coolness deter him. The more she pulled back, the more intrigued he became. He placed his hands on her boot. "Let's see if we can get this off."

Lacy wasn't having it. Letting him remove her footwear smacked of an intimacy she didn't want to encourage. "I got it," she said evenly.

But she didn't. Not only did her neck hurt when she leaned down to reach the boot hidden beneath her long brown suede skirt, but the ankle was so swollen the attempts to remove it brought her nothing but pain. Hurting, she exhaled an angry, frustrated sigh and leaned back against the chair.

"Let me try," he said gently.

She nodded for him to go ahead, but his actions only made the pain flare again, so he stopped and told her, "We may have to cut it."

Lacy sighed with frustration. The black boots had cost her eighty-five dollars on sale at Marshall Field's. Although the mayor's suggestion made sense, the reality of having to slice through the soft leather only added to an already messed up day.

Denise came back, papers in hand. "Can't get it off?"

Grim, Lacy said, "No."

Denise took what appeared to be a capped pen from her pocket, but when the cap was removed, a small silver scalpel caught the light. She handed the instrument to Drake. "Dr. Carson is on his way," she said, then shook her head sadly. "Those are killer boots, girlfriend."

"Were," Lacy corrected her, and raised her suede skirt to her knee.

The boots were knee high, so the incision began at the top. Drake worked slowly and carefully until the halves of the leather fell away to reveal the sheer black-stockinged leg beneath. He drew the boot off. Silently admiring her leg and the purple polish on the toes of her well-formed foot, he keep his face impassive, concentrating instead on the large knot that had once been her ankle.

Grateful to be free of the confining boot, Lacy gingerly moved her toes, only to wince at the pain.

"Sorry about the boot," he said.

"I'll add them to your bill."

Drake shook his head at her wit, then wheeled her out of the room and down the hall to where Dr. Carson and the X-ray machine waited.

Two

A short brother decked out in green scrubs and carrying a set of crutches entered the room. He was what folks in the south called *"red-bone."* Red hair, freckles, and a winning smile. He shook the mayor's hand enthusiastically. "You slumming, Your Honor? We poor doctor types don't see you around here much these days."

Drake laughed. "Reggie, I know you're not calling yourself poor. You make more money than the Ford family."

"I wish." Reggie then looked to Lacy and stuck out his hand. "Name's Reggie Carson."

"Lacy Green."

"How'd you hurt your ankle?"

"Car accident. My Escort met the mayor's limo. The Escort lost."

Reggie shook his head. "You'd think His Fineness would have a better way of meeting women."

"You'd think," Lacy quipped, enjoying Reggie's sense of humor.

The mayor rolled his eyes.

Reggie chuckled. "Let's see what you have here." After a few twists and turns of her ankle, he said, "Yep. A prime candidate for my services. Denise said your neck hurts too?"

"Yeah. Seems to be getting stiffer and stiffer."

He did a short, gentle inspection of her neck and shoulders, then said, "Let's take some pictures and see what's going on."

Afterward, while Lacy waited in the examination room for the mayor and Dr. Carson to return with the X-ray results, she took out her cell phone and punched up her mother, Val, in Atlanta. The call was answered on the second ring, and the familiar southern voice soothed Lacy's frayed nerves. "Hey, Mama."

"Hey, baby. How are you?"

"Had a car accident."

Val gasped. "Are you okay? I can hop on a plane and be there before dark."

Lacy smiled. "I'm okay, but I'm at the hospital having some X-rays on my neck and ankle. My car looks totaled, though."

"I'm sorry, but it was time to get rid of that wreck anyway."

Lacy laughed softly. "Leave my car alone."

"Are you sure you don't want me to come?"

"I'm sure. Soon as I'm done here, I'm heading home. How's Daddy?"

"Fine. I'm still trying to get him to retire, but you know your father. He and that mail bag will be buried together."

Lacy's father, Martin, had been carrying the mail since before her birth. The postal service was his life. "He'll retire when he's ready."

"I know, I know, but the doctor says his back won't get any better until he does."

"Well, give him my love and tell him I'm okay."

"I will, but he'll want to hear that for himself, so call him back tonight if you get a chance."

"Okay."

"Now, tell me about the accident."

Lacy spent the next few minutes relating her tale of snow and woe.

Val's response was, "Told you not to move to that wasteland. If the Good Lord had wanted us to live in snow, She would've given us fur."

Lacy laughed. Val firmly believed the Almighty was female.

Her mother then asked, "Do you know who hit you?"

"Yep. The mayor's driver."

For a moment there was silence on the other end, then, "Your mayor? Mayor Randolph?"

"The one and only."

"Was he in the car?"

"Yes. In fact, he's here with me at the hospital."

"Well, now," her mother said in a knowing voice. "He's a real cutie."

Lacy said through her smile, "Don't start, Mama."

"I'm not starting anything. Just saying you could do worse, baby."

"Already been there, done that. Remember?"

"All I remember is me telling you not to get married in the first place, but you knew more than anybody back then. Remember?"

Lacy's smile was now tinged with embarrassment. "I remember." Val had all but begged her daughter not to marry the much older Wilton Cox, but Lacy had dug in her heels and refused to listen.

"Is Randolph as fine as he is in his pictures?"

Lacy looked over at His Fineness standing just outside the door, talking on his own phone, and reluctantly admitted, "Yes."

"If he asks you out, say yes."

Lacy raised her eyes to heaven for strength. "He isn't going to ask me out. He's just here because of the accident. If we go anywhere, it will be to court."

"Be nice. Just because you fell and skinned your knee once doesn't mean you can't get back on the bicycle."

"I'm not looking for anyone right now, Mama."

"I know, baby. I know. Studley's enough to make any woman celibate."

They both laughed. Studley was Val's name for Lacy's ex, Wilton Cox. According to the media, Wil was one of America's most trusted Black leaders, but Lacy knew him to be an arrogant, self-promoting son of a bitch whose manipulative and adulterous ways led to a very public—all over the newspapers—divorce. She didn't think him qualified to lead anything or anybody, anywhere.

Her mother didn't either, and Lacy could hear it in Val's voice when she said, "He was here in Atlanta last weekend rallying folks for something or other. Had the streets all tied up. But enough about him."

Lacy agreed.

"Let me know how the X rays turn out. Like I said, if you need me, I can come."

"I'll be okay, don't worry."

"I'm supposed to worry. I'm your mama."

Lacy chuckled. Through the exam room's open door she could see Drake and Carson heading her way. Carson carried a large brown envelope that she assumed held the film. "I have to go, Ma. The mayor's coming."

"Okay, baby. Tell that cutie I say hello, and don't forget to call back and talk to your father."

"Will do. Love you."

"Love you more," Val replied affectionately. " 'Bye."

" 'Bye." Lacy closed the phone.

The X ray showed no broken bones but lots of bruising. While the mayor looked on, Reg Carson explained, "The injury to your ankle was probably caused by you standing on the brake when you spun out. It's a natural reaction in situations like that to want to stop the car. Your neck's fine too, but the soreness and stiffness may be with you for a while."

Lacy was relieved that the injuries weren't real serious.

"I'll prescribe something for the pain. A few days of staying off of it and some ice should have you back on your feet good as new."

"Thanks," she said genuinely.

"You're welcome. Excuse me a minute. Need to talk to Denise."

As he and Denise consulted outside, Lacy discreetly checked out the mayor standing across the room. He was checking her out too, which made her look away. All the hype surrounding how fine he was certainly was warranted. His well-cut hair, medium brown skin, and sexy moustache, coupled with his height and build in the black suit and the long, black, GQ cashmere coat, added up to a man any sister would be proud to call her own. Any sister but Lacy. Her marriage to Cox had left her gun-shy. Even though the divorce had been five years ago, she hadn't allowed herself to get emotionally involved with another man since.

Dr. Carson reentered the room and said, "Before I wrap your ankle, let me write the scrip. Denise needs to get back to her other patients but she'll have one of the aides run it up to the pharmacy."

Lacy was then asked a series of doctor-type questions about her allergies and so forth. When he seemed satisfied with her answers, he scribbled on the white prescription pad he'd pulled from his pocket and ripped the sheet free. He handed it to Denise, who took off to find the aide.

Reg said, "I'll get some tape and be right back."

His exit left her and the mayor alone. Neither said anything at first. Lacy sent a few glances his way, only to find him watching her intently. She quickly turned away again, then said, "Um, how long have you been a doctor?"

"About ten years."

"Which do you like more, being mayor or a doctor?"

Drake shrugged. "Not sure. It's a question I've been asking myself a lot lately, though."

She waited for him to explain.

"I miss helping patients, but I also like helping the city." He then asked, "Where are you from originally?"

"Atlanta."

"Thought I heard the South in your voice."

She smiled. "My parents still live there. What about you? Are you a native Detroiter?"

"Yep. Born, bred, and raised. Just like my mother and my four sisters."

Lacy couldn't hide her surprise. "You have four sisters?"

He nodded. "I'm the baby."

"Baby boy. They must be real proud of you."

"They are. Between them and my brothers, I get plenty advice on how to run the city."

"You have brothers too? How many?"

"Two."

"Seven kids. That's a big family."

"My brothers are steps. They didn't live with us."

"Oh."

"Doesn't stop them from telling me what to do, though."

Lacy replied knowingly, "Everybody has an opinion, I take it?"

"Exactly."

"If I was mayor, I know my mother would call me every morning telling me what I should be fixing."

He chuckled. "That's my mother. Every morning around eight-thirty. Most times she's right, though, so I don't mind."

The story made him more human in Lacy's eyes. There was now a bit of substance added to her image of the rich and handsome bachelor mayor.

"My apology again for the accident," he offered genuinely. "Burton was driving entirely too fast."

"Yes he was." She wondered how many women would have already given him their number by now. Thousands, probably.

"How's the ankle?"

"It's awake and yelling."

His lips thinned. "Hopefully the pain meds will put it to sleep long enough for you to get home and relax."

"I hope so."

Dr. Carson returned. He stooped in front of Lacy and once again gave her ankle a few gentle twists. "We'll have to cut off the foot of your stocking."

Resigned, she nodded her approval.

Once her foot was cut free of the nylon, he proceeded to tape and wrap the bare ankle as if she were an injured athlete. When he finished, only the tips of her purple painted toes were visible. "How's it feel?" he asked.

"Like it's wrapped up."

"Good. Stay off of it for the next three days. No

work. No nothing but laying up like Cleopatra." He then gave her the crutches. "Do you know how to use these?"

"Yes, broke the same ankle about five years ago."

"How?"

"Went out for a pass and stepped in a hole," she explained before adding, "But I have to go to work."

"Not for the next three days you don't. Did you catch the pass?"

She nodded. "Yep, and took it in for the score. Had to go straight to the E.R. after that, but hey, my team won."

He looked over at the mayor. "Fine, *and* plays football? I see why you ran into her car."

Drake chuckled softly.

Reg asked Lacy, "So, can we have dinner?"

Lacy shook her head and tossed back, "I never date my doctors."

Mischief twinkled in his eyes. "How about I give you a *week* off of work?"

She laughed. "No, in fact I can't even afford these three days. I have meetings and—"

"I'll talk to your boss," the mayor said.

Lacy started to protest that she was the boss, then thought about being home for three blissful days and decided to take the gift and hush up. "Okay." It occurred to her then that she should try and call work again and let them know she wouldn't be coming in. "I need to call the office."

The mayor nodded. "Go ahead. Reggie and I'll

wait outside." The men left the room to give her some privacy.

The phone in her office rang six times before it was picked up by her fire-plug-shaped administrative assistant. "Hey, Ida."

"Girl, where are you?"

"I was in a car accident. I'm at Henry Ford, and the doctor's making me take three days off."

"Are you okay?"

"Mostly. I'm waiting on a pain prescription. I jammed my ankle."

"How's your hoopty?"

"Totaled, looks like."

"Well, no great loss. You needed a new car anyway."

"You sound like my mother."

Ida laughed before asking in a more serious tone, "Was anyone else hurt?"

"No."

"Was it your fault?"

"No. I'll call you tonight and give you the 411."

"Okay. I'm going to cancel everything for the rest of the week."

"That's fine. I should be back by Wednesday the sixth."

"Do you need a ride home? I can come get you."

"No. I'll take a cab or something. Nobody should be on the roads today."

"Okay," Ida replied, "but make sure you call me when you get home."

"I will. 'Bye." Lacy closed the phone. She'd deliberately downplayed the details surrounding the accident because, like Val, Ida would start fantasizing on her hooking up with the mayor, and right now she wasn't up to it. She gingerly moved her neck. The stiffness was getting worse and she could feel it spreading into her spine and shoulders.

Denise's aide finally came back from the pharmacy with the prescribed meds. The mayor handed Lacy a paper cup of water, and as he placed the pills in her hand, his skin brushed against hers, sending a sweet shock up her arm. Her surprised eyes flew to his. His eyebrow arched speculatively. Grabbing ahold of herself, Lacy tried to play the whole thing off, but her hands shook a bit as she put the pills in her mouth and washed them down with the water.

She placed the empty cup into his outstretched hand but was careful not to touch him again.

Dr. Carson gave her his business card and a yellow instruction sheet detailing care for the ankle once she was home. "If the swelling doesn't go down or if it gets worse, you call me."

Lacy glanced at the sheet. "I will. Thanks."

"Nice meeting you."

"Same here."

He then shook the mayor's hand. "Your Honor, I'll see you soon."

"Thanks, Reg."

Dr. Carson waved as he exited.

Once she and the mayor were alone again, Lacy could feel whatever was going on between them rising in the silence. She tried to talk it away. "Do you think Denise has a city phone book around here somewhere?"

"Probably. Why?"

"So I can call a cab to take me home."

"I'll take you."

The richness of his tone coupled with the depth of his gaze made her voice softer than she intended. "That's not necessary."

"As your attending physician it's my duty to make sure you get home."

That said, he walked over, took hold of the handles on her wheelchair and slowly propelled it forward.

They both waved good-bye to Denise.

Lacy picked up the conversation while he rolled her down the hall. "Your duty?"

He stopped the chair. "Yes. My duty."

Lacy studied him for a long moment. She didn't mind that he was trying to charm her; the man was fine. However, she hoped he didn't think this whatever-he-was-playing-at would go any further than her front door. She tried to downplay the fact that every time she met his eyes her heart did a weird kind of samba. "As my attending physician, *and* as one of the people responsible for me being here in the first place, giving me a ride home is okay, I suppose."

He flashed that legendary smile. Admittedly, it touched her, but she shook it off. He was a heartbreaker for sure, and she was too old to be picking herself up and dusting herself off.

As he wheeled her toward the exit, she spotted a

gaggle of reporters and TV camera crews waiting by the door. Someone must have dropped a dime on the mayor's presence in the hospital. Lacy wasn't pleased to see them. Neither was he, if the soft curse he gave was any indication.

He stopped the chair. "I'm real sorry about this."

She shrugged and smiled. "It's what I get for hanging out with you."

He smiled back. "Let me see if I can convince them not to put you on the six o'clock news."

"Good luck," she answered.

His approach to the reporters was met by a hail of shouted questions and flashing cameras. Some of the cameras were aimed in her direction, but she quickly shielded her face with her hand. The scene brought to mind the whirlwind that had swirled around her during her divorce. Because Wilton was an influential city councilman at the time, every news outlet in Atlanta had been in her business, and no matter where she went, the press hounded her like pit bulls gone wild. One of the benefits of getting Wilton out of her life had been having the press lose interest too.

But because of today's car accident, she assumed that disinterest would change. The mayor was popular. He was also handsome, rich, and single. Any woman associated with him on any level was considered fair game by the city's reporters because everything about the mayor was news. Lacy could already see her face plastered across the front pages of the papers and hear the television anchors filling their viewers in on her past links to Wilton Cox. Then if they dug deep enough, out would come the story of her having been fired from her last job. Insubordination, her supervisor had called it. She sighed.

Drake, on the other hand, was trying his best to keep the press hounds at bay. He answered each question truthfully. "Yes, my driver accidentally hit her. Yes, he will be ticketed."

When another reporter asked Drake to give up the victim's name, Drake refused. "You'll have to talk to the lady. I don't have her permission to tell you that."

He then ended the mini press conference by saying, "Ladies and gentlemen, I need to get her home."

A flurry of questions followed that statement, but Drake turned on his heel and went back to the grim-faced Lacy. "You ready?"

She glanced at the eager pack of reporters. "No, but let's go anyway."

He nodded and pushed the wheelchair forward. Lacy shielded her face with her big tote as best she could. Cameras flashed and questions were shouted, but she didn't respond. Instead she let the mayor roll her outside into the cold, where the limo sat waiting with its engine running. As she and her crutches struggled into the warm sanctuary of the backseat, next to the mayor and one of his bodyguards, she continued to ignore the reporters, their cameras, and their questions.

By the time the car pulled away from the curb, Lacy's pain meds had kicked in and she was floating in a land that was all fuzzy and soft. The mayor asked her for her address. She remembered replying, but a heartbeat later she was asleep.

She awakened slowly in response to someone calling her name. Then there was the mayor's handsome face hovering from above. The drugs in her system made her smile up at him and say, softly, "Hi."

He grinned. "Yes, you are. You're also home."

Lacy struggled to clear her head. A look to the window showed that they were indeed in the snow-filled lot of her building, but truthfully, she didn't want to move. Feeling no pain because of the meds, she was content. However, spending her three day hiatus in the backseat of the mayor's limo was not an option, so she forced her brain to concentrate on gathering her belongings and her crutches.

Burton, who hadn't spoken a word to her since their initial conversation, turned and said, "You take care of yourself now, and again, I'm real sorry about what happened."

Lacy nodded. What more could she do?

Drake looked at the snow piled up between where the limo was parked and the front door of the apartment building's. There was no way she'd make the trek across the huge parking lot on crutches, and the drifts wouldn't let them park any closer. "You may need some help."

Lacy asked, "Why?"

"Too much snow for those crutches."

She looked around and had to admit he was right. Trying to negotiate the wintry mess would probably result in her spraining more than an ankle. She paid a pretty penny in association fees for services like snow removal. The crews were usually prompt and did a good job, but because of the suddenness and severity of the storm, she wasn't surprised to see that the walks and parking lots were still choked with snow. The last thing she wanted was to be carried to her porch by the playa mayor, but she didn't have much choice.

"I can carry you,"

"Let me," the guard sitting beside her in the backseat offered. "Name's Simon Lane, Ms. Green."

Drake looked at Simon as if the man had lost his mind.

Lacy said, "Nice to meet you, Mr. Lane." He was as big as the other man, Cruise, but his skin was lighter and his hair had just a touch of gray.

Drake said to him, "How about you go get the wheelchair out of the trunk?"

Lane grinned. "Yes sir," he said, and got out.

Drake looked at Lacy. "As I was saying, I can carry you, if you want."

Lacy didn't comment on the men's exchange but she was inwardly amused. "Only if you promise not to drop me."

"I promise."

A second later she was lifted up into his strong, coat-cushioned arms. Her face only inches from his, she studied him, and once again felt herself touched by his nearness. Then a strong wind came up and effectively shut down the moment. She turned her face into his coat and yelled, "How do you people live here?"

He chuckled and, with Lane preceding him began a slow trek toward the building. "You'll get used to it."

"But I don't want to!" she wailed. As the icy wind continued to swirl, she kept her face against him and heard the deep rumbles of laughter in his chest.

Drake was enjoying her. She didn't weigh much, and he thought she fit perfectly in his arms. His enjoyment aside, wading through the heavy, deep snow was like walking through knee-high liquefied cement. His feet were freezing in his thin wet gators but he concentrated on each step. She would never talk to him again, for real, if he dropped her, and he wanted her to talk to him, more than he cared to admit.

He finally made it to her walk and nodded at Lane to open the door. Inside, the shadowy foyer was a testament to the building's age. The Towers, as they were called, had housed only rich White widows when Drake was young. Now the residents were mostly young and middle-age Black professionals.

Lane unfolded the wheelchair, and Drake set Lacy gently on the seat. "I can take it from here, Lane."

He nodded. "Nice meeting you, Ms. Green."

"Same here," Lacy said genuinely.

While Lane went back out to the car, Drake followed Lacy's directions to the elevators.

She lived on the fifth floor and when they reached her door, she handed Drake her keys so he could open the locks.

Lacy was glad the place was clean, so he wouldn't

know what a slob she was, but she was proud of her apartment. Although the building was old, the place had good bones. She had two bedrooms, a large kitchen, a spacious open living room, and a step-down area off the living room that she planned to turn into an office one day. There was also a dishwasher and her own personal washer and dryers. But best of all, there were seventeen windows, and the bulk of them looked out onto the river.

Drake wheeled her into the quiet and looked around. "I like this." The space was large and unfurnished except for one yellow upholstered chair and a TV sitting on a turned-over red milk crate.

"I haven't had time to get furniture, as you can probably see, but soon."

He walked over to look out at the river. "You have a patio."

"Yes. Can't wait to sit out there in the summer. Read, do some grilling. Those flower boxes were there when I moved in, so I threw in some bulbs in October."

"Something's coming up in this red one."

"Tulips." She watched him look up at her high ceilings then check out the gleaming hardwood floors.

"Real nice place."

"Thanks. I'm looking forward to making it my own soon as I get the chance." There were a few framed pieces of African art on the walls, but that was it. "Thanks again for the ride."

"No problem. Do you need anything before I leave?

Need me to run to the store? Do you have enough food?"

She shook her head. "I'm fine." She hobbled over to the lone yellow chair and sat.

"You sure?"

"Positive."

"I don't mind."

"I'm okay," she said with a soft laugh.

"Sorry," he said, an embarrassed grin on his handsome face. "It's the gentleman in me."

Lacy smiled. "I see. Tell your mama she raised you well. But now I want you to go."

"But—"

"Go home, Mayor Randolph. You have a city to run, remember?"

Drake didn't want to leave. The meeting he'd been racing back to attend had been cancelled because of the weather, and the other work waiting for him at the office would be there no matter how long it took him to arrive. He reached into his coat and removed his silver business card holder. Pulling out one of his embossed, fine as linen CITY OF DETROIT business cards, he scribbled a number on it and handed it to her. "Here's my home number. Call me if you need anything."

Lacy glanced at what he'd written. "Thank you," she said, then added truthfully, "but I probably won't call."

"Why not?"

He looked so stunned, she almost laughed. She

wondered if he'd never had a woman turn him down before. "Your Hippocratic duties are over and appreciated," was all she allowed herself to say.

Lacy wasn't made of wood. The raw power of him radiated over her like heat in July, but because he probably affected women worldwide the same way, she knew better than to read anything deep into his interest. "Thanks again, Mayor Randolph."

He smiled. "All right, I can take a hint." But he didn't move. Instead he stood looking at her sitting on the yellow chair while the need to know more about her filled him in ways that for the moment he couldn't explain.

"Take care of yourself," he said, then moved to the door. "Let me know what happens with your car."

"I will."

He nodded and was gone.

Lacy hobbled over to the window to wait for him to appear in the parking lot. After a little while, there he was. The man was definitely fine, and what she'd seen of his personality, she liked, but according to the gossip, His Fineness had more women than Keebler had cookies, and she had no desire to be one of many. So she watched until the big Lincoln drove from sight, and then she and her crutches went into the bedroom so she could lie down.

Three

On the ride back downtown, the dark-eyed Lacy stayed on Drake's mind. She was witty, sharp, and fine. He most definitely wanted to see her again, but getting her to agree might be difficult, considering her lukewarm reaction to him. He never had to pursue women. For as far back as he could remember girls had always lined up for his smile. If he said, "Jump," they'd ask, "How high?" But this Lacy Green, with her fine ebony self, didn't impress him as the how high type.

Burton asked, "Thinking about her?"

Drake nodded.

"Pretty lady."

"Very. Not that she seemed real impressed by me."

"Well, we did run her off the road," Simon Lane remarked sagely.

"No. *Burton* ran her off the road," Drake pointed out.

"You said you were late for the meeting," Burton said.

"And I told you three or four different times to slow it down." Drake loved Burton. He was his great-uncle and had always been Drake's hero, but after today's wreck, blood or no blood, he had to go. His bat out of hell driving was exposing the city to unnecessary lawsuits, not to mention the safety issue. Burt's need for speed came from driving the Negro race car circuit back in the forties and early fifties. Few people knew about the postwar, Black pioneer drivers like Burton Randolph, but Drake and his sisters had grown up hearing the stories and marveling at all the trophies and ribbons he'd won.

Drake also knew how much Burt enjoyed being the mayor's official driver, so it pained him to say, "I'm going to have to let you go, Uncle Burt."

Burt turned and stared at his nephew. "What? Why!"

Drake gave him an incredulous look. "Why? This is your third accident in the last year."

"Firing me's not right," Burt grumbled.

"Neither is running a woman into the ditch," Billy Cruise tossed out from behind the steering wheel.

"I didn't do it on purpose."

"I know that, Unc, but you're endangering everybody on the road, including yourself, driving so fast all the time."

"Can't help it. Race driving's in my blood."

"I know that too, but as much as I hate to say this, your reactions aren't what they used to be."

"You saying I'm old?"

"Yes."

The seventy-two-year-old Burt sat up angrily. "Boy, I was driving hot rods before you were born."

"Bingo!"

Bested, Burt slumped against his seat and groused, "You always were smarter than I could stand."

Drake smiled. "Thanks. And you are the best uncle in the world hands down, but your driving days with me are over. Sorry."

Drake glanced at his uncle's sullen face. "Look at it this way—not driving for me leaves you free to drive those hot little church widows around on their errands."

"All those crows want is my pension."

Drake chuckled. "You may need one of those crows one day."

"Maybe, but it'll only be at night."

The men's laughter filled the car.

As they entered the heart of downtown, Drake looked out at his city. On the left was the Detroit River shining blue in the cold sunshine, and on its far bank the Canadian city of Windsor, Ontario. Visitors to the area were often amazed by the city's close proximity to its international neighbor, and those with an interest in the fabled underground railroad could see why the abolitionists in Detroit were able to ferry thousands of escaped slaves to freedom; Canada was just a short boat ride away.

The limo passed the huge, green marble sculpture of the man known as the Spirit of Detroit. Whenever any of the local teams made the playoffs, the Spirit was always dressed in a matching jersey to show his support. Red for the NFL Red Wings and blue for the NBA Pistons. Thinking about how cool the Spirit looked decked out in a Piston jersey during the team's last championship run made Drake smile. In spite of the city's negative reputation, Drake, like the nearly one million citizens within its borders, loved the city for its vibrancy, spirit, and tenacity. Many of the suburban naysayers spent their lifetimes telling anyone who'd listen their take on why the city was the way it was, but Drake didn't care. The city was coming back. His administration was adamant about restoring the neighborhoods, fixing the schools, and giving the taxpayers a city that worked.

Cruise pulled into the city garage. After parking, he got out and gave the keys to the attendant, Malcolm Ford, a former boxer who worked the garage by day and studied to be a lawyer at night. Drake liked the man a lot.

"Hey, Mayor Randolph. Looks like you had an accident."

Drake checked out the damaged bumper and busted headlight. "Hey, Malcolm. Yeah, we did. Old Speedy Gonzales here strikes again."

Malcolm smiled over at the stony-faced Burton and said, "You okay?"

"Yeah, but His Honor's firing me."

Everyone could hear the anger and the hurt in his voice.

Malcolm, trying to act as peacemaker, said, "Well,

Mr. Randolph, what if you crash and really hurt somebody one of these times?"

Burton looked his nephew in the face and said, "I suppose." Then added, "I'm going to file my report and clean out my desk."

He walked away.

Drake felt bad, but the decision was a necessary one. "I had to let him go."

"I know you did," Lane said. "Everybody around here wanted to know why you didn't do that the last time. We all like Unc, but not behind the wheel."

The last ticket Burton had received came courtesy of a trooper with the Michigan State Police. He'd clocked the limo at 95 mph on one of the city freeways. Burton blamed the excessive speed on blowing the carbon out of the cylinders in order to keep the engine in tip-top shape. The trooper hadn't believed a word of it. Burton was given a huge fine, and some points on his license for good measure.

Malcolm asked, "So, Mayor Randolph, who's going to be your driver now?"

Drake shrugged, "Oh, I don't know. How's your driving record?"

Malcolm stared, then said, "It's great. Excellent. I, uh, even have a valid chauffeur's license from when I drove for the limo people at the airport last year."

"Think you can come up to my office later so we can talk about pay, duties, etcetera?"

Malcolm nodded like a horse. "Yeah, yeah. Who else you considering?"

"No one."

Malcolm stood speechless.

Drake smiled and said, "I like to help a man who's getting his life together." He patted the amazed-looking Malcolm on his back. "See ya later."

Drake and his body guards were halfway across the garage and on their way to the elevator before Malcolm found his voice and yelled, "Thank you, Mayor Randolph! Thank you!"

It was almost two o'clock in the afternoon when Drake stepped off the elevator onto the mayor's floor of the building. His hopes of finding the corridor outside of his office empty were dashed by the line of people awaiting his arrival. Today was Friday, and Fridays were Talk to the Mayor Day. Most times the citizens were lined up like they were at one of the neighborhood clinics, coming to complain about everything from bus service to the time the libraries closed in the evenings. Every now and then someone would show up and say, "Good job," but those people were rare.

Today's snow must have kept the citizenry at home. In line instead were a few department heads, a representative from the Chamber of Commerce, and two administrative assistants who worked for members of the City Council. He didn't recognize the other seven or eight people. He gave them a nod but didn't stop moving; he knew better.

He entered and waved to the bevy of secretaries. Out of one of the side offices stepped his chief assistant, Rhonda Curry. She had a body by Fischer and a brain by MIT, her alma mater. Today she had on a hot red suit guaranteed to singe a man, but Rhonda was lesbian and proud. "Lots of calls about the snow. Parents are mad that the schools weren't officially closed, and Councilwoman Draper and her buddy Councilman Parker want you to call them."

Drake had no intentions of putting either one at the top of the list. All they wanted to do was argue. "What're they pissed off about now?"

Rhonda followed him into his main office. He tossed his coat on the couch and went behind his desk to look at the stack of messages waiting for him to read. He glanced up at her.

"They want to know if you're really rehiring Dr. Shaw."

Drake stared. "Do they have my office bugged? How'd they find out?" Dr. Denise Shaw was his pick for the new school superintendent job. She'd had the job with the last administration but was fired for shaking things up too much. Drake wanted her back because she was the kind of superintendent he thought the city schools needed.

Rhonda shrugged her red-suited shoulders. "No idea."

"What did you tell them?"

"That the mayor hasn't made a decision yet."

"Thank you. What else is burning on the stove?"

Rhonda looked down at her yellow legal pad and read off a list that started with a broken water main flooding a street on the west side, a call from the governor concerning a conference she wanted Drake to attend next week, and finished with notes about a story in the morning paper concerning a city bus driver who not only had no valid operator's license, but had been involved in fourteen accidents in the last two years.

Drake shook his head hearing that one.

Rhonda added, "I've handled most of them. The water department has been on the break since late this morning, and I called the bus garage and told them to put that driver on suspension."

"Good job." Drake had no idea where he'd be without Rhonda's unflappable assistance. "And the mob outside?"

"They all have appointments but shouldn't take long."

"You always say that."

She gave him a smile. "Makes you feel better."

"Yeah right," he cracked. "Let me change out of these wet shoes and then send in the first one." Before she could leave, he said, "Oh, and call Triple A. Find out if they've towed the car we hit this morning, and where they took it."

"How's the victim?"

"Hurt her ankle. She should be up and around in a few days." Lacy's dark face hovered in his memory while he shuffled through the messages and sorted them into piles according to importance. He put the one from his mother on top. "Name's Lacy Green. Works downstairs in the Environmental Office, I think. Do you know her?"

"Nope. Is she going to sue?"

"No idea."

"Well, we'll keep a good thought. I'll find out about her car."

"Thanks, Rhon."

"You bet. I'll send in the Chamber brother first."

"Fine."

And so Drake's day began.

It was after nine when Cruise pulled up to the circular drive of the east side mansion that served as the mayor's official residence and let Drake out. A few feet away sat the unmarked police car holding the two police officers who made up the night shift. As mayor, Drake had 24/7 protection. He thought it unnecessary. His police chief didn't agree, and because she carried a gun and Drake didn't, the bodyguards stayed. He gave them a wave and went inside.

The dark silence of the house's interior washed over him as he hung up his coat in the foyer closet. He turned on a lamp with a bulb that glowed just enough to beat back the shadows. The place was large and elegantly furnished. The huge windows that ran the length of the house offered a spectacular view of the river and the lights of the Windsor skyline. On the mansion's professionally painted walls hung framed art from his personal collection and a few pieces on loan from the city's largest museum, the Detroit Institute of Arts. The residence was one of the city's jewels, but for all the joy it gave Drake he may as well be living in a cave.

For him, the mansion was just another reminder of

his responsibilities as Detroit's CEO. In a perfect world, he'd have someplace to go where he could be off the clock. If only for a little while. In this mythical someplace he would ditch the bodyguards, the pager, the chauffeurs and the press, and just be Drake. Plain old Dr. Drake Randolph.

He clicked on the lights in the state-of-the-art kitchen and walked past the gleaming, brushed metal appliances and over to the fridge. He pulled out the food his mother had sent over before he left for San Antonio and wondered if it was safe to microwave and then eat seven-day-old macaroni and cheese? He set it on the counter nearby and pulled out the remains of the turkey. Pulling back the foil showed a dried and shriveled carcass that looked as questionable as the macaroni. He deposited it all into the trash, closed the fridge door and sighed. *Pizza again.* He toyed with the idea of jumping into his car and making the ten minute drive down Jefferson to his brother Mykal's house. Myk's wife, Sarita, would feed him until he couldn't move, but Drake nixed the idea. Myk and Sarita were married a little over a year ago, and he'd eaten there at least four days a week when he was in town. Neither minded his company, but lately, with Sarita's baby on the way, he was beginning to feel like a third wheel, and was trying to keep his visits to a minimum.

With that in mind, he pulled out his phone, called the policemen outside to alert them to the pending delivery and to ask if they wanted anything. He then punched up the pizza place and placed his order. Done with that, he headed for his bedroom and the relief he knew would come from a long hot shower.

Somewhere in Lacy's dream the phone was ringing. Determined to ignore it, she burrowed deeper under the blankets, but the insistent sound wouldn't go away. When she opened her eyes and realized it wasn't a dream, she groaned and reached for the handset on the nightstand. "Yeah?" she said groggily.

"Girl, why didn't you tell me it was the mayor who hit you?"

Ida.

"Ida, I'm trying to sleep."

"Well, wake up, because you're on the eleven o'clock news."

Lacy closed her eyes, cursed silently, then said, "Call me tomorrow." And hung up.

The next morning, Lacy awakened with aches and pains in places that had never had aches and pains before. The backs of her shoulders, the edges of her thighs. She guessed it came from being tossed around in the car during the accident. Every inch of her body radiated soreness. Especially her neck. She moved it gingerly and the tenderness made her wince. Figuring a hot shower might do her some good, she struggled to sit up. The voice in her mind asked how she planned to shower on crutches and with a wrapped-up foot. Since she had no answer, she settled on washing her face and brushing her teeth.

With her feet up and a bowl of microwave oatmeal in her hand, Lacy turned on the morning news. It was a little after 8:00 A.M. and usually by now most of the local news programs had come and gone, but Channel 2 ran news until nine. She dreaded the idea of seeing herself on the tube, but needed to see what everyone else in the city had seen. After a commercial for vinyl windows, one for a local casino, and a preview of the Montel Williams show, the female anchor came back on, saying, "Now, here's a look at our mayor at Henry Ford Hospital yesterday. According to sources, the woman in the wheelchair was struck by the mayor's limo during yesterday's storm and forced off of I-94 . . ."

Seeing herself hiding behind her tote like a mafia don while the mayor pushed her to his limo made Lacy lower her spoon and shake her head. The camera showed the press yapping like a pack of excited terriers. The mayor looked grim. While the footage ran, the anchor added, "So far, the woman remains unidentified, but an unnamed source at the hospital said the victim may be a city employee. No reports on whether the mystery woman will sue the city. In other news. . . ."

Lacy clicked off the remote. At least they didn't have her name. Yet. She had the sinking feeling that the outing of her identity would only be a matter of time. Not pleased, she went back to her bowl of oatmeal.

Later, a call to the tow company only added to her mood. She was told by a gum-chewing young woman on the other end of the line that the Escort had been towed to four different body shops, but due to the totality of the damage and the advanced age of the vehicle, no one wanted to waste the time running down the ancient parts, let alone fix it. A grim Lacy thanked her, then punched in the number of her insurance agent, who said right off the bat that because so many cars had been in storm-related accidents, it was going to be Thursday at the earliest before they could even send an adjuster out to look at the car. Not happy, Lacy related to the agent what she'd been told by the body shops.

The woman replied, "Then we may have to go ahead and total your Escort out, Ms. Green."

Lacy liked the sound of that. "If you do, when can I expect a check?"

"Six to eight weeks."

Lacy was appalled. "What am I supposed to drive in the meantime?"

"Well? Oh, sorry, I have a call on another line. I'll get back to you."

And she hung up.

Lacy was so outdone, all she could do was stare at the phone and promise to find a new insurance company as soon as this mess was resolved. "Six to eight weeks my ass," she said out loud, and tossed the phone onto the bed beside her.

Following Dr. Carson's advice, she did her best to play Cleopatra, but the phone kept ringing. By mid-afternoon she'd talked to her mother, then her father, who was on lunch break, Ida—twice—and now she was talking to the building manager, who'd called to let her know she had a package waiting downstairs. "I'm on crutches, Wanda. Can you have somebody bring it up?"

"Sure can."

When Lacy heard the knock, she grabbed the crutches and crossed the bare floors to the door. Once she got it open, the sight of Drake Randolph standing there holding a huge vase of roses almost made her fall over. She knew she was staring like an idiot, but . . . "Hi," she finally managed to say. "What are you doing here?"

"Was on my way to a luncheon. Thought I'd check on you and bring you these."

He held the vase out, but Lacy raised a crutch. "My hands are full, come on in."

He entered behind her, asking, "Where do you want them?"

She nodded at one of the windowsills. "Over there is fine. Thanks."

The pale yellow roses were tipped with a blush of pink. They were gorgeous.

He checked her out from across the room. "Didn't know if you liked flowers or not."

"I do." Lacy then asked, "Do you always bring flowers to your victims?"

He smiled. "You make me sound like a vampire or something, but the answer is no." Then he said directly into her eyes, "I've never wanted to take any of them to dinner either."

The soft words were powerful. Lacy drew in a steadying breath and swore the room was getting warm, but even as she reacted physically, the logical parts of herself were a bit skeptical. She'd heard all the gossip. The man's game was legendary, so was he setting her up to be his next conquest? Did he think taking her to dinner and charming her would keep her from suing the city? Because she knew next to nothing about him, she couldn't answer either.

He asked her then, "Yes? No?"

Lacy tried to put him down as gently as possible. "I think, no. The flowers are more than enough. Thanks." The offer was flattering but she didn't know him from the man in the moon.

"Okay," he said with a smile that didn't meet his eyes. "Well, guess I should get going. Like I said, just wanted to check on you."

"And I appreciate it."

He walked back over to the door. "Take care now."

"I will. 'Bye."

He exited and the door closed softly behind him. As the silence resettled, Lacy smiled.

Down in the parking lot, Drake got back into the limo and slammed the door. "Let's go."

Malcolm Ford looked back at his boss and asked, "What happened?"

"I gave her the flowers. She said, 'Fine, thank you very much, good-bye.' "

Malcolm chuckled. "She didn't want to go out?"

"No."

Lane, seated beside Drake, chuckled and asked, "Does she know you're the mayor?"

Drake shot him a look.

From the front seat, Cruise said, "Ms. Lacy doesn't impress me as your average mayor type lady. You might have to work a little on this one."

Drake drawled, "Your advice is noted. Malcolm. Drive."

"Yes, sir."

Drake had never been turned down for a date in his life. Ever. Not in high school, college, med school, or anyplace else. If anything, the women were stepping over each other trying to get invites from him. He wasn't boasting or arrogant; it was the story of his life. He was a good-looking, hardworking, sister-loving man, and he never lacked for company. Apparently, Lacy Green didn't know that. What kind of woman says no to dinner with Mayor Dr. Drake Randolph? he wondered, then smiled knowingly. He reminded himself that he had the blood of the Vachons in his veins, which meant he was just going to have to find out.

When Reynard Parker saw the news story on the mayor's accident, he hoped the incident would damage Randolph's credibility and reputation. After all, the driver involved was Randolph's uncle. But Parker doubted the wish would come true. Detroit's pretty boy doctor mayor was so popular he'd have to be caught in bed with either a live boy or a dead girl to bring him down. Instead, Randolph was threatening Parker's power base by seeking to change the way members of the City Council were elected. Council members ran citywide, and voters elected everyone from one slate. Randolph wanted the council to be elected by district. His hope, or so he said, was to make the council more accountable and open the process to new blood, because as it stood now, the same core of council members were elected again and again, some having been in office nearly thirty years.

Parker didn't want the system changed. The impact on his bribes, special contracts, and kickbacks would be detrimental if he weren't able to control the whole pie. How could he ask for under-the-table payments from companies doing business on the west side of the city if the only part of the city under his direct control was just a sliver of the east side? Parker and his ally on the council, Lola Draper, had made a pact to stall the mayor's initiative for as long as necessary. Draper didn't want her funds affected, and neither did he.

Parker didn't usually work on Saturday, but he'd come in this evening not to handle city business, but to take care of a problem related to Parker Environmental. The lush, plush corporate office was a sharp contrast to the bare bones, ancient space he maintained down the street in the City Council wing, and it showcased just how far he'd come. There were secretaries, the latest electronic office equipment, and a desk imported from Spain. At the sound of the knock on the door, Parker called, "Come in."

Benny "Fish" Madison came in, nodded to his boss, and took a seat near the desk. Nicknamed Fish because of his bulging eyes, his official title was VP of Special Projects. The thirty-six-year-old former felon handled jobs for the corporation that had to be kept on the down low.

Parker asked him, "Is the Wheeler situation taken care of?"

Benny's fish eyes gleamed with sharklike satisfaction. "Yeah. Put the body in a truck and sent it to one of the landfills. By now he's in such little pieces even the gulls won't be able to find him, let alone the police."

Parker thought about the hundreds of gulls that constantly circled his three landfills in search of food. He hoped Fish was right. Wheeler had been the company treasurer but hadn't been a team player. His outraged refusals to cook the books, followed by threats to bring in the FBI, made Parker send him on a permanent vacation. Parker hoped he was happy. Wheeler's ethics had left his wife a widow and his two young sons fatherless. "When's the next shipment due in from Montreal?"

"Tomorrow evening."

Parker's waste haulers had been smuggling drugs across the Michigan-Canada border for years. His three rural landfills worked perfectly as dropoff and distribution points because the out-of-the-way locations made them less likely to be under surveillance by the feds. The less attention the smuggling operations drew, the more product Parker could move. "When Wheeler's wife files the missing person's report the police will probably come sniffing around."

"Let 'em," Fish responded confidently. "We made sure everything was cleaned up. We also searched his office and his car to see if we could find anything proving he'd already made contact with the feds, but nothing."

"Too bad we can't search his house too."

"I'll try and get in there on Monday. She works and the kids are in school. She has to wait forty-eight hours before she can file, so we have a little bit of time."

Satisfied, Parker nodded.

Fish looked at his watch, then asked, "Anything else for me? I got a date with a lap dancer in an hour."

Parker didn't hide his distaste. "No, nothing else. Just don't let your dick make you lose your mind."

Fish stood and didn't hide his distaste either. "Don't worry. Everything's under control."

"So you keep telling me, but remember what happened last time."

"I do," he responded, his fish eyes cool. Six months ago one of Fish's favorite pole dancers had spiked his drink, and while he lay passed out in the motel room, she'd stolen his wallet and briefcase. "I also remember that I got everything back, and eliminated the problem *permanently*." The trash-compacted remains of the woman and her pimp were now mixed in with the soil beneath one of the company's newly constructed subdivisions.

"It never should have happened in the first place."

Fish's face tightened. "You play your way and I'll play mine. Are we done?"

Parker nodded grimly and watched as Fish made his exit. Perhaps it was time to find a new VP of Special

Operations. But because Fish knew where all the skeletons were buried, replacing him would be easier said than done. He had to come up with a solution, however; he didn't want any baggage cluttering up his life when he made his run for mayor.

Four

Monday morning Drake sequestered himself in his office to go over budget requests from some of his department heads. For the first time in two administrations there was money in the bank. Drake and his people were concentrating on cutting fat and streamlining services to turn the ship around, and slowly but surely the city was moving away from the abyss.

Picking up his cup of still hot coffee, he took a sip and scanned a few of the requests. There was one from Parks and Rec to reinstate the SwimMobile. Drake had nothing but good memories of the mobile swimming pool rolling up to his neighborhood, and the fun he and his friends had made him smile. The SwimMobile had been out of commission for a good six or seven years and he'd love to bring it back. He set the proposal off to the side. For the next hour he scrutinized proposals on infrastructure repairs, requests for reopening the city aquarium, and many other projects and programs that were feasible candidates. By lunchtime he had two piles—one for proposals worthy enough to consider now, the other for the requests he'd have to hold on to and deal with later, when more money became available.

One of the best and workable proposals had come from the Environmental Office. It sought reinstatement of the neighborhood Toxic Watch programs and included a very interesting plan to go after polluters. Past administrations had been stuck with a bunch of outdated laws that gave convicted polluters and slumlords little more than a slap on the wrist as punishment. One of Drake's campaign promises had been to clean up the city. The demolition of abandoned buildings was well under way, and litter along the highways had all but been eliminated, but getting a handle on all the old tires, junk cars, and illegal dumpings was necessary if the cleanup was to be a true success. Drake read a few more pages and was intrigued by the proposal to institute a court that handled nothing but pollution crimes. Impressed by the well-thought-out and documented presentation, he flipped to the back page of the packet to see who had put the proposal together. When he read *Lacy Green and Staff*, he smiled and turned to his appointment calendar. He knew she wasn't due back to work until Wednesday. He wondered if she could present the proposal to his cabinet on, say, Friday morning. Yes, he wanted to see her again, but it was her proposal that had him excited now.

Rhonda knocked on his partially opened door and said, "Turn on Channel 7."

Drake picked up the remote and pointed it across the room at the TV. The picture came on showing council members Reynard Parker and Lola Draper—or as Drake called them, "*Crooked and Crookeder*"—seated around a table with one of the local news male anchors. "What are they up to?"

"Listen," Rhonda said quietly.

Lola was saying, "So that's why Councilman Parker and I want to put this issue before the voters. The mayor wants to change the way members of the City Council are elected. Why fix something that isn't broken? The system already in place works fine."

Drake sighed grimly. The only reason they were opposed was because there'd be less bribe money crossing their greedy palms. Both were suspected of being on the take, but so far had been slick enough not to get caught. NIA, a group of people dedicated to ridding the city of drugs and corruption, was trying to change that. Lola was small potatoes; it was Parker they wanted to bring down. He had enough tentacles in the pockets of area politicians and developers to be called the Doc Oc of Detroit. Although no one was brave enough or stupid enough to point a finger directly at him, Parker killed people. Or at least his flunkies did. Rumors of murder for hire, kickbacks, bribes, and peddling his influence to the highest bidder had dogged him quietly for years, but nothing stuck. Parker was an old school politician and had a large constituency. His supporters heralded his humble beginnings and cheered him each and every time a charge was dropped. They didn't seem to care that he was crooked as a four dollar bill.

On the TV, Parker was saying, "Tomorrow we'll begin gathering signatures to support a ballot proposal."

The reporter asked, "Are you two going to run against Mayor Randolph in the next election?"

Parker spoke first. "Ms. Draper and I have discussed it. Although we agree that the city under Mayor Randolph is not heading in the right direction, my constituency is larger. With that being the case, I'd be delighted to have her as my chief assistant or deputy mayor."

Rhonda laughed and pointed at the screen. "Look at Lola's face!"

Drake knew the former beauty queen had no intention of playing second fiddle to Parker or anyone else, and the fake smile on her furious face said it all.

Draper responded tightly, "And I would delighted to have Councilman Parker as my deputy as well."

Drake clicked the remote and the picture vanished. "I'm so tired of those two," he said.

"So, you're going to run again?"

Drake eyed Rhonda's serious face. "Don't know," he said honestly. It was a decision he'd been grappling with for weeks.

"You can't leave the city to them. They'll gut it and we'll be right back where we started."

"I know, Rhon."

"The citizens need you, Drake."

He knew that too, but the idea of running again

and plunging himself back into the fishbowl wasn't real appealing.

"Just think about it, please?"

"Promise."

"Okay. I'm going to send out for lunch. What do you want?"

He picked from the choices she offered, cleared his mind of the problems of Draper and Parker, and went back to Lacy's proposal.

By Tuesday evening Lacy felt confident about returning to work. She'd weaned herself down to just a few over-the-counter pain pills a day and tossed the remaining prescription drugs into her medicine cabinet. She'd made arrangements to get a rental car, but with her ankle still real sore, she knew it was going to be impossible to press down on the gas pedal, so driving was out for at least another few days. Calling a cab seemed to be her only option until Ida called.

"I'll swing by and pick you up on my way in. I have to drive right by you anyway."

Lacy didn't want to be a bother and tried to talk her out of it, but Ida was determined. "No, I'm coming to get you. Your mama and I are sorors—I'm supposed to make sure you're okay. I'll be there at seven-fifteen sharp. Be ready."

"Yes, ma'am." It was all Lacy could say.

True to her word, Ida Mae Richardson drove up in her chocolate-gold Cadillac at precisely 7:15 A.M. Lacy, all ready to go, crutched her way out to the parking lot just as Ida stepped out of the still running vehicle.

"'Morning," Ida said with a smile. "Need some help?"

"'Morning," Lacy called back, her voice sounding loud in the morning quiet. "No, I'm okay. May take me a minute to get there."

The rise in temperatures over the weekend had reduced the piles of snow to dirty little bumps here and there, so Lacy didn't have to worry about falling. Ida met her halfway and took the tote and long-strapped leather bag Lacy sometimes used as a briefcase.

"How you feeling?" Ida asked, keeping a slow pace at Lacy's side.

"Not bad."

Lacy maneuvered her way into the soft warmth of the leather-encased interior while Ida took the crutches and stuck them in the backseat along with the bag and tote.

After the short ride down Jefferson Avenue, Ida pulled into the city's employee garage and swung the car into the space. "Sit here a minute. My sister Maxine sent you something."

A puzzled Lacy turned to watch Ida go into the trunk, but the raised lid kept her from seeing what Ida was up to.

What Ida was up to was bringing a small trikelike scooter around to the passenger side of the car. Lacy had seen seniors driving the motorized vehicles in the mall and at the grocery stores.

"Max bought it last year when she broke her foot," Ida explained. "She said to keep it for as long as you need to."

An elated Lacy studied the cute little red machine. Sizewise, it was smaller than a golf cart, and there was a wire basket attached to the front. "Give Max a big kiss for me. This is perfect."

It took Lacy only a few moments to master the controls, and then she and Ida headed for the elevator.

The city's Environmental Office consisted of Lacy, Ida, and their young secretary, Janika Doyle. Felton Adams, the former director and the man who'd interviewed and hired Lacy, had taken a job in New Mexico back in February, and no one had been hired to replace him. The people in H.R. kept promising to find a replacement, but when the mayor's hiring freeze went into effect a few weeks later, all bets were off.

It hadn't taken Lacy long to get acclimated, though. Thanks to Ida and Janika, she learned to negotiate her way through the maze of city offices and regulations. It took her even less time to realize that although her office reported to the Department of Public Works, the director had his hands full coordinating garbage pickup, demolitions, and infrastructure headaches like broken water mains. It left him little time for much else. Her office was a fly on the butt of a rhino in terms of importance, so she and her staff had no champion for any proposals they wanted to bring to the table.

Lacy found her bottom rung position on the city's totem pole frustrating because she truly believed in what she was doing. Although her zealous campaigns against polluters had gotten her fired from her last job, she'd accepted the Detroit job because, one, it was the only one offered, and two, she thought her ideas could make a difference. Since the birth of the environmental movement in the seventies, most of the focus had been on clean water and air, virgin lands, and animal populations. Only lately had urban areas like Detroit, Philadelphia, and Chicago come under scrutiny. Illegal dumping, abandoned factories, and toxic waste were affecting its citizens in ways that demanded action, and Lacy wanted to bring the fight here. Landlords who refused to rid their houses of lead paint should pay. She felt the same way about illegal dumpers and business owners who walked away from their dying enterprises leaving behind barrels of toxic chemicals or contaminated sites for the cities to clean up. She was girded for battle but still waiting for a sword.

Around ten that morning, Janika stuck her head into Lacy's office. "Girl, check your makeup, His Fineness just came in!"

Lacy's eyes widened then she got hold of herself. No sense in being crazy, Janika already had that covered, so she took a deep breath, composed herself, and waited for him to appear. A few seconds later he was knocking on her open door.

"Ms. Green?"

Lacy looked up into that blinding handsomeness and fought to sound nonchalant. "How are you, Mayor Randolph?"

"I'm okay. You?"

"Doing fine. Fine. What can I help you with?"

He held up a green folder. "This. You sent up a budget request?"

She recognized the folder now. "Yes, for the Blight Court."

"Can you present this to the cabinet Friday morning?"

Lacy went still. "Yes. Why?"

"This is exactly what I've been looking for. It's cheap, effective, and fresh."

"Really?"

"Really. Now, if Friday's too soon . . . ?"

"Oh, no. Friday's fine." Lacy was having trouble breathing. Were her ideas really going to be considered? Then the skeptic inside kicked in. "You are basing this on the merits, right?"

He chuckled. "Yes. This isn't a move to get you to have dinner with me, although I haven't given up on that."

Lacy met his eyes. No man had the right to be that fine. No man. From his boyish charm to his tailored gray suit to the matching gators on his feet, he was handsomeness personified.

"I've never had a woman turn me down before."

"Never?"

"Ever."

"Makes me memorable, then."

"Very." He smiled, then added, "I'm really harmless, you know."

"That's not what I heard."

"No?"

His eyes and smile were working her overtime, and Lacy could feel the temperature in the air rising. "I heard you have as many women as Chrysler has cars."

"Not anymore. I'm older now. The booty call days are over."

The sincerity in his tone rang true. "That's good, because I don't like to share."

"Neither do I."

"Then maybe we can talk dinner."

"Your call."

Lacy swore her brain was filled with static. "I'll let you know."

"That's fair."

Lacy took in a deep breath and decided it might be time to change the conversation to something less volatile. "Um, what time Friday?"

"Nine A.M.?"

"Okay."

Drake sensed her thawing, so he didn't push. He wanted her to feel comfortable around him, and if that took a bit more time, he could wait. "How's the ankle?"

"Better. I'm hoping I'll be able to drive by the end of the week."

"How're you getting to work?"

"Ida."

"Ah."

"Her sister also loaned me that scooter."

He turned and looked at the machine. "Nice of her."

"It's better than the crutches."

They were making small talk so as not to end the encounter, and they both knew it, but he eventually had to go back to his own office. He held up the folder. "Good work, Ms. Green."

"Thank you."

"See you Friday."

"See you Friday."

And he was gone.

It took Lacy a few moments to collect herself, and then she yelled, "Ida!"

Ida strolled in. "His Fineness left here smiling. You two going out?"

"No. You sound like my mother." Lacy then explained the visit.

"He wants you to present it?"

Lacy nodded excitedly.

"Hot damn."

"You ready?"

"Been ready. Janika and I will start pulling the packets together and get the charts printed out."

Lacy was grinning. "This is so cool!" *Finally!* Their work down here on the bottom of the totem pole was being noticed, and now she had to put on a good show. "Well, as my mama says, let's rock and roll!"

"All righty now!"

The ladies spent the next two days getting ready for Lacy's presentation. Reports were typed, printed, and collated. Charts were drawn up and statistics compiled. Lacy reread her materials and placed a few calls to her counterpart in Chicago to verify some facts.

By the time she got to her desk on Friday morning,

the butterflies in her stomach were whirling like they were on steroids. She had on her best black power suit and a brand new silk blouse. Unfortunately, she had to wear sneakers because her ankle refused to go into the pumps she'd wanted to wear. The shoes spoiled the overall look, but hey, it was all she had.

Since it was still early, Lacy took advantage of the quiet surroundings to scribble a few notes and to get her head into the game.

At eight-thirty Ida stuck her head around Lacy's door. "Ready?"

"Yep."

Ida grabbed the packets while Lacy maneuvered herself onto the scooter, then the two women headed back out to the elevator for the ride up to the mayor's office.

The conference room was crowded. Lacy recognized some of the women and men as heads of various departments, but most of the faces were unfamiliar. She thought he said he was bringing in his cabinet. There seemed to be a lot more people here than that, but the confident Lacy eased the scooter to the front of the room.

Drake was having a conversation with one of the legal beagles about the upcoming contract talks with the city's bus drivers union when Lacy and her scooter appeared in the doorway. Keeping the conversation going, he followed her progress through the crowded room with his eyes. She looked good in the black suit, and the open-necked white blouse looked expensive.

The long string of gray pearls around her neck gave the outfit even more elegance. Seeing the high-top Nikes on her feet made him chuckle inwardly. Evidently she'd chosen practicality over fashion, but even so, the lady had style.

Drake wanted to stroll over and talk to her, but forced himself to remain where he was. The graceful way her jaw melted into her neck, and the sparkle in her onyx eyes as she and Ida chatted, entranced him. The way the small twists in her hair framed her face and the curves of her sweet-looking mouth also drew his visual attention, but he'd promised himself he wouldn't crowd her, and she was here to work. She probably wouldn't appreciate him distracting her right now. So he gave the lawyer his undivided attention. There'd be time and opportunity to enjoy Lacy's company later.

At precisely nine o'clock Lacy said to the gathering. "I'd like to get started. I know many of you have other appointments and meetings today and I don't want to keep you here any longer than necessary."

Someone called out, "I like her already. I vote yes for whatever she's asking."

The quip brought laughter, then the room slowly quieted.

Lacy saw the mayor standing at the back of the room. "Mayor Randolph, do you have anything you want to say before Ida and I get started?"

Drake liked the way she'd included Ida's name in the presentation. For him, it said a lot about Lacy's lack of ego. "No, Ms. Green. Go ahead."

Lacy began by explaining the basics. "Basically, what I'm calling Blight Court is a set of administrative hearings devoted specifically to civil infractions committed in four areas. Property Maintenance, Zoning, Solid Waste Removal, and Illegal Dumping. In the past all of these citations and summons went through the Thirty-sixth District Court, but they're so backed up on bigger cases they can only hear maybe fifty blight cases a week. Maybe. But with this plan the city could handle as many as seventy thousand cases a year." Lacy could see the surprise on some of the faces and, at the back of the room, the mayor nodding his encouragement.

She continued. "The court would have three full-time members presiding over the hearings, and they could be attorneys, independent contractors, or citizens. That will be up the mayor."

Someone asked, "What about enforcement? Right now, we can summon, but they don't have to show up at court because they know their case isn't high priority."

"We'll garnish their checks. We'll slap liens on their homes or businesses. The legal precedents used successfully by other cities have been included in the packets I'll pass out when we're done."

"Wow," a woman said from the back.

A skinny balding man up front concurred. "Sounds like you've really done your homework, Ms. Green."

"Thank you."

Lacy talked about the Chicago model the Detroit

court would be modeled after and then, on the overhead projector, put up the stats showing the effectiveness of their measures. She talked about how steep the fines might be and the need for more city inspectors for the whole picture to work. In all, the presentation took thirty minutes.

When she finished, she turned off the projector and applause broke in the packed room. Surprised and somewhat embarrassed, she beamed. She could see people nodding their heads in agreement and smiling.

"Are there any questions?" she asked from her seat on the scooter.

There were plenty. Some came from the court officers present, others from the city's lawyers. Lacy answered as best she could, though inside she was a giddy fool. Her program looked like it was going to be a go, and she couldn't ask for more, except for maybe wanting this meeting to be over so she and Ida could go back to the office and celebrate.

Drake watched Lacy taking questions. She'd given an impressive performance. The material she presented had been clear and concise. Judging by the group's response he wasn't the only one excited about the plan. He had to go to the state capital later that day for a meeting with the governor, and he was looking forward to reading her materials in depth on the ride. In the meantime, while she shook a few more hands and accepted more smiles and congratulations on a job well done, Drake watched her with appreciative eyes. *Beautiful, sassy, and bright,* he noted to himself. It was a wicked combination in a woman. A wicked combination.

As the room emptied, Drake spent a few moments talking with various people and fielding their enthusiasm for Lacy's proposal. When the last person exited, he was left alone with Ida and Lacy. They were gathering up their materials to go back to their office. "Great job, ladies," he said walking to the front of the conference room to join them at the table.

They replied in unison, "Thanks."

"Real good job. Don't be surprised if this winds up on the fast track."

He sat on the edge of the table just close enough for Lacy to feel his warmth slowly mingle with her own. Ida was replacing the slides in a folder and trying to act as if she weren't checking out Lacy and the mayor, but Lacy knew better.

"Didn't Lacy do a good job?" Ida asked.

"Yes, she did."

"She should be director instead of assistant," Ida declared.

"You think so?" he asked Ida, but his eyes were locked on Lacy's.

"I know so."

Lacy wondered if this was how it felt to be mesmerized. She couldn't seem to do anything but look at him. As a result, her voice came out a lot softer than she'd intended. "I don't need to be director. I—"

"Lace. I'm going to take this stuff upstairs."

And before Lacy could tell her to wait, Ida

snatched up the box they'd brought down and was gone. *Traitor!* she wanted to yell, but instead found herself trying not to concentrate on the vivid nearness of His Fineness. It was difficult. She wondered what it was about this man that made her feel so *aware*? His presence seemed to enhance her senses, making her note the faint scents of his cologne, the strong sound of her heart, and the feel of her lungs as she breathed in and out.

"I like the Nikes," he told her.

She raised her foot and checked out her shoe. "Pretty jazzy, huh?"

"Yep, and they match your suit."

Their smiles met.

He said then, "I heard about your car."

"Then you know the bad news."

"I do." Learning from Rhonda that Lacy's Escort was too cracked up to be repaired only added to the guilt Drake felt over the accident. "The city will compensate you. I'll have Rhonda send you the forms. It may take a while for them to cut the check, so the sooner you get the paperwork done, the sooner you'll get your money."

"Okay."

Silence settled again before Drake said, "I meant what I said about the presentation."

"Thanks for liking the proposal. When I first started working here, I wasn't sure anyone knew our office existed."

"We do now."

"And I can't wait to get going."

He paused for a moment, then asked, "When are you going to let me take you to dinner?"

She chuckled softly and looked up into his face. "Oh, I don't know."

"I keep telling you, I'm harmless."

"No man with your reputation is *harmless.*"

He threw back his head and laughed. After composing himself, he told her, "You got me on that one."

"Uh-huh," she replied. "I need to go back downstairs so we can both get some work done."

Once again their eyes locked, and Lacy could feel her blood begin to samba. After a moment she confessed without shame, "You're very hard to say no to, Mr. Mayor."

"Good," he whispered.

As he reached out and slowly ran a gentle finger down her cheek, time seemed to slow. Lacy's eyes fluttered closed in response to the power of his touch. "Very hard . . ."

He smiled softly.

Rhonda leaned into the door. "Mayor Randolph, I—"

Lacy jumped like a teenager busted kissing in the high school hall.

Rhonda saw the embarrassment on the young woman's face and instantly apologized, "I'm sorry. I thought you were alone."

He eased himself to his feet. "Rhonda Curry. Lacy Green."

Lacy nodded, then said, "Hello."

Rhonda smiled. "Hello." Then she said to Drake, "Malcolm has the car ready. He said give him a ring when you're ready to leave for Lansing."

She turned to Lacy and said genuinely, "Nice meeting you."

"Same here."

Her departure left them alone again.

Lacy picked up a few papers Ida had overlooked and placed them in the scooter's basket. "I should go." Her senses were still blooming from his whispered caress across her cheek. "Thanks again for the support."

"You're welcome."

Drake watched her drive out of the room. It took everything he had not to call her back.

Back in her office, Lacy joined Janika and Ida in a Hallelujah celebration. They were excited about the proposal going forward and proud that the mayor had rewarded them for all their hard work. Lacy sprang for pizza for lunch, and they ate the hot slices of pie around the big smiles on their faces.

At about three that afternoon City Councilman Reynard Parker stormed into Lacy's office and threw a folder down on her desk. "Did you write this?" he demanded.

She checked out his angry round face for a moment, then picked up the folder and leafed through the pages. It was a copy of her Blight Court presentation. "Yes, my staff and I put this together. Is there a problem?"

"Yes. Under whose authority did you do this?"

"The mayor requested projects for the upcoming budget, so I gave him one."

"This is a waste of taxpayer money."

Lacy remained calm. "How so?"

"This will do nothing but harass small businesses."

"Only if they're breaking the law, councilman."

"Is the mayor so hard-up for funds that he's now targeting small businesses with petty fines?"

"That is not the intent." Lacy wondered what this was really about. She didn't know much about Parker other than that he opposed all of the mayor's initiatives and had ties to the waste hauling interests in the area. "People who poison the city, or refuse to keep up their property, or don't answer summons, are the only people being targeted."

His brown face was grim. "Well, I don't like it, and I'm going to do everything in my power to stop it!"

"That's your choice, sir, but I'd hope you'd wait for it to be implemented before condemning it."

He snatched up the report. "This is not good for the businesses of my constituents. You're new here, aren't you?"

"Yes, I am."

"Then you need to learn the rules before getting into the game. You'll be hearing from me."

And he left.

Lacy realized she was shaking.

A wide-eyed Ida rushed in. "What happened?"

"I don't know, but I think I just made an enemy."

Five

Drake's meeting with the governor took up most of the afternoon, but before he could leave the capital he had to meet with a few of the Detroit legislators. By the time he and Malcolm finally headed back to Detroit for the last meeting of the day, he was running late.

When he entered the large conference room of Chandler Works, the lights were already dimmed and the members of NIA were seated around the table waiting for the slide show to begin. NIA was Drake's brain child. When he first became mayor, the city had been so overrun with drug-related violence that every time he picked up a newspaper or turned on the nightly news, there were stories of death. Because the country had spent billions fighting drugs in the major cities with only minimal results, Drake decided to try a different and yes, controversial approach. That approach was NIA, which in Swahili, means purpose, and Drake's purpose at the time had been to rid his beloved city of the drugs and its ancillary pestilence by any means necessary. It was an ongoing battle. They'd had success on some fronts and were still knocking on closed doors on others, but Drake refused to give up.

Relieved that the briefing hadn't started, he quickly found a chair in the back and tossed his overcoat onto the empty chair in front on him. The first slide came up. The color shot was of a middle-age Black man Drake didn't recognize.

"This is Lloyd Wheeler. For the past ten years he was the accountant at Parker Environmental, City Councilman Reynard Parker's company. For the past six months Wheeler has been feeding info on Parker to our friends over in the Federal Building."

The voice of the narrator belonged to Drake's half brother, Mykal Chandler, the no nonsense CEO of the architectural firm Chandler Works and the titular head of NIA. Myk stood then, and Drake could see his tall frame in the light of the projector.

"According to Wheeler," he continued, "Parker has been using his trash haulers to distribute drugs. That was verified this afternoon. One of his trucks was stopped by the border patrol at the Ambassador Bridge which connects Detroit to Windsor, Ontario. The agents found thirty-five trash bags of pot, or roughly about a thousand pounds."

Somebody whistled.

"The driver's in custody, but he's asked for a

lawyer, so we have to wait and see if he implicates his boss."

A woman seated in front of Drake interrupted. "How much more information does this Wheeler have? Various agencies have been trying to nail Parker for years."

"No idea, because Mr. Wheeler went missing a few days ago."

Drake asked, "Do we think he's missing or dead?"

"Unfortunately it may be the latter," his brother responded. "His wife has filed a missing persons report. For the moment, the feds are treating the disappearance as a missing persons case. She's agreed to let them look at his home computer, and they'll probably want to do the same for the one in his office."

"What's Parker saying?"

"He's been talking back and forth with Wheeler's wife, offering to help her look for him, telling her not to worry because he's sure her husband will show up."

"Are we looking at him as a suspect?"

"Yep, but proving he's responsible is going to be the hard part. Especially with no corpse."

Drake asked, "You'll keep us posted?"

Myk nodded.

Drake wondered if Parker knew about the Wheeler partnership with the feds and had him killed because of it. He wouldn't be surprised. He also wouldn't be surprised if indicting Parker took a long time. The man was smart; too smart, it seemed. He was shaping up to be NIA's most challenging foe since the deadly Clark Nelson, who had been a major player in the

Midwest drug rings. That case ended with Myk's wife, Sarita, being shot and Nelson killed. Sarita had been hospitalized for weeks but made a full recovery.

Myk closed down the discussion on Parker, then reported on some of the other investigations NIA was involved in. One that caught Drake's attention was a request from Adam Gary, an old friend of his from med school. Gary was now a celebrated metallurgist working on a revolutionary polymetal that had the Defense Department salivating over the metal's unique properties. Apparently, the Defense Department wasn't the only group interested. According to Myk, a few weeks ago Adam Gary had almost been abducted in Madrid after giving a lecture on his preliminary findings. The DOD wanted him protected until he finished his final analyses and they took possession of the prototype.

Myk opened the floor for comments, and Drake asked, "How about sending Max Blake?"

"Is she back from the Middle East?" someone asked.

No one knew. Maxine Blake was one of their best operatives. They decided to check on her status, and if she was available send her to protect the scientist. After that, the discussion moved to the next item on the agenda.

An hour later the meeting ended and Drake and Mykal were the only ones left in the room. Like their third half brother, Saint, they shared the same father but had been raised apart. Growing up, though, Myk and Drake spent summers together in Louisiana with their paternal grandmother. They hadn't known about Saint until a few years ago.

"So," Drake asked, "how's the little mama?"

Sarita was due to deliver in September. "She's doing fine. Me, I'm a basket case," he admitted as he put away the projector.

"Why?"

"I worry about her 24/7."

"Pregnancy is a natural thing."

"Maybe for women."

Drake grinned. "How are the Lamaze classes coming?"

Myk shrugged. "Okay I guess. I just hope I remember what I'm supposed to do."

"You'll be okay. Older men than you have come through it."

Myk shot Drake a look.

Drake just grinned.

Myk said, "Speaking of old men, what is this about you and Burton running some poor woman off the road?" He began gathering up his papers and reports and sticking them in a black leather briefcase.

Drake told him the story.

"Is she gonna sue?" Myk asked.

"I don't think so, but man . . ."

Myk looked into his brother's eyes. "What?"

"She is so fine."

Myk chuckled. "Oh, really."

"Yes, Lord, but getting her to talk to me is like trying to put shoes on an orca."

Myk's handsome face showed his smile. "Any

woman who can resist His Fineness is one I want to meet. Wait until I tell Sarita."

It was Drake's turn to shoot Myk a look.

"Wait until I tell Sarita and our little brother," Myk teased.

Not sure he liked being teased, and hoping to turn the conversation to something else, Drake asked, "Speaking of little brother, how're Saint and Narice doing?"

"She hasn't put him out yet, so I guess they're doing okay. Last I heard, they were looking at a villa in Tahiti."

"Tahiti?"

Myk shrugged. "You know Saint. But he promised they'll be here for Gran's birthday party next month."

Gran was their father's mother and the woman who had raised Myk from infancy.

Myk added, "If you can get that woman to talk to you, you should bring her along as your date. Can't wait to meet her."

"I'll bet."

Myk laughed. "Have you had dinner?"

"Nope."

"Sarita's making jambalaya."

Drake paused a moment. "Let's see, Sarita's jambalaya or pizza? Hmm."

Myk grinned. "Get your coat and let's go."

Drake didn't have to be told twice.

After sending Malcolm home, Drake joined his brother for the ride to Indian Village, where Myk and

Sarita lived. "How old is Gran going to be?" he asked.

Myk shrugged. "Two hundred."

Drake laughed. "She's going to get you for that."

"Only if you tell her. Which you probably will."

They shared a look. Myk had amusement in his eyes.

Drake asked, "You're never going to forgive me, are you?"

"Nope," and he chuckled. "You cost me a night with Charlene Reynolds."

"Yeah, yeah," Drake replied, unimpressed. "You were what, twelve that summer?"

"Thirteen."

"Charlene the Bed Queen would've *hurt* your skinny little thirteen-year-old behind."

"Maybe, but thanks to you, we'll never know."

The story revolved around Myk's attempt to sneak fifteen-year-old Charlene into his bedroom one night, only to have the eleven-year-old Drake rat him out to their grandmother. Myk stayed mad at Drake for the rest of the summer.

"I wonder what happened to her?" Drake asked.

Myk looked over. "No idea."

Drake thought back on the well-built Charlene. "Hindsight? She was fine."

"Oh, now you admit it?" Myk laughed accusingly.

"Chalk it up to me being young. I was eleven. Didn't care a thing about girls."

"I know," Myk answered sagely.

An amused Drake settled back and watched the streets go by.

Reynard Parker wasn't happy. In addition to having to hold the hand of the Wheeler's clueless wife, one of his haulers had been busted by the feds, and now the driver was in jail and the truck and its load impounded. Parker used his well-paid blond lawyer to disavow any knowledge of the hidden contraband. He also promised to help the authorities with their investigation. He looked at his watch: 10:00 P.M. Where the hell was Fish? He had paged him over an hour ago, and so far Fish hadn't called him back. *Probably between some woman's legs,* Parker groused inwardly. He needed Fish to pay a visit to the jailed driver and let him know he'd be taken care of as long as he kept his mouth shut.

Ten minutes later the phone rang. It was Fish, and from the sounds in the background, he was at a club. The high-pitched laugh of women competed with the sounds of tinkling glasses and thumping music blaring over speakers. Parker shouted over the din, "When are you coming in?"

Fish yelled back in a slightly slurred voice, "Come in for what?"

"Something's gone down that we need to discuss."

"Can't it wait until tomorrow?"

"If it could've, I wouldn't have called you now."

"Okay, let me say 'bye to the ladies and I'll be right there."

He never showed.

By 2:00 A.M., Parker had come to a decision. Fish had become unreliable, and an unreliable team player was a potential liability. He was too old to have his ship sunk by a fish-eyed fool who couldn't keep his pants on. Sooner or later—more than likely sooner—Fish, in his effort to impress one of the topless dancers or streetwalkers he couldn't seem to resist, was going to give up some vital information about his business, and who knew what might happen next. The incident with the pole dancer and the briefcase was a prime example. Women made Fish careless, and Parker knew that in his business, such carelessness could get a man fifteen to twenty years in the state prison. "And I'm not going down like that," he said aloud. Not after all he'd done.

He hoped Fish had had fun tonight, because if he had his way, it would be Fish's last. Parker picked up the phone to make the call, then set the phone back in the cradle. With the accountant Wheeler supposedly missing, it wouldn't look good to have another employee disappear. Even though Fish had no immediate family, he had friends on the street, and having him suddenly vanish might bring more scrutiny. It would be better to postpone Fish's fate. Only fools rush in, or so the song went, and Reynard Parker had never been a fool.

His encounter with the Green woman had also tested his patience, but he didn't think he'd have any trouble making her see the light. The last thing he and his constituents needed were more inspectors nosing around in their business. According to the report,

Green was recommending six new people be hired. Fines for citations topped out at fifty grand and she wanted to put citizens and environmental representatives on the hearing board. No, she had to be schooled before this idea became a reality. He had enough on his plate; he didn't need a tree hugger complicating his life.

Drake was in the office Saturday morning trying to catch up on the never ending paperwork that went with being mayor. His plan was to get as much of it off his desk as he could in the four or five hours he and Rhonda planned on being around, so he'd have less to face come Monday morning. Tonight he had a formal event to attend at the Charles H. Wright African American Museum—a scholarship fundraiser for one of the city's high schools—and he was looking forward to it. Right now there were papers to be signed, contracts to scrutinize, and City Council minutes to read and review. But the sun was shining, it was April warm, and just like a kid, he wanted to be outside. He thought about cruising over to Belle Isle and taking in the fresh air off the river. He thought about driving over to his sister's and taking the kids for ice cream. He thought about a lot of things that had nothing to do with being cooped up inside on a gorgeous Saturday morning, but he had work to do, so he dove in.

But he couldn't concentrate. The sunshine kept calling, and his mind kept turning to other things, like Lacy Green. He swung his chair around and faced the window that looked out onto Jefferson Avenue and the sunlight playing on the river. The memory of how soft her skin had been was still a vivid one. Had Rhonda not interrupted, who knew where that short moment in time might have taken them? It was not like him to be so obsessed with a woman. Usually, if a woman didn't want to be with him, he'd shrug it off and move on. Not this time. He thanked the brother above for giving the lovely Lacy such an impressive brain, because had she not come up with the proposal, he might never have been given the opportunity to know her better.

He turned back to his computer and brought up Google. He typed in Lacy's name and hit *Enter*. Drake knew searching her out on the Net wasn't a very gentlemanly thing to do, but he wanted to know as much as about her as he could before starting his campaign to woo her, as Uncle Burton was famous for saying. Drake didn't really expect the search to turn up anything, so when hundreds of hits came up, he stared, amazed, then began to read.

The articles tied to Lacy proved to be real interesting. No wonder she was so standoffish. If the info was accurate, she had good reason. She'd been married to Wilton Cox, and their divorce had been all over the Atlanta papers. Drake had met Wilton Cox a few years back at an NAACP fund-raiser in D.C. The man had been so full of himself Drake had politely excused himself from the conversation and did his best to avoid Cox for the rest of the evening. Cox was one of those men whose view of himself and his own importance far outweighed anything else. The man was a legend in his own mind, as his mother was known to say. *What in the world had Lacy been thinking, to marry such an arrogant SOB?* There were no answers in the hits on Google, but he did find another interesting fact. Her mother was the well-known artist Valerie Garner Green. Unlike most artists, who operate in only one field, Lacy's mother was known for creating in a variety of mediums. Watercolors, oils. Jewelry. She even sculpted. Many of her pieces were on loan to elite museums all over the country. Drake was impressed. Although he'd never met Mrs. Garner Green, he was aware of her celebrity status. *So, she's Lacy's mama,* he thought. He wondered if Lacy had inherited any of her mother's talent. Again, he had no answers, but thanks to Google, he knew a lot more about Lacy than he had before.

When Rhonda walked in with a small stack of papers, he looked up. "Her mother is Valerie Garner Green."

"Whose mother?" Rhonda asked, setting the paper on his desk.

"Lacy's."

"Valerie Garner Green, the artist?"

"Yeah."

"Are you smitten with Ms. Lacy?" Rhonda asked slyly.

"Smitten?"

"Yes, like—"

"I know what smitten means, Rhon. It's just not a word you hear this side of the nineteenth century."

She smiled. "'*Smitten*' is the Word of the Day on my calendar."

"Ah," he said, understanding now.

"So, are you?"

"I think I am, but the verdict's still out on her."

Rhon looked impressed. "Really? I like her already."

He gave her a look.

"Hey, any woman who can be around you and still remember her name is my kind of girl."

"Don't you have something to do?"

"Yep, but teasing you is much more fun."

He grinned and pointed to his glass doors. "Out."

The amused Rhonda went.

During Lacy's Cleopatra hiatus after the accident, she decided the time had come to break down and buy some furniture. She'd seen apartments of poor college students with more furnishings than one yellow chair, so she and her credit card went shopping by phone and on the Net. This morning it began arriving.

For her living room, she'd ordered a leather couch in a color the website called "warm vanilla butter," and when the delivery truck showed up promptly at 8:00 A.M., the leather was soft as butter to her admiring touch. The dining room set, courtesy of a sale on Pier One's website, arrived at nine-thirty. For the rest of the morning various odds and ends she'd ordered came to the door, and by late that Saturday afternoon, Lacy was seated on her vanilla butter couch admiring the way her once empty apartment had come alive. She had a couple of lamps, a coffee table, and two end tables. Her mother had already promised to ship her some of the art Lacy had stored at home, and when it arrived, her furnishings would be complete. None of the objects were heirlooms, by any means, but they were comfortable and, more important, affordable for a girl who worked a nine-to-five. She also had a place for Drake to sit and eat when she invited him over for dinner. It been in her thoughts off and on ever since that close encounter in his boardroom. Had Rhonda not appeared, would the moment have led to a kiss? It certainly felt that way, and even now, a day later, Lacy could still feel how thick the air had been and the fleeting weight of his finger across her cheek. In reality, it made no sense to keep fighting the feeling. It wasn't as if the man was an ogre, smelled bad or had some other obvious physical flaw. She knew he was intelligent, witty and had shown her nothing but concern since the accident. He was also supporting her programs. She had no reason not to have dinner with him, but she wanted it on her terms. That way, she could enjoy his company and not wind up losing her heart to a man rumored to be the ultimate collector.

The last person Drake wanted to see when he walked into the museum for the scholarship gala was Lola Draper, but there she stood, holding court in a too tight black gown that let folks know she was no longer the svelte young woman who'd represented the state in the Miss America pageant back in the eighties. Lola was also daughter of one of the city's first elected Black city councilmen. Politics was in her blood, but she had a habit of backing the wrong horse. She also had a habit of drinking too much. As her eyes caught his through the crowd, Drake could see that hers were already glassy and red. He made a point of heading to the other side of the packed room. He didn't need any drama from her tonight. Spying the museum's new female director, he went to say hello.

On the way, he nodded greetings and shook hands with the area's movers and shakers. He made a special point to stop and speak to as many of the high school students and their parents in attendance as he could and offer congratulations. He even posed for a few pictures taken by proud parents. He enjoyed this part of being mayor.

After spending a few minutes with the director. Drake and the rest of the attendees moved to the big hall set up for the dinner. Before he had a chance to scope out his seat, Reynard Parker, dressed in a well-tailored tux, walked over.

"Councilman Parker. Where's your lovely wife?"

"Mexico."

"Ah."

They both nodded at the people flowing around them, then Parker asked with a cold smile, "What do you know about this new program coming out of the Environmental Office?"

Drake didn't think now was the time. "How about we talk on Monday? This isn't the place."

"Fine, but I'm letting you know right off the bat that I'm opposed."

Drake didn't ask for whys, he'd hear them soon enough. "Thanks for letting me know. Enjoy your dinner." And he went to find his table.

On the way, he made a discreet call to his brother. "Hey. Parker's here. The crew has maybe an hour. The wife's in Mexico." He ended the call and pocketed the phone.

On the ride home after the dinner, Drake sat in the darkened back seat of the limo. He hadn't heard back from Myk on how the covert search of Parker's home had gone, but he had no doubts they'd gotten in and out successfully. The mission was nothing more than a preliminary search to learn the layout of the place, get a look at the security system, and pinpoint items like safes, computers, and any other items that might be of interest if a legal search needed to be conducted. A few years back, when NIA's focus had been on bringing down suburban drug importers, the organization had relied on the small group of day workers and gardeners in the NIA ranks for inside info on the interiors and alarm systems of their wealthy employers' residences. Parker and his wife didn't employ any full-time or part-time help at their home, so a NIA squad had been dispatched to take a quick look around. Drake hadn't been sure Parker would be in attendance tonight, but he'd told Myk to expect a call if he showed, and to put the squad on alert.

He hoped they'd uncovered something. Parker needed to be brought to justice, and Wheeler's family deserved closure.

Drake had just gotten into bed when his phone rang.

Mykal. "How was the dinner?"

"Not bad. How was your adventure?"

"Not bad."

"Any gold?"

"Some. Not enough to stake a claim, but we might hit the mother lode if we keep digging."

Drake was pleased. "Good. Kiss Little Mama for me, and I'll swing by tomorrow after church."

"Will do."

Drake set the phone on the nightstand, then drifted off to sleep.

On Monday morning, Lacy drove the rental car to work. Although she'd healed enough to trade in her crutches for a cane, she still had to wear sneakers because her ankle didn't like real shoes. It also protested every time she pressed down on the accelerator or brake pedal, but she gritted her teeth and drove downtown. Her insurance company had totaled out the Escort, so now all she had to do was wait for their check and go buy a new car.

Janika was at her desk with her computer booted up when Lacy entered the office. "Hey Lacy, how's the ankle?"

Leaning on the cane, Lacy smiled. "It's coming along. How was your weekend?"

"Got my nails done," Janika replied proudly, showing off the hot pink acrylic tips accented with a thin swirl of rhinestone glitter. "Had more baby-daddy drama too."

Twenty-two-year-old Janika had a four-year-old daughter named Lisa. Samuel Kane was Lisa's father. Although Lacy had never met the man, Janika's stories were enough to convince Lacy that Janika's old high school sweetheart was now a twenty-something jerk. Even though Samuel had made it quite clear he wasn't going to marry Janika, he didn't want her seeing anyone else either.

Janika continued tightly, "If my mama would stay out of my business, this might get settled. But no. She has to tell him where I'm going, who I'm with, then his silly behind shows up on my dates and clowns."

Janika's mama, Thelma, was crazy about Samuel and always had been. Janika had had many arguments with her mother about the meddling, but Thelma wouldn't stop.

"So what happened?" Lacy asked.

"He showed up at Lisa's birthday party Friday night, drunk, loud, and acting stupid, so Rick asked him to leave."

Rick Stowe, Janika's new boyfriend, was a city cop. "So did he?"

"No. He wanted to fight."

"What?"

"Yeah. And as soon as he threw the first punch, Rick took him down. Samuel's been in jail all weekend."

"Maybe he'll learn this time."

Janika didn't look convinced. "Rick wants to press

charges, and that's fine with me. I just hope my baby girl doesn't grow up to have her daddy's stupid genes."

Lacy chuckled, then used the cane to help her cross the remaining distance to her office.

Six

When Lacy was first hired, one of the ideas she discussed with the director of Public Works centered around getting the city's block clubs and neighborhood associations to buy into an Environmental Watch program. In her opinion, the more eyes the city had on the problem, the better. Though citizens were already reporting environmental crimes like illegal dumping, Lacy was convinced that the city could help the residents do more. Pole-mounted cameras had been put up by a previous city administration to monitor areas known for illegal dumping. In the years since—and when the cameras were working—numerous illegalities had been caught on tape, but with the slap-on-the-wrist punishments the city was known to give, the cameras might as well have been filming the new polar bear exhibit at the Detroit Zoo. Lacy wanted to get all the cameras working and to use the tapes to help the magistrates when her proposed Blight Court was ready to go. She also wanted to hand out disposable cameras to the neighborhood groups so that residents could take pictures too.

Unfortunately, there was no extra money in the budget for the disposable cameras, but last week she'd signed a work order for the repairs on the pole cameras, so one out of two wasn't bad. Having her Blight Court proposal approved was also a victory. Councilman Parker's visit to her office on Friday still concerned her, though. She had no idea why he was so upset about the implementation of a program that could be beneficial to the city's health. He'd given every indication that he would be back, and she was not looking forward to it.

After lunch, Lacy and her staff went about preparing the handouts she'd be passing out at the meetings with the block clubs to promote the Environmental Watch program. The first meeting was slated for later in the week at the Northwest Activities Center. Although she'd made numerous calls to the major camera manufacturers, so far not one was willing to donate their disposable products for the campaign. She refused to be discouraged, however. She wondered if the mayor had any ideas, and decided that even if he didn't, he might like to have that dinner he'd been campaigning to have with her.

She picked up the desk phone and called upstairs. Rhonda Curry answered and sent the call right through.

The mayor came on a heartbeat later. " 'Morning, Ms. Green."

His phone voice was as sexy as it was in person. "Good morning, Mayor Randolph," she said. "How are you?"

"Better now that I'm talking to you."

It was an old player line, but he said it as if he'd invented it. He then asked, "How's the ankle?"

"Healing. I've traded the crutches for a cane."

"You'll be Ballrooming in no time."

"I don't know about all that," she responded with amusement, "but I'm doing okay."

"Did you call just so I could hear your sweet voice, or is this business?"

His sensual tone forced Lacy to take a calming breath so she could answer. "Business. I'd like to talk to you about buying cameras for the Environmental Watch program."

"That doesn't sound like much fun."

"How about talking over dinner?"

"Just the two of us?"

"Yes."

"When and where?"

"Tomorrow evening. My place."

He was silent for so long, Lacy asked, "Are you still there?"

"Yeah. You caught me by surprise. Your place?"

"Yes," she answered, her voice softening. "What time is good for you?"

"I'm free tomorrow evening, so whatever is good for you."

"Let's make it seven then."

"Seven it is."

For a moment there was a thick silence, as if they both wanted to say more. Lacy finally asked, "Is there anything you're allergic to?"

"Just bad cooking."

"Then we should be fine."

"Can I bring anything?"

"How about some wine?"

"Will do.

"See you then."

" 'Bye baby."

That last part made her senses ring. Her hand was trembling when she put down the phone.

Up on the mayor's floor, Rhonda walked into Drake's office carrying two documents that needed his signature. She found him leaning back in his chair. The broad smile plastered on his face made her stop and ask warily, "What's the matter?"

"Nothing. Why?"

"You have that pleased male look on your face."

"Ah. Lacy's invited me to dinner."

"Well now. When?"

"Tomorrow. Seven. Her place."

"Her place? Whoa. This is moving along."

"Yes, it is."

"Well, bring your A game, Mr. Mayor. Ms. Lacy doesn't impress me as your usual conquest."

"No, she isn't, and I think that's part of the reason I'm attracted to her. I don't meet many challenging women."

"You're right. Most of them start licking your shoes two seconds after giving up their name and number."

He laughed. "You're a cold sister."

"But a truthful one, which is one of the many reasons why you keep me around."

"If you say so."

Rhonda got his signature. As she walked out, Drake went back to smiling and thinking about Tuesday evening.

Tuesday evening, Drake looked at his watch. If he didn't leave his office in the next three minutes, he would be late for his dinner with Lacy, but City Councilwoman Lola Draper kept talking. She didn't know about his evening plans, and if she did, she wouldn't have cared. Her only concern was getting him straight on how he ought to be running the city. He'd invited her up to his office over an hour ago, hoping to find some common ground on their differences, but his olive branch wasn't working, mainly because she wasn't interested in common ground. Right now, she was telling him why his pick for superintendent wouldn't fly.

"Denise Shaw is not the person we need for the schools," she told him haughtily, "and if it comes up for a vote, I'm voting her down. Then I'll make sure the rest of the council does the same."

Drake held onto his temper. "And as I said, I'll take your opinion under advisement. I haven't decided who's going to get the job, one way or the other. Now, I really—"

"The last time she had the job, she was rude and—"

"I have another meeting."

Lola looked at her watch. "I only have a few more things to discuss."

Rhonda opened the door and stuck her head in. She had Drake's coat over her arm. "Your car's waiting, Mayor Randolph."

Though the interruption had been preplanned, Drake still could have kissed his assistant. "Thanks, Rhonda. Lola, it's been good talking to you."

"We're not done," she said emphatically. Had she been standing she would have stomped her foot like a spoiled child.

Drake went to the door and took his coat from Rhonda. He then told Lola, "Leave the rest of your concerns with Ms. Curry. I'll get back to you."

If anyone wondered why the mayor was running to the elevator, no one asked.

Lacy took one last look around her apartment. Everything was ready: the table was set, the bread was in the oven, she was dressed, and now she just had to wait for him to arrive. She was nervous. She told herself to calm down. Drake might be the mayor but he was still just a man. *Right!* she corrected herself sarcastically. According to Janika, the man had dated everything from beauty queens to movie stars, and now he seemed to be interested in a skinny, dark-skinned girl who used to wear Coke-bottle glasses. The butterflies in her stomach were flapping in hyperdrive.

The door buzzer blared. Forcing herself to be calm, she went over to the intercom. "Who is it?"

"Me. Drake."

"Come on up." She hit the buzzer and took another deep breath.

She opened the door to his firm knock. Seeing him standing there in his gray suit, and with that patented boyish smile on his face, all she could think was how absolutely gorgeous he was. "How are you?" She stepped back to let him in.

"Doing good," he said, entering. "Smells good in here."

He gave her the wine.

"Thanks. I'll take this in the kitchen."

Once there, Lacy took in yet another breath before sticking the bottle into the ice bucket. *Lordy!*

"You got furniture?"

"Yep," she called back. "Needed something for you to sit on if I was having you over for dinner."

Next thing she knew, he was in the kitchen, standing close enough for her to smell his cologne. His scent was becoming as familiar to her as her own signature scent. Lacy looked up into his eyes and saw both interest and amusement. To give herself something to do besides be overwhelmed, she opened the oven door to check on the twin loaves of French bread.

Drake liked the view. She had on a flirty little black skirt that outlined the tantalizing curve of her sweet behind. The skinny knit top was short-sleeved and had a low scoop neckline. There were two delicate gold chains around her neck, gold hoops in her ears, and matching bangles on her right wrist. When she straightened and closed the door, his eyes were drawn down her shapely body to the black satin slippers on her feet, and then to the brown medical wrap on her right ankle.

"Thanks for the invitation," Drake told her while admiring her hair and her beautiful ebony face. He found it hard to just stand there politely looking at her when what he wanted to do was find out if her lips were as soft as they appeared.

"You're welcome."

"So you've been planning to have me over for a while?"

"No, just since Saturday," Lacy tossed back lightly, "when the furniture was delivered."

"So much for me being irresistible."

She laughed. "Bread will be ready in a few. Then we can eat. How about we go sit down?"

"Lead the way."

As she did, the sway of her skirt teased Drake's eyes.

He sat on her new couch. "I like this."

She took a seat on the yellow chair. "Thanks. The place is starting to look like a home instead of just an apartment."

"Yes it is."

Silence crept in between them. Lacy kept shooting quick little glances his way, only to find his eyes waiting to meet hers each time. He looked very comfortable sitting on her couch. She, on the other hand, was trying to breathe slowly and not act like the nervous wreck she felt inside.

He said, "So. Here we are."

"Yep," Lacy replied, in an effort to sound nonchalant.

Drake sensed her nervousness. In spite of his cool exterior, he was too. He wasn't sure why, but being here with her made him feel like a sixteen-year-old in a too small suit on his first date. "Can't remember the last time a date gave me a case of the butterflies."

Lacy was glad to hear that. "I thought it was just me."

"No."

Their smiles met.

"Then, just so you'll know—I don't bite. Well, maybe sometimes."

He cocked his head and studied her.

She smiled serenely.

"Are you flirting with me, Ms. Green?"

"I'm not sure. It's been a while since I've been on a date. My flirt game's kinda rusty."

"Doesn't sound rusty to me. In fact," he said, enjoying her, "I think this is going to be a real interesting evening."

"I think you might be right." Lacy had never considered herself a flirt, but he seemed to be opening places in her that released a woman she didn't really know. "How about some music?"

"Sure."

She walked over to her small system and looked through her CDs. She could feel his eyes on her every move. She held up one of her favorites. "Boney James?"

"You like jazz?" Drake asked, impressed. He got up

and joined her, then checked out her collection. "Beethoven?" he asked, holding up the CD.

"I listen to a little of everything. That's one of the great things about your fair city, Mister Mayor."

"What is?"

"The music. It's 24/7, and you can get everything from classical to jazz to classic rock, to old school, to techno. I've never lived anyplace that jams like Detroit."

"We are Motown. The more music, the better."

Then, just like in his conference room, time seemed to slow and they found themselves caught up in the sight, scents, and nearness of each other. Unable to resist, Drake reached out and slowly traced a finger over the dark satiny skin of her cheek.

In response, Lacy's eyes closed and her inner woman began to quake.

Drake whispered, "How about we get this first one out of the way. . . ."

Lacy didn't pretend not to know what he was asking. Anticipation filled her. Trembling, she let him kiss her, and she went weak inside. As the warmth rose and the heat of their bodies mingled, she kissed him back, moving her hand up to his clean-shaven cheek. He drew her in closer and the kiss deepened. She thought she'd wanted to keep him at a distance—after all, she'd known him less than two weeks—but she was wrong. No kiss had ever filled her this way. No man had ever held her so tenderly yet possessively. Just when she thought she might drown in the new, rising sensations, he reluctantly and slowly drew away.

Her eyes were closed and her legs were like jelly. "Glad we got that out of the way," she whispered.

"Me, too." Now that Drake had the taste of her on his lips, he wanted more.

Her eyes met his. Seeing the humor in her gaze, he decided then and there that if he had to walk through hell in gasoline drawers, this woman was going to be his. "I want to kiss you again."

Lacy was still trying to recover from the first one. She turned away and began looking at CDs. "We're supposed to be picking out music."

He fit himself behind her and slipped his arms around her waist. The warmth of him against her back sent her senses spinning.

"I know," he confessed against her ear, "but kissing you is far more exciting."

She turned and looked up. "Are you always so tempting?"

"Depends on the situation."

"Anybody ever tell you you're too good-looking for your own good?"

He reached out and languidly traced the curves of her mouth. "Anyone ever tell you you were a challenge, Lacy Green?"

Her singed lips parted passionately. "No."

"Well, you are."

Lacy wondered if this man was some kind of alien. No earthborn brother had such a dazzling touch. The contact was like being shocked with short, pleasure-filled pulses of electricity. *Reason number fifty-seven why women went gaga over him*, she thought.

Watching her lips part in response to his slow touch, Drake's groin tightened at the thought of making love to her, slowly and totally. He knew it wouldn't be tonight, but for her, he could wait.

Lacy fought through the haze surrounding her and finally asked, "Why am I a challenge?"

"Because you're not only fine, you're smart."

"Smart?"

"Yes," he said in a voice that caressed her from her twists to her toes. "I think brainy women are very sexy."

"I've never had a man lust after my mind before."

"Then you've been hanging around the wrong men."

The frankness in his eyes shook her senses again, and it came to her that he was way more dangerous than she'd initially believed. The smells of the bread wafted past her nose, and she was glad for the momentary distraction, if only so she could pull herself back together. "Bread's done. Ready to eat?"

"I suppose."

Truthfully, Lacy didn't want to end the moment either, but knew if she didn't put some distance between herself and this man, she was going to melt into a puddle on the floor.

Drake said to her, "I'll put the CD in, wash my hands, and meet you at the table."

She nodded. And as she walked away, he watched the sway of her hips with appreciative eyes.

The bold yellow and orange tablecloth was one Lacy had purchased on a trip to Ghana a few years back. The new black plates on top of it were gleaming, as were the glasses. When Drake returned from washing his hands, he took a seat, and Lacy placed the serving dishes in the center of the table. The serving dishes and platters held blackened salmon brushed with a teriyaki sauce, wild rice, a salad, and her homemade French bread.

It was Drake's experience that not many women cooked this way these days. Personally, he had trouble boiling eggs, so the sights and smells of what she'd prepared added yet another intriguing facet to the dark-skinned jewel seated on the other side of the table. "This looks good."

"Hope you're hungry."

"I am."

In his eyes Lacy read more than a hunger for food, and he didn't hide it from her at all. Her core tightened as if answering his unspoken desire. "Would you bless the food?"

"Sure."

He recited a short blessing, then after their "Amens," they helped themselves to the meal.

In the background the saxophone of Boney James played softly and sweetly. Drake couldn't believe how good the food was. His mother could burn, and so could his sister-in-law, Sarita, but Lacy had stuck her toe in this. The salmon was succulent, the wild rice perfect, and the bread? He couldn't get enough of the hot fresh loaf. "You made this?"

Lacy looked up from her plate. "Yep. My mother

said every woman should know how to make bread, so she taught me."

"A man could get fat hanging out with you."

She laughed softly. "If there's any bread left, I'll let you take it home."

"Thanks."

They were both aware of the attraction humming like electricity between them and that it was difficult to ignore. Drake found himself watching her graceful table manners and speculating on when he might kiss her again. Needing to distract himself from his rising desire, he forked up a bit more of the tasty blackened salmon, then said to her, "Talk to me about these cameras."

So she did, and when she finished, she added, "There's no money in our budget to buy disposable cameras so I was hoping you had a few ideas?"

"Not off of the top of my head," he said truthfully, "but I'll have Rhonda look into it. I'm pretty sure there was a similar campaign a few years back. Maybe someone will know how the city acquired the cameras."

"I'd really appreciate the help. My first meeting is the day after tomorrow."

"How many people are you expecting?"

"Hopefully, a lot."

He looked skeptical. "Don't be discouraged if only a few show. The environment is important but it's not a hot button issue in the city right now."

"With the lead paint problems and the results of the new asthma studies, it should be."

"What asthma studies?"

"The ones tracking the startling spike in asthma in inner city kids. I'll send it to you in the morning."

"Appreciate it." Drake then asked a question he'd been wanting answered. "What made you decide to do environmental work?"

"The Girl Scouts."

That surprised him. "Really?"

"Yep. When I was twelve, our summer camp was closed down because fertilizer and pesticides from a golf course down the road contaminated the camp's creek. I'd been going to camp there since third grade, and no one in our troop was happy when it was closed."

"So did the Scouts take them to court?"

"No, we made signs and started picketing the golf course."

Drake laughed. "What?"

"Yes. We marched. We sang."

"What did the golf course owners do?"

"Got an injunction that made us stop, but by then we were rolling. We wrote letters to everybody we could. The governor. President Reagan. We called radio stations and television reporters. We even made buttons with pictures of sad-faced Girl Scouts on them to sell to the public and get them involved."

Drake was impressed. "You all were serious."

"As a heart attack."

"So did it finally get resolved?"

"Sort of. The course owners were fined, but the camp couldn't be used anymore. The judge ordered the owners to buy the Scouts some land in another part of the county. We were pretty excited because we felt we'd won. I've been hooked on environmental issues ever since."

He raised his wineglass to her in salute. "And the city of Detroit is glad about it."

The compliment brought heat to Lacy's cheeks. "I hope to be around a long time."

"That's good to know."

From the look in his eyes and the timbre of his voice, Lacy sensed he was talking about more than the job. The memory of the kiss rose again, and she forced her breathing and her heart to slow down. "If you're done, I can take your plate."

"Thanks."

She came around to where he was seated and he handed her his plate. The nearness set her blood to thumping again, but she took the dishes to the sink and set them inside.

Boney James was still playing.

"Are you ready for dessert?"

"If it's kisses, yes."

She almost swooned right there. "No. It's not kisses."

He stood and slowly walked over to where she was standing. "Why not?" His eyes were a mix of temptation and playfulness.

The shaking Lacy was finding it hard to breathe. "Because I'm making Bananas Foster instead."

"If I'm a good boy, can I have both?"

Lacy's senses spiraled like a kite. "Greedy man."

He bent down and kissed her softly, whispering, "You don't know the half of it."

The kiss that followed melted Lacy back against the hard edge of the sink, but she was too caught up in the passion to care. She slipped her arms around his waist, and the contact singed her everywhere. He held her close with one arm and used his free hand to explore the shape of her back. All the while his expert lips trailed from her mouth to the edges of her jaw, setting fires along the way. "The only dessert I want is you. . . ." he husked out against the edge of her arched throat.

Lacy was pulsating and shimmering like heat on asphalt. She'd never experienced this before. She'd been a virgin when she married Wilton Cox, and he'd convinced her that in spite of all she'd read, and all that she'd seen in the movies or on TV, *good* women didn't enjoy sex. But as Drake's kisses threatened to make her insane, and her nipples were hard and the heat between her thighs was spreading through her like warmed honey, she knew Wilton had lied. The realization made her back away so she could catch her breath.

Drake was aware of Lacy's marriage and divorce, but he tasted an innocence in her kiss that was as surprising as it was firing. When he nibbled on her ripe bottom lip or slid his tongue over the parted corners of her lips, she'd trembled like a virgin. It was easy for him to see that she was trying to compose herself. *Is she a virgin?* "If we're going too fast, tell me."

"It's not that. It's . . . Let's just say I don't have a lot of experience at this."

"Virgin?"

She shook her head, but didn't tell him that the sweet magic of his kisses made her feel like one. "Just inexperienced."

He studied her closely. "Then we can go slow," he said, easing her back in against his chest and wrapping her up with his arms. He kissed the top of her head. "As slow as you want."

Lacy could hear his heartbeat. "Thank you."

"And lucky for you, I'm an excellent teacher."

She laughed softly. "Oh, really?"

Drake looked down and once again committed her dark beauty to his memory. "The best. Would you like lessons?"

"You are a mess, do you know that?"

"It's genetic, so it's not my fault. All the men in my family have a romance bone."

Lacy knew she was about to enter a mine field, but couldn't stop herself, "A genetic romance bone?"

"Yes, it's a trait the Vachon men have."

"Is Vachon your family name?"

"Yep. My brothers and I are descendants of a man named Galen Vachon and his dark-skinned wife, Hester. She was almost as beautiful as you."

Lacy let that compliment fill her, then asked, "So tell me about this trait."

"It's a spoil-your-woman-to-death trait."

"Which makes you do what?"

"Just what it says. We spoil our women. And you didn't answer my question," he pointed out softly.

"Which question?"

"If you wanted lessons or not . . ."

Somewhere inside of Lacy a flare burst into flame, and she was instantaneously placed back in the sensual spot where this whole conversation began. The woman he'd unleashed answered for her, "How much are they?"

Drake raised an eyebrow and grinned. "For you, free."

"Are you a hard professor?" Once she heard herself, Lacy couldn't believe she'd said what she had.

The double entendre was not lost on Drake. He chuckled. "Oh, you're good, baby."

"I can't believe I said that." She looked up. "This is your fault."

He pointed to himself. "Me? You're the one asking if I'm hard or not, and the answer, Ms. Green, is hell, yes."

Embarrassed to her toes, a mortified but tickled Lacy buried her face in his shirt. "Stop it."

"You started this," he reminded her with amusement, then gathered her in against him again and said softly, "You're fun, Lacy. I like that."

She looked up. "You're fun too, Drake."

He kissed her softly, letting her know just how much he was enjoying her, then pulled back. He stared down at her silently for a moment, wondering if that was really their future he saw shining in her eyes. "CD's over," he told her, noticing the silence around them. "What do we hear next?"

She smiled and shrugged. "Let's go see."

Seven

*They decided to follow the saxo*phone of Boney James with the signature piano tunes of Joe Sample. Once the music began floating melodically through the apartment, Lacy said to Drake, "Will you come watch the sunset with me? Or is that too corny for you?"

He shook his head. "Nothing you want is corny, Lacy."

Pleased by that, she opened the big French doors and they stepped out into the fresh air of the evening. The small bricked-in balcony faced the water, giving them an unobstructed view of the sun hovering above the river like a blazing orange ball of fire. Now that they had acknowledged their attraction for each other and were cool with it, they stood side by side, leaning with their forearms on the brick in a companionable silence. Five floors below, the expansive parking lot was filled with cars and the comings and goings of the other residents, but Drake and Lacy were only conscious of the sunset and the quiet piano jazz playing behind them like their own private soundtrack. Lacy drew in deep breaths of the cool air off the river and decided life was perfect.

She looked Drake's way. He appeared deep in thought. She'd be willing to bet his boyish good looks had been driving women crazy since the day he was born, and she didn't even want to think about the dimples or that sexy moustache framing his full lips. According to Ida, Drake Randolph, with his vivid dark eyes and high wattage white-toothed smile, worked out regularly, and it showed. Not even the expensive suit could totally disguise the cut of his lean arms and shoulders. Everything about him was gorgeous, so she wondered how a woman like herself was supposed to deal with a man who claimed to have a woman-pleasing gene. *And what exactly what did that mean?*

Lacy asked, "What are you thinking?"

He grinned into her eyes. "You don't want to know."

"I do."

"Okay, I was thinking about jacking one of my brother Myk's private jets and whisking you away to a secluded island so I could spend all the time I wanted learning everything there is to know about Lacy Green."

Lacy stilled.

"And after that I'd tempt you with passion fruit and candlelight, undress you slowly and take you under the stars. . . ."

Lacy just knew she was going to faint.

He gave her a seductive wink. "Told you you didn't want to know."

She somehow managed to toss back, "I never do islands on the first date."

"I can wait."

Her heart was flying. "Is that your romance gene talking?"

"Yep."

Every inch of Lacy's body had come alive in response to his overwhelming self. Her nipples were hard, and she didn't even want to think about what was going on between her thighs. "You are way too good at this, Your Honor."

"I know."

Lacy chuckled and shook her head.

He had playfulness in his eyes, but beneath it there was an intensity that touched her senses like fire. It was like being near a hot stove or an open flame, both of which could be dangerous if a girl wasn't careful. Lacy found him fascinating, and tempting, and all those other *ings*. She thought being involved with him might be way over her head, but she didn't care.

The breeze lifted her perfume to Drake's nose. He couldn't remembered ever being so enchanted by a woman so quickly. In many ways it was downright scary, but not scary enough for him to back off. No, he wanted Lacy Green, and like all the Vachon men, he was looking forward to the challenge.

"Do you still want the Bananas Foster?" she asked, though all she could think about were his kisses and his island fantasy.

He turned his head her way. "As much as I'd like to say yes. I should get going."

Lacy hid her disappointment by gazing back toward the river. "Okay. Maybe next time."

He reached over and gently turned her chin back so he could see her eyes. "If I stay, I may turn this apartment into that island, and you're not ready for that. At least not yet."

She dropped her eyes for a moment. He was right, of course.

When she looked up again, he added softly, "If and when we come together, I want it to be because you want to, not because your inexperience gets the best of you. Does that make sense?"

"Yes." She reached up and placed her palm against his cheek. "You're a very special man, Drake Randolph."

He covered her hand with his, then placed a soft kiss against her palm. "Some men would probably call me stupid, but I think this is the beginning of something real special, and I don't want to mess it up just because I couldn't keep my pants zipped." The seriousness in his eyes mirrored his tone. "You and I will know when the time is right."

She offered up a little smile.

He said to her then, "My grandmother is having a

birthday party in a few weeks. Would you go with me?"

"Might be a little soon for me to meet your family."

"It's not like that. This is just my gran's party."

Lacy wondered how long his kisses would echo. "Let me think about it, okay?"

"No problem."

"Do you still want that bread?"

"Of course."

They went back inside. She wrapped the bread in a large piece of foil and handed it to him.

"Thanks."

"You're welcome."

He seemed reluctant to leave, and Lacy knew that she didn't want him to go even if it was the right thing for him to do. "I'll walk down with you."

"No. I want my visits kept just between us. Once the news gets out, you won't have any privacy." He thought about all the Google clippings of her divorce. "The guard on the gate thinks your building manager, Wanda, is one of my part-time aides, so I give him her name when I drive up."

"Very clever. Do you do this super-spy stuff often?"

"No. You're the first lady I've ever wanted to protect."

Lacy saw the truth in his eyes and felt the current that flowed between them surge. "I'm honored." And she was.

"You might not be once the press sets up in your hallway."

"I'll be okay."

"Good."

He touched her cheek tenderly, then kissed her good-bye. "See you later."

"Okay."

She walked with him to the door. They stopped. He looked down into her eyes and whispered, "One more . . ."

His lips teased themselves against hers and she didn't protest. She wanted one more too, and it was as sweet and wonderful as the rest. Then he was gone.

A dazed Lacy closed the door and then braced her back against it. She stood there for a moment remembering, pulsing, longing, then slowly melted down the wood to the floor.

In the dimly lit main office of Parker Environmental, City Councilman Reynard Parker was in a panic. According to the fax he'd received an hour ago from his new accountant, he was about to have cash flow problems. It seemed the reason his former accountant Wheeler had refused to go along with the plan to cook the books was because he'd already cooked them! The balance sheet showed a seven figure deficit that would soon start impacting his ability to meet his financial responsibilities to payroll, taxes, and all the ancillary fees that had to be paid out in order to run his business. Were Wheeler not already gull food, he would have killed him with his bare hands.

Parker threw his coffee cup against the wall. The burst of violence helped drain some of his anger. Calmer now, he sat back down at his desk and tried to figure out what to do first. First he had to cut corners. His trucks would have to start dumping a portion of the loads someplace other than the landfills. He couldn't afford to send in fully loaded trucks because he was charged by the ton. *Damn Wheeler!* The little accountant had certainly extracted his own revenge. He couldn't wait to meet the bastard in hell.

Grabbing the phone, Parker called in some of his most trusted drivers. Most of his workforce were former felons. He offered the men who were serious about staying on the right side of the law a steady job that allowed them to pay their bills, be gainfully employed, and give good reports to their parole officers. On the other hand, Parker had enough down low operations going on that the men who wanted to supplement their legitimate paychecks with side hustles were accommodated, too. The hustlers knew that if any of their outside work brought the police to his door, they'd be fired and on their own. Currently working beneath the radar were a group of drivers who sold nonshredded identity items to a bogus credit card ring operating overseas. Others cased homes for B&E specialists, and new cars and trucks for chop shop owners. They did drug drops, transported illegal immigrants, and smuggled stolen art and artifacts for a well-known, Toronto-based art dealer.

None of that mattered right now, though. What did matter was bringing all of his special drivers in for a meeting so they could discuss where and how to dump their loads. With their help, he might be able to stay above water until he could figure a way out of this mess.

* * *

By the time Drake got back to the mansion, he was kicking himself for not getting Lacy's number. He supposed he could use NIA's databases to find it, but he'd already gone behind her back and checked her out on Google, and he didn't feel good about intruding on her privacy again. Not to mention she might not take it too well if he called her up out of the blue. If he were a single female living alone, he knew that he'd want to know how he'd gotten the number. And he wouldn't be able to tell her because he couldn't tell her. Not about NIA. So he opted for seeing her at work tomorrow and getting it then. On a whim, he checked to see if her name was listed in the phone book, but like most big city single women, she wasn't.

He decided that maybe not having her number was a good thing, at least for tonight. He had a NIA meeting later, and talking to Lacy might be a distraction. He vividly remembered how much trouble Mykal had, keeping his NIA life and its secrets from his Sarita when they first got married, and how many meetings his brother had missed being "distracted" by Sarita. Drake planned to keep his secret life from Lacy for as long as necessary, because the less she knew, the better it would be for everyone involved. But he wished he'd gotten her number.

Soaking in a tub of vanilla-scented bubbles, Lacy had her cell phone in one hand and the mayor's business card in the other. He'd written his number on it the day he brought her home from the hospital, and she was debating whether to call him or not. She had intended to give him her number but had been so dazzled by the evening, she'd forgotten. Now, looking at his terrible handwriting, she couldn't decide. On one hand, dinner had been fabulous and it would take her years to forget the power of his kiss, but on the other, she didn't want him to think she was trying to be all over him, because she wasn't.

In the end she set the card and the phone on the short table beside the tub and sank back into the warmth of the water. She'd give him her number at work tomorrow. Right now she just wanted to replay everything that had happened between them, and smile.

Who knew the touch of a man could make a woman want those touches everywhere? Wilton had never spent much time on kissing or any other kind of foreplay, at least not with her. He'd saved whatever creativity he'd had in the bedroom for his many mistresses. His interactions with her had never lasted more than a few minutes because he'd been so rough and boorish on their wedding night, she came to look upon sex as a marital duty that had to be endured. Add to that his belief that wives weren't supposed to be enjoying themselves anyway and you had one mixed-up young wife.

And she'd stayed mixed up for a while. After the divorce, the few men she had relationships with found her stiff and wooden in bed. One man in particular said a dead fish was more responsive. As a consequence, Lacy had avoided intimacy, convinced her aversion to getting busy stemmed from a problem within herself.

A frank discussion with her mother put much of that insecurity to rest. Val's take on the matter pretty much mirrored Drake's. She had been hanging around the wrong men, Val said, and assured her that one day she would meet a man who would make her climb mountains for his touch. As always, Mother knew best. Drake seemed to be the *right* man, and Lacy wanted to learn everything Professor Drake had to offer, even if it meant staying after school. She laughed out loud at this new bold side of herself, then went back to the sensual memories that wouldn't leave her alone.

When Lacy came into work Wednesday morning, the dinner with Drake was still reverberating through her like the faint sensual beat of an African drum. Just the thought of him put a silly smile on her face. Not even the day's pouring rain or having to use the cane kept her from feeling particularly alive

Passing Janika, Lacy waved and went on into her own office. She was booting up her computer when a smiling and sly-looking Ida slid into her office and closed the door.

" 'Morning," Lacy said cheerily. "What's up?"

Ida took a seat and replied casually, "That's what I came to ask you."

Lacy was confused. "What do you mean?"

"You and His Fineness had dinner last night."

Lacy didn't say a word. She was too stunned. Finally, she said, "Uh, no. I heard he was in the building to see Wanda, the manager. She does some kind of secretarial work for him on the side."

Ida shook her head. "I go to church with Wanda Jean, so what's your next story?"

Lacy dropped her head to her desk and banged it softly on the edge. When she first moved to Detroit, Ida told her that everyone in Detroit was connected to everyone else in some form or fashion, and now Lacy believed her. *Her business was out in the street already!* She looked at Ida. "Who told you?"

"My cousin Remmie."

"Oh, shoot."

Ida's cousin Remmie lived across the hall from Lacy. In fact, if it hadn't been for Remmie, Lacy would never have known that the apartment was for rent. "Will she keep my secret?"

Ida laughed. "Remmie? She can't keep a secret to save her life. Always been that way, always will be that way."

"Can't you talk to her?"

"Too late. With all the people she knows through church and her volunteer work, I was surprised your date wasn't on the front page of the *Free Press* this morning."

Lacy banged her head again for a few more moments, then straightened up. "Okay. I'll just have to deal with it, I guess."

"Prepare yourself for a few pieces of hate mail too, then."

"Hate mail?"

Ida nodded. "Some of the women in this town are cuckoo for Cocoa Puffs, as we used to say back in the day. They're not going to be happy seeing you with the mayor."

"What?" Lacy asked incredulously.

"I'm not kidding. When he first got elected, women tried to break into the mansion to see him. They hid in the bushes, waited for him in the baggage claim at the airport. That's part of the reason he has the police detail with him most of the time. One crazy broad even went to the papers and said he was the father of her five kids. She was a woman from his church. Supposedly his mama took care of that one."

Lacy couldn't believe what she was hearing.

"Do you know about the magazine spread he was in?" Ida asked.

"No. When was this?"

"It was right before the election so must have been early '02."

"What was the article about?"

"It was called the 'Fifty Most Eligible Black Men on the Planet,' and His Fineness was one of them. Rhonda said he got 35,000 letters after the magazine came out."

Lacy was speechless, then asked, "Who writes to men they see in magazines?"

"At least 35,000 women do."

"Oh my goodness. Ida, that's crazy."

"That's what I'm telling you. Enjoy his company but expect the unexpected."

"Yes, Mama."

Ida smiled, then asked, "So how was the date?"

Lacy swooned against the back of her chair. "Fabulous. He is so wonderful."

"Good. I think you two will do good together."

"Why?"

"Just a feeling." Ida stood, then said, "Let me get back to my desk. If the *National Enquirer* calls, we'll tell them you're in Paris with Tupac."

Lacy laughed. "Appreciate it."

Once the silence resettled, Lacy mulled over what she'd been told. She found the 35,000 letters pretty amazing. It had never occurred to her that dating the mayor might be hazardous to her health. He had run her off the road, but that was different. Ida was convinced there were some pretty Mad Hatters out there, and Lacy knew that as crazy as the world was today, it behooved her to take Ida's warnings seriously. *Lordy!*

Lacy supposed she should call him and let him know that thanks to Ida's cousin Remmie, the cat was out of the bag.

Rhonda put her call right through.

" 'Morning, baby," he said in that sensual voice of his.

"How are you?"

"Doing okay. Thought about you after I got home. Wanted to call you but I don't have your number."

"Do you have a pencil?"

"Ready."

Lacy recited the numbers.

"Thanks," he said. "So, what's going on with you?"

"Just wanted to let you know, Ida's cousin lives across the hall and she saw you leaving my place."

"Damn. Can she keep a secret?"

"According to Ida, not even if her life depends on it."

She heard Drake sigh with frustration. "Okay," he said. "How are you feeling about maybe being on the front page?"

"I'll just deal with it. Can't do anything else."

"I'm sorry," he offered quietly.

"You don't have anything to apologize for and besides, I had a really good time."

"So did I. How about dinner at my place next time?"

"Just tell me when."

"I'll call you tonight and see what we can work out."

"I'd like that."

He then said, "Can you hold on a minute, please?"

"Sure."

She heard his muffled voice and assumed their call had been interrupted by someone wanting to discuss something with him. A few seconds later he was back, saying, "Sorry. Had to talk to Rhonda a minute."

"No problem.

"So, we agree on dinner at my place."

"We agree."

"Good. I'll call you tonight."

"Okay. 'Bye."

" 'Bye."

After she put the phone down, Lacy sighed. She now

knew what women like her mother meant by a *"dream boat."* Drake was all that and a bag of chips, too.

That night he did call. "What're you doing?" he asked.

Lacy picked up the TV remote and muted the television. "Watching a documentary on snow leopards on the National Geographic channel."

"Is it any good?"

"Yes, but I'd rather talk to you."

"Watch out. You're going to give me the big head."

"I think your head's already there. Ida told me about the magazine spread you did back in '02. Did you really get 35,000 letters?"

He laughed. "Sure did, and I've been sending them all thank-you letters."

Lacy shook her head. "That's insane. They're insane."

"Come on, now. Some of them were very nice ladies. I got pictures from Guam, France, Switzerland. I still have about five thousand to go, though. Give or take a few hundred."

Lacy was amazed. "I'm sure they all appreciate you writing back, but 35,000? I told Ida I'd never write a man in a magazine."

"Not even me?"

She laughed. "No."

"I'm hurt."

"Life is rough sometimes."

"If I were there, I'd kiss that sassy mouth of yours."

"And I'd let you."

"Be careful now. I'm only a few minutes away."

"I dare you."

He laughed then. "You dare me?"

"Yep."

"All right, Miss Girl. You're on."

And he hung up.

Lacy stared down at the phone with wide eyes. Had they been cut off? She punched his number into the phone. It rang but he didn't pick up. She lowered the phone. Was he really on his way over? She'd been kidding. It was after ten and she was in her pjs, for heaven's sake. "He wasn't serious. He's not coming here," she said to the silent apartment.

But what if he was? The thought made her giddy. Jumping up, the now grinning Lacy ran to her bedroom and struggled into a clean set of sweats, checked her hair, quickly brushed her teeth, then went back out to the snow leopards to wait.

Sure enough, fifteen minutes later the buzzer sounded. Making herself walk slow, she strolled to the intercom. "Who's there?"

"Me."

"Do I know you?" she asked saucily.

His humor-laced voice came back, "Let me up, woman. Don't make me call the fire department. I'll have a cherry picker drop me right down on your balcony."

Laughing, Lacy hit the buzzer and awaited his arrival.

When she opened the door to his knock, the smile on his face told her all she needed to know. He was dressed in a pair of jeans and a tattered Lions shirt. He closed the door behind him, then said possessively, softly, "Come here, you. . . ."

And Lacy went.

He pulled her in against him and gently held her there. Looking down into her eyes, he said, "Now, about this kiss . . ."

Lacy's eyes glowed with sensual challenge. "Took you long enough to get here."

He threw back his head and laughed. "What am I going to do with you?"

She remained silent.

"Guess this is all I have," he whispered, then lowered his head to give her the kiss they'd both been craving.

He brushed his lips over her in silent invitation, and she replied in the same wordless fashion. They teased each other with hypnotic gives and takes until they were both breathing loud and their hands began to roam. His palms burned through the thin cotton of her sweats to her skin, and she reveled in the feel of the hard smooth strength of his bare arms beneath her caressing hands.

They kissed their way across the room and then down onto the couch. He ran a worshipping hand up the outside of her thigh over her hip and up her ribs until he found a small hard-nippled breast. He nibbled at it, and Lacy arched and let out a sound of pleasure. Somewhere a phone buzzed. It was Drake's, but he chose Lacy over it and let his voice mail get it. But the buzzing came back, again and again. Finally,

Drake snatched the phone off his belt and looked at the number. Myk.

He sighed. "Sorry, baby." Then he barked into the phone, "Dammit. What?"

"Where are you?" Myk asked on the other end.

"None of your business."

"Testy, are we? Well get your mayoral behind to the meeting. We're waiting on you." Then he hung up.

Drake sank back against the couch. He turned to Lacy. The look of her passion-lidded eyes made him even harder. "I have to go. It's what I get for having so much on my plate."

"It's okay."

"No, it isn't." And it wasn't. In his eagerness to get over here and taste her sassy little mouth, he'd forgotten about tonight's eleven o'clock NIA meeting. Now he had to leave her.

Lacy understood that he had responsibilities, and for her to get upset because of it made no sense. He was the mayor, after all. She moved closer and kissed him softly. "Go take care of your business."

Resigned, Drake kissed her back so thoroughly and completely they both wished they had more time. He ended by giving her a series of short parting presses of his lips against hers before drawing away from her tempting mouth for good. He then ran a slow finger down her soft cheek. "I'll call you in the morning."

She nodded.

He kissed the tip of her nose then stood.

While Lacy watched from the couch, he left, softly closing the door behind him.

* * *

Drake walked into the conference room at Chandler Works, and the five NIA board members already at the table applauded his arrival. Embarrassed, he shook his head and took a seat.

"Glad you could make it," Myk told him.

"Just start the meeting," Drake tossed back.

So the smiling Myk did just that.

They were reviewing the video made by the crew that snuck into Parker's house on the night of the museum dinner. The only points of interest were the two safes they'd found. There was one in the basement and another built into the wall in what appeared to be the wife's bedroom. There hadn't been time to open them and search the contents. They'd save that for the next trip.

Drake asked, "Any new news on finding Wheeler?"

"Nothing new so far. The feds are going to search his computer sometime in the next few days. They're hoping it'll shed some light on what might have happened to him."

The next item on the agenda was a report on Maxine Blake and the scientist Adam Gary. "She's at his compound, but the two of them aren't getting along."

"What's the problem?" one of the female NIA board members asked, adding, "Please don't tell me the man has gender issues?"

Myk nodded. "That's part of it. Apparently he's not comfortable having Max as his security advisor, and he's not feeling her dogs either."

Max worked with two very intelligent rottweilers

named Ruby and Ossie. Drake knew that the dogs were more intelligent than a lot of people, so he was confused by Adam's reactions to them. "Is he allergic to dogs? I don't remember seeing anything about that in the info the Defense Department provided us on him."

"No. According to Max, Gary just doesn't like dogs."

"How's she handling it?"

"You know Maxine. She told him to get over it."

The NIA board members went over a few more agenda items then called it a night.

Drake and Myk were in the elevator going down to the garage when Myk said, "Not like you to miss a meeting."

"I was busy."

"I see," Myk replied knowingly. "She must be speaking to you now."

Drake smiled but didn't answer.

"Remember all the grief you gave me when I missed NIA meetings because Sarita was all I could think about?"

"Yes."

"Well, payback is a dog, my brother."

"Shut up," Drake told him, trying to keep a straight face.

Then they laughed.

Eight

Lacy's Thursday evening meeting at the Northwest Activities Center started off slowly, mostly because there were only ten people in attendance. She quickly got over her disappointment with the low turnout and dove into her presentation. She began with the Blight Court proposal. It was basically the same talk she'd made at the mayor's meeting, and like the mayor, the environmentalists found her ideas exciting.

A light-skinned Black man named Rick Klein represented a group called Detroit Rehab. When Lacy finished her report, he pumped his fist in the air and called out, "Finally, somebody downtown gets it! Thank you, thank you, Ms. Green!" His organization, one of the city's most visible groups, refurbished abandoned homes then sold them for a profit.

Lacy was glad for his support but still wished there were more than ten people at the meeting.

A lady who said she represented one of the block clubs nearby asked, "So what can we do when we see somebody dumping? I've stopped calling downtown because nobody ever does anything when I do."

Lacy noted that many of the others nodded in agreement. "I want you to call my office," she said. "We'll be setting up a hotline. It should be up and running in a few days. We're also in the process of fixing the surveillance cameras. Once they're working again, we can use the pictures on the tapes as evidence. In the meantime, I'm trying to get funding for disposable cameras people can use at their homes, especially people on the southwest side. Most of the real dumping happens there."

The same woman asked, "When do you think you'll get them? We have a lot of seniors in our area who'd be real helpful with this since they're retired and home most of the day. Lot of them don't do nothing but look out the window anyway."

A few people chuckled.

Lacy told her, "Depends on if there's any money available. The mayor has promised to look into the matter. I'm not sure if the City Council has to approve the purchase first."

Rick Klein tossed out sarcastically, "Hell will freeze over before Council acts. What about private money?"

Lacy shrugged. "I've tried to get donations, but so far nothing. You have any ideas?"

So for the next hour, Lacy and her small group of volunteers brainstormed ideas on how to get the home camera program privately funded. Someone wanted to bombard the camera manufacturers with letters and phone calls, others wanted to hit up the auto manufacturers, or the Big Three, as they were known in Detroit: Chrysler, Ford, and General Motors. Someone else thought getting the local churches on board might be the way. Lacy liked that idea. She hadn't thought about enlisting the city's very powerful church base in the battle.

Once the initial discussion began to wind down, she asked, "Anyone else?"

"Yeah!"

Startled, she looked up. A young man was standing back by the doorway. He appeared to be in his late twenties, had a large 'fro and wore a leather jacket and scruffy jeans. Beside him were three similarly dressed men of about the same age and a lone young woman with an Ipod jack in her ear. Her winter white skin stood out against the dark skin of the men.

But the man who'd spoken was the one Lacy was watching, just like he was watching her. He had an average dark-skinned face, but the light brown eyes seemed to glow like flames.

"Are you here for the environmental meeting?" she asked.

A light of amusement appeared in his blazing eyes. "Don't I look like an environmentalist?"

The small band of new arrivals made their way to the front seats. "Name's Lenny. Lenny Durant. This here's my main crew. We call ourselves, BAD—Blacks against dumping. Hey Rick."

"Lenny." The tightness on Rick's face made Lacy wonder what the history between the two men involved. Rick didn't look happy to see Lenny at all.

Lenny and his crew sat.

"Thanks for coming," Lacy said.

"You know about us?"

Lacy shook her head. "Sorry. I've only been in Detroit six months."

He took a moment to look her up and down. "So, what have I missed?"

"Quite a bit, actually. I'll catch you up when we're done."

"Don't worry about it. I just came to say me and BAD aren't waiting on the city anymore. The next dumper we find is gonna wish he'd stayed his ass in the suburbs," and he looked around at Rick.

Rick seemed to take offense. "And that means what?"

"Nothing, but if we bust a few caps in a few fat suburban butts, they'll think twice about polluting our neighborhoods again."

Rick shook his head. "This isn't the sixties. You can't go around blowing people away."

"Why not?" The anger in Lenny's eyes was apparent to everyone in the room. "I say we declare open war on these busters and see how they like it."

Lacy shook her head. "I feel you, but we aren't advocating violence."

"They're advocating violence on us. Have you seen the statistics on how much crap is dumped in our communities nationwide every day? Want to know how many kids and seniors die each year from these toxic murderers? I heard you talking about cameras. Forget that. What the city ought to be giving out are guns."

Lacy blew out a breath. "How many members are in your organization?"

"Depends. If I put the word out, I can call on maybe two, three hundred people."

Lacy wondered how much truth lay behind that boast. If he could really depend on that many people, maybe this coalition would work. "Would they be willing to come to a meeting so I can get their addresses and add them to our alert phone trees and mailing list?"

"They're not much on meeting and talking. BAD is about action."

"I have no problem with that, but can I have your number in case I need your people?"

"I'll give you my mom's number. She'll know how to track me down."

Lacy had him write the number on her pad, and as he wrote, he looked up at her and asked, "You got a man?"

"That's none of your business."

"You gay?"

Lacy just looked at him.

He chuckled, then handed her back the pad. For a moment those burning eyes seemed to stare into her soul. It was like looking into the eyes of a predator who intended to play with the prey before killing it. She shivered involuntarily.

He asked then, "You got a card?"

Lacy gave him one from the stack she had on the table. His eyes never left hers as he put it into the pocket of his coat. "I'll be in touch," he said quietly.

The woman with him cut Lacy a cool look but didn't say anything. Lenny waved a tight good-bye to the scowling Rick, then left the room.

"Well," Lacy said.

"Stay away from him," Rick told her. "He's bad news. Real bad news."

Lacy got the sense that she might not have a choice. She knew as sure as her name was Lacy Green that she would run into Lenny again somewhere, soon. "How do you know each other?"

"Was introduced to him about five years ago. He was just starting BAD. Wanted our board's help in getting them some funding. We were happy to help. When the funding was denied because they hadn't been in existence long enough, he blamed us. Said we deliberately sabotaged the application."

"Did you?" Lacy asked.

He looked shocked. "Of course not. The next day some of the houses we were working on burned to the ground. The fire marshal said it was definitely arson."

"And you suspected BAD."

"Yes. But we couldn't prove it and the arsonist was never caught."

Lacy studied Rick's face for a moment. She wasn't sure if she believed his version of the story. Something in his eyes just wasn't right. She didn't have time to delve into it now though, so she filed his story away for later. Right now she wanted to wrap up the meeting and go home.

She made sure she got everyone's contact information and then thanked them for coming. They decided to meet once a month for now, and after setting a mutually agreed upon date, grabbed their coats and belongings and headed for the door.

When Lacy got back to her apartment, she helped herself to the Chinese food she'd picked up on the way home, then turned on the NBA and sat down to eat.

Then she called her mother. Lacy had deliberately not told her about the dinner with Drake beforehand, because knowing Valerie Garner Green, her mother would have hopped a plane and been knocking on Lacy's door that very same night, eagerly wanting the 411. Lacy loved her mother dearly, but all that creative energy could be overwhelming at times. Her own personality was more in tune with her mailman daddy, Martin, or at least that's how she viewed herself—very down to earth, and even boring at times, though she could be moved to passion when it came to something she cared deeply about. Like cleaning up the environment.

Lacy's father answered the phone. "Hey there, baby girl."

"Hi, Daddy. How's the mail business?"

"Not bad," he said with a smile in his voice. "How're things up there in the Murder City?"

"Stop that. Lots of folks being shot in Atlanta too. So don't ever start. I feel real safe here."

"Well, I'd feel safer if you got you a gun."

"Daddy?"

"I'm serious. When was the last time you went to the range?"

Lacy thought back.

He told her, "If you have to think about it, then it's time."

Her father, like most of the men in the South, grew up around firearms for hunting and protection purposes. To her mother's dismay, Martin's gift to Lacy for her thirteenth birthday had been a brand new bb gun. He'd set up a small range on the fence in their rural backyard, and over the next few weeks taught Lacy to shoot, and shoot well. She thought shooting was cool for a while, but like most teenage girls, moved on to more gender appropriate activities, like gawking at boys.

Her father asked, "You still have a valid permit, don't you?"

Silence.

"I'll take that as a no."

"Daddy?" she whined.

"Get your license renewed. Now, here's your mother."

Lacy felt twelve years old all over again.

"Hey baby. What was he fussing about?"

"My not having a valid gun license."

"He's just worried about you. Do what you think is best. Now, what's going on with my child?"

"Remember when you told me if the mayor asked me out, I was supposed to say yes? Well, I invited him to my place for dinner instead."

A profound silence followed.

"Mama? You still there?"

Val finally answered. "I am. I just had to find a chair so I could sit down."

Lacy laughed. "Are you ready now?"

"I think so. Go ahead."

So, Lacy told her about the dinner date. She left out the kissing parts, though. "What's he like?"

"Genuinely nice. Said we'd take it slow, and I liked that."

"Praise the Lord."

Lacy laughed. "Why'd you say that?"

"Because maybe you've finally found somebody worthy of you, baby. You're a real complex woman, and some men these days can't handle complex."

"Amen to that."

"So the fact that he wants to go slow and isn't pushing himself on you says a lot to me."

"Me, too."

"Good. I hope I'll get a chance to meet him. Hint. Hint."

"If it gets that far, you will definitely meet him. I promise."

"I'm going to hold you to that. What else is going on?"

Lacy gave her mother an update on her ankle and what was going on at work. She also related her encounter with City Councilman Parker.

Val asked, "Did he say why he was so mad?"

"Not really. It was weird. Kind of surprising too."

"Did you feel threatened?"

"In a way, yes, but not really. Does that make sense?"

"I suppose. Well, keep an eye on him. People are crazy these days."

"Don't worry."

"Oh, one last thing. Did you ever get a car?"

"Haven't had time."

"That's what I figured, so I ordered you one from one of the dealers up there."

"Mama—"

"Lacy, you're no longer the little girl I can spoil anytime I like, so let me do this. Just this once?"

Lacy was thirty-two years old, and she had a good job. She didn't need her mama buying her a car. "Mama, I don't—"

"Lacy, my art has made me so rich, there's no way your father and I can spend it all before we die. You know that. Since the bulk of it will be coming to you anyway, think of the car as an advance on your inheritance. Oh, and an early birthday present too."

Lacy knew when she was fighting a losing battle with her mother, and this was one of those times, so she surrendered. If her mother wanted to buy her a car, so be it. She was independent, but she wasn't stupid. "Okay, what's the name of the dealership?" she asked.

Val gave her the name, and the name of the sales person she needed to contact.

"Thanks, Mama."

"You're welcome. Enjoy the car, and tell that fine man of yours I say, hello."

A smile filled Lacy's face. "I will, and you tell that fine daddy of mine I'll get my licensed renewed so he can sleep at night."

Val chuckled. "Good. I'm on my way to Amsterdam in the morning. I'll be back at the end of the month. Keep me posted. Love you, baby girl."

Lacy wasn't surprised to hear her mother was leaving the country. For Valerie Garner Green, traveling was a way of life. "Love you too, Mama. Be careful traveling. 'Bye, now."

Lacy clicked off.

"So, I have a car," she said out loud. She shook her head at her beautiful flower child mother and went back to the game. Drake had called her this morning at work. He was flying to San Antonio tonight for a mayor's conference and would be returning Sunday afternoon. Thinking about them both getting onto planes, Lacy said a quick prayer that their journeys would be safe ones.

"You're kidding, right?"

"No, miss. This is the car your mother ordered."

It was Saturday afternoon and Lacy was looking at the black Chrysler Crossfire Coupe her mother had purchased to replace her Escort. The car resembled a fine piece of art. From the black clear coat finish, to the stylish wheels, to the satin silver finished interior, it was beautiful. According to the salesman, the Crossfire had 215 horses under the hood, and a six speed manual transmission to set them free. The sleek coupe was way flashier than anything she would have purchased, probably the main reason her mother had chosen it. Val had always been after her to be more cutting edge, more extravagant, and this Crossfire was definitely both.

The well-dressed salesman was saying, "It has a 3.2 liter engine, bucket seats, and your mother has added a state-of-the-art alarm system, a Bose sound package, and even a GPS navigational aid."

Lacy was amazed. Val drove a Porsche Boxster, but this being Detroit, she'd picked out an American name plate for her, and she certainly appreciated that.

The man was still talking about torque and spoilers when Lacy politely cut him off. "Okay. Let's finish up the paperwork and I'll take her home."

As she followed him across the showroom to his desk, she took a long look back at the unbelievable car. New car, new city, new life. New man. Maybe the time had come to let herself live a little.

Lacy signed all the documents, made arrangements for the rental car to be picked up at the dealership, then took the keys. On the ride home her ankle complained about the pedals, but she didn't care. There weren't many Crossfires like hers on the streets, and she received many toots of appreciation and even more looks of WOW! on the faces of the drivers she passed. The black car was hot, and being behind the wheel made her feel like a million bucks. She would definitely be calling her mama to thank her for the gift.

Sunday morning, Councilman Reynard Parker sat leafing through the day's paper in his sun-filled breakfast nook. He was searching for anything related to the dumping his crews were doing. Since he was an equal opportunity polluter, the suburbs were getting their fair share of the waste too. The snooty residents of Oakland County were going to pitch a fit when the barrels started turning up in their manicured neighborhoods and in the parking lots of their pricey strip malls, but why should Detroit have all the fun?

He smiled at his own drab humor, even though the situation wasn't humorous at all. Were it ever proven that his company trucks were responsible, his political career would be over. Wheeler's thievery necessitated this plan of action. The feds were coming in on Tuesday to look at Wheeler's computer. They were still treating the disappearance as a missing persons case, or so they told him, but he was no fool. He'd done his best to cover his ass. The day Wheeler was made into gull food, he'd had one of his employees—who'd done five years time for computer crimes—sweep Wheeler's hard drive. Parker wanted to make sure Wheeler hadn't already made contact with the law, as he'd claimed. No smoking guns were found. Luckily, the accounting spread sheets were left intact, giving Parker hard proof that Wheeler had been an embezzler. When it became known that he hadn't gotten wind of the embezzling until after Wheeler disappeared, the feds would have to look elsewhere for clues, and he could fix his problems without anyone looking over his shoulder. Or so he hoped.

On the back page of the paper's first section, a small item caught Parker's eye. The story was on the recent sighting of yet another mysterious black van. The vans first showed up in the city about two years ago. No one knew who the occupants were. The only thing folks could agree on was that the teams wore all black, wore ski masks to hide their identities, and targeted drug houses. They kicked in doors, stole product, made dealers disappear, and weren't afraid to shoot it out with anyone silly enough to fire on them. The residents called them the Drug Busters; the police and mayor called them vigilantes.

There were all kinds of urban rumors attached to the group: that they were responsible for bringing down all those rich White suburban drug dealers convicted back in '03; that, even though the feds kept claiming they weren't involved, the group was a covert government operation; and that the police had a stack of missing persons reports filed by families of teens who vanished after being caught in the raids, but the police weren't processing the paperwork. The nightly takedowns of crack dens and drug dealers occurred so frequently, there'd been reports on the local news and in the papers almost daily. Then the sightings tailed off.

The small article in today's paper was the first Parker had seen on the vans in the past eighteen months. Were they back, or had they just gone underground for a while? Supposedly, the city's police department hadn't been able to find, let alone arrest, anyone connected with the vans, but he hadn't believed it back then, and he certainly didn't believe it now. He was convinced that the police and the current Randolph administration knew way more than they were telling. Although he didn't have a shred of evidence, his gut said he was right. For him, it was just too much of a coincidence that the vans began showing up right after Randolph took office.

Parker folded up the paper. He had an appointment with Randolph in the morning. Maybe he'd ask the mayor a few questions. If he could prove his theory, Randolph would certainly be charged and then disgraced, and he could win the upcoming election with no problems at all. And as mayor, he wouldn't have to worry about cash flow problems, Wheeler, or anything else, because he would be in control of the board.

Sunday evening Lacy was out on the balcony watering her plants when she heard her phone ringing. She put watering can down and ran to catch it. She hadn't heard from Drake, and feeling like a teenager, she prayed it was him. "Hello."

"Hey, baby."

Her knees went weak. "Hey. How are you?"

"You can judge for yourself. I'm downstairs in the parking lot."

Her heart began racing. "Okay."

He hung up, and Lacy ran around the apartment like the super heroine Storm, picking up the junk the place had accumulated over the weekend. The buzzer sounded just as she threw a pair of dirty socks into the bedroom and closed the door. She hit the button to let him in, then ran her fingers through her twists and took in a deep breath.

"Hi," he said, and his smile seemed to brighten the fading daylight.

"Hi," she said back, and hoped she wasn't grinning like the village idiot. "Come on in."

He was dressed for business in a fine gray suit and a gray, lightweight, all-weather coat that didn't appear to have a wrinkle in it. The very air in the room seemed charged with his presence.

"How was San Antonio?" she asked him.

"Hot," he said, taking a seat on the couch. "And humid. How'd your thing go at the Northwest Activities Center?"

Lacy took a seat beside him and gave him a rundown on her meeting and her introduction to Rick Klein.

"I've worked with him and his people on a few projects," Drake said. "His group's doing good work. Making a nice little profit reselling those refurbished homes, too, but hey, whatever the market will bear. I'm just glad they're bringing residents back into the city."

"Do you know about a group called BAD?"

"Lenny Durant? Yes. The young brother is angry *all* the time. I had a couple of meetings with him when I first took office. He wanted to shoot the polluters like rats, was how he phrased it."

"Well, he still does."

"He didn't give you any trouble, did he?"

She shook her head. "Nah. He wanted to know if I had a man."

His eyebrow rose. "What did you tell him?"

"None of his business."

For a moment he didn't say anything, then asked in that low rich voice, "Are you taking applications?"

The hushed tone made her dizzy for a moment. She tried to play it off, but failed miserably. "It—the job hasn't been posted."

He reached out and very gently stroked her cheek. "When it is, I want to know. . . ."

Lacy's breath was stacked up in her throat. She was shaking like a virgin on her wedding night. "Drake . . ."

He leaned in and kissed her softly. "What . . . ?"

She couldn't think.

He kissed her again, slower this time and with more intent. "I'm the best man for the job, hands down. . . ."

Her eyes closed and she sighed, moaned, with pleasure.

Drake enjoyed the sound of her surrender almost as much as he was enjoying the slow, seductive kisses. Her lush lips seemed to have been especially made for him. He brought a hand up to cup her jaw and slid his tongue into the warmth of her mouth. Her tongue played provocatively with his. When the passion inched up in intensity, he felt her tremble and felt his own shuddering response. *Lord, he wanted this woman.*

Lacy had never been kissed with such lazy passion before. There was no rushing here. This was a lingering, languid exercise that made her run her hand up the side of his neck so the two of them could come closer.

The encouraging gesture made Drake want her closer still, and with a low growl of passion, he pulled her onto his lap. The heat of her teased him everywhere. He sought her lips once more, moving his hands up and down her back. The male in him wanted to carry her to the nearest bed, right now, but the man in him wanted this relationship to be more than an occasional booty call. The man in him knew that she'd need time to get back in the relationship game.

Fitting actions to thought, Drake took his time. He let his kisses cajole her, tempt her. He invited her to explore passion at any pace she desired. He assured her in the only way he knew how that it was okay to come out and play because he would treasure her.

Lacy was so filled with desire, her eyes were covered by a veil of sensation. He hadn't even touched her inside of her clothes, but she already knew the touch would be hot and true. She could feel his hard response beneath her hips, and that added to the fiery sensations. When he moved his hot lips down her jaw and over the thin gold chain circling her neck, she just knew she would dissolve and blow away. She could hear the laugh track on the TV, and her hand searched blindly for the remote to shut it off. In the silence that followed, their passionate breathing sounded magnified.

Drake raised his head and recaptured her mouth. He was hot and hard and wanted to do more than kiss her. "If you don't want me to touch you, you need to tell me. . . ." She responded by teasing her tongue against the corner on his mouth, and it sent him spiraling. His hand explored her curves and the flare of her behind in her loose sweats. On fire, he filled his hand with her small breast and played with it until she purred. Only then did he lower his head to bite the marble-hard tip. Lacy arched and cooed. He teased the nipple until it stood out against the thin fabric of her short-sleeve blouse before moving his attention to its twin.

Lacy could feel her buttons being undone, but she didn't stop him; she didn't want him to. His touches and kisses were as reverent as they were fiery; she felt treasured, priceless, not a sensation she'd ever experienced with a man before.

Then the buzzer sounded.

Drake raised his mouth to hers and kissed her with a gentle possessiveness that let her know they'd continue this next time. "Probably Malcolm."

Every cell in Lacy's body was singing with lust. She was hard in some places, swollen in others, and breathing like a woman who'd just run a race. "I should go to the door. . . ."

Drake couldn't seem to stop kissing her. "You button up. I'll go."

Drake gave her one last powerful kiss, then got to his feet. He hit the intercom.

"Your twenty minutes are up."

Drake hung his head. "Okay, be there in a minute." He looked over at Lacy. "Being mayor is overrated."

Lacy was absolutely rocked by his loving. The passionate haze encasing her shimmered, and was also pulsing through her body. She wanted him to come back and make her purr some more. It was a scandalous wish, but she didn't care.

Drake noted that her blouse was still undone, exposing portions of her small dark breasts as they moved in tandem with her breathing. He made a mental note to make love to the brainy Lacy Green as soon as it could be arranged. "I promised Malcolm I'd be back in twenty minutes. He just picked me up from the airport, and he promised to take his wife to the movies tonight."

Lacy looked back at his dark intense gaze and knew it wouldn't be long before she invited him into her bed. "Tell Malcolm he owes me one."

Drake's smile showed as he studied her kiss-swollen lips and still lidded eyes. He was as hard as he'd been a moment ago. "I'm going to stand over here because if I come back over there, I'm going to start kissing you again."

Fueled by a sensual mischief she was beginning to enjoy, Lacy walked over to him and stopped a few inches away. "Is that a bad thing?"

"You're not right," he said, chuckling and taking in the sensual disarray of her blouse.

She waited.

He placed a finger beneath her chin so he could commit her midnight beauty to his memory once again, then leaned down and gave her a poignant kiss good-bye. "See you, Lacy."

She kissed him back with a quiet fervor. "'Bye, Drake."

When the door closed, a pulsing Lacy stood in the silence for a long time.

Nine

Later, she took a quick shower and put on some clean pjs. Her body was still tingling from the mayor's special handling, and just thinking about him made her shimmer. She was just about to crawl into bed when the phone rang. The caller ID gave up Drake's name, so she picked it up and asked with mock warning, "Am I going to have to take a PPO out on you?"

He laughed. "The newspapers would love that, wouldn't they?" Then, in his best television anchor voice, he mimicked, "City administrator files for Personal Protection Order against the mayor. More news at eleven."

She stretched out on the bed and enjoyed the sound of him.

"I just called to see if you want to have dinner with me Saturday night."

"Sure. Where?"

"My place."

"Okay. So, where are you now? Home? In the car?"

"Home. In bed. Alone."

"Then you have time to knock out another thousand of those thank-you notes to those crazy women from the magazine."

"Hush," he said with humor in his tone.

Lacy giggled.

Silence settled for a moment, then he said, "I was serious about applying for that job."

His declaration thrilled Lacy, but she thought she owed him a few truths before allowing this relationship to move any further. "I really, really like being with you, Drake, but I had such a messed-up marriage and divorce, I'm a little gun-shy."

"Like I said, slow is fine with me."

She appreciated that. "You know who Wilton Cox is, right?"

"I do. Your ex."

Lacy was stunned. "How'd you know?"

"I'm going to apologize up front. I checked you out on Google."

"You did?"

"I wanted to know who you were, and I didn't really expect to find anything."

"Got the surprise of your life, I'll bet."

"True dat. Hundreds of hits."

"Only hundreds?" she asked sarcastically.

Drake heard the coolness in her voice. "Are you going to hang up on me now?"

"I should, but you did tell me the truth about it."

"With you, always."

The richly spoken promise slid over her like silk. "My parents tried to tell me Wilton was too old, too arrogant, too everything, but I was twenty-four, hadn't known a lot of men, and frankly, thought I knew every damn thing."

"My grandmother says that God gives us youth so we can make mistakes."

"Marrying Wilton was a whopper."

She heard him chuckle softly, then he said, seriously, "Getting your heart broken is no fun, but you're too vibrant a woman to hide yourself away, Lacy."

That too touched her heart. "I also didn't like the press in my face during the divorce, and I definitely won't like them in any business you and I might have, but I'll deal with it, like I said." The rigors of the divorce had taken a lot out of her soul, and she'd been carrying around a measure of that emptiness ever since, but Drake Randolph was just the medicine she needed, it seemed. He was a fascinating, smart, dedicated, and caring man; all the things Wilton was not.

"Lacy? You still there?"

"Yes. Sorry, I was thinking."

"'Bout what?"

"You applying for the position."

His voice softened. "And? Do I get the job?"

"I think yes, but you'll have to serve a ninety day probation period before we talk long-term, though."

He laughed. "Probation?"

She tossed back playfully, "A girl can't be too careful, you know." She turned over onto her stomach.

He chuckled and asked, "So, will you go with me to my gran's party?"

"Yes."

"It's the weekend of May twenty-first."

"I'll put it in my calendar."

Then he added, "Since I don't want to hang up, what do you want to talk about now?"

Lacy grinned. "I don't know. What do you want to talk about?"

"Everything. Nothing."

She wished he were there. "Tell me about your sisters."

"Okay. Let's see, the oldest is Madeline. She's a principal at Cass Tech. Then comes Denise. She teaches English at Wayne State. My third sister, Angela, owns a bakery over on Griswold. Last is Sharon. She's a stay-at-home mom. Her husband James is a GM executive and he treats her like a queen."

"She's very lucky. Are the others married?"

"Madey has been married for a hundred years to another real nice guy named Raymond. Angie and Denise are divorced. Did you ever want sibs?"

"Sometimes, but my mother said one child was enough. And since you Googled me, you probably know who Mama is, too."

"I do. I've seen many of her pieces."

"She calls me her and Daddy's greatest work. You'd like her. She's all about spirit and creativity and energy. Keeping up with her is like trying to cage the wind sometimes, but I've never met anyone she didn't like. Well, except Wilton, of course. She calls him Studley."

There was a silence for a moment, then he said, "I could talk to you all night."

"Me too." She looked over at the clock on her wall. "But it's past midnight, Drake. I have to get up in the morning."

"I know. Just a little longer, okay?"

"Okay."

So they talked on. The conversation took many twists and turns. He told her about medical school, and she told him about being fired from her last job. "One of the polluters I wanted to prosecute was a fifth or sixth cousin to the governor, so they fired me instead."

"Their loss is the city's gain. Not to mention mine."

"I'm glad I wound up here, too."

There was silence for a few more moments, then Drake said, "I should let you go to bed."

Lacy yawned. "Yes, you should. I need my beauty sleep."

"You get any prettier and you will have to take out a PPO on me."

"Flattery will get you your own loaf of bread next time you come for dinner."

"Really?"

She laughed at his eager tone. "Go to bed, Your Honor."

"I'm going. 'Night, Lacy."

" 'Night, Drake."

She put down the phone, turned off the lamp beside the bed, and climbed beneath the covers. She was still smiling when she drifted off to sleep.

Drake stood at the windows of his office and watched the city come to life. It was Monday morning and folks were scurrying over the sidewalks and filling the lanes of Jefferson Avenue with their cars on their way to work. He didn't know why he'd agreed to meet with Parker first thing this morning, because all the encounter would do was ruin the rest of his week. He didn't like the man and Parker didn't like him. They had sort of a mutual hate society thing going on. To him Parker was a parasite feeding off the city with his bribes and dirty deals. And Parker dismissed him as being nothing more than a lightweight pretty boy.

As much as Drake would have loved to see Parker snatched up by NIA and dumped in a rain forest somewhere, Parker was a duly elected representative of the city, and as such, Drake had no choice but to deal with him.

Turning from the windows, he leaned over his desk and hit a button on the intercom. "Ms. Curry, you can bring the councilman in now."

Drake took a deep breath and waited for Parker to arrive.

When he walked in, Drake noted that Parker could've been Mike Tyson's daddy. Parker was taller than the former champion and lacked the bizarre facial tattoo, but both men shared the squat powerful body type. "Have a seat, councilman. Can I get you coffee? Water?"

Brusque as always, Parker said, "No," then sat down in one of the plush leather chairs ringing the front of Drake's desk.

"How've you been?" Drake asked, making small talk.

"Fine. You?"

"I'm okay. Now that we've gotten that out of the way, let's talk about your concerns with the Blight Court proposal."

"We can get to that in a minute."

Drake shrugged nonchalantly. "Take the conversation wherever you want it to go."

"According to yesterday's paper, one of those vans showed up over the weekend."

"What vans?"

"Those Dope Buster vans."

Drake had received a coded text message on Sunday from Myk about the story. "Ah, yes. Ms. Curry mentioned it to me this morning when I came in." Drake didn't say more. He waited for Parker to further the conversation, or not.

"What do the police know about these people?"

"Not much. Usually before the police can be dispatched to the scene, the vans are gone. The detectives say it's like trying to catch smoke."

"Are you sure this isn't some kind of federal group?"

"They say they're not involved."

"Do you believe them?"

"Doesn't matter what I believe, the feds are going to do their thing."

"That's not an answer."

Drake studied him, then asked, "Are you trying to put me on the spot for any particular reason?"

"No. Just curious, that's all. I'd think the mayor would be more concerned about a lawless gang of vigilantes terrorizing citizens."

"Who says I'm not concerned? Law enforcement is doing all it can. I have every confidence in them. What else?"

Parker studied the doctor mayor. It was Randolph's arrogance that he hated most, he decided. That and the fact that Randolph was pretty, rich, and acted as if his shit didn't stink. Parker couldn't wait to bring him down. "About this new Blight Court."

"Yes?"

"Why are we wasting money on it?"

"If you read the report you'll see that it isn't a waste. I've talked to some of the magistrates in Chicago—"

"I don't care about that. We need improved streets, schools, and city services like improved buses, and you want to nickel and dime the last few viable businesses in the city with these new fines? It stinks."

"We'll only nickel and dime them if they violate the codes. Have you seen the stats on asthma and other respiratory diseases for kids in our communities? The numbers are off the charts, and it's from what they're breathing. You don't want to oppose this, councilman. You'll lose. I can get the churches, the hospitals, and the schools to jump on the bandwagon. Won't look good at election time."

Drake paused a moment to gauge Parker's reaction, but in reality he didn't care. "Now, I certainly understand if you have friends worried about getting caught doing whatever they are doing, but that's not my concern. My concern is cleaning up this city. Period."

"You really think you got the world by the balls, don't you?"

"No, but I am the mayor, and I don't like being challenged just because you don't like my suits. Now, you got anything else? If not, I have work to do."

Parker stood. "This isn't the end."

"If you have any sense, it will be."

"You threatening me?"

"No. I'm trying to school you."

Then Drake said to him, "Whatever schemes or machinations you believe you have up your sleeve—you'd better think twice about exposing them, because you really don't want to mess with me. The suit is only a facade."

"Oh really?" Parker said with a challenge in his eyes. "Well, we'll see. Won't we?" He walked to the door and said over his shoulder, "Have a good day, Your Honor."

"You too, councilman," Drake tossed back. It didn't take a rocket scientist to know Parker was up to something. He could smell it.

"Hey you."

Lacy was startled to see the angry Lenny Durant in

her office doorway. Since she didn't like being addressed as "Hey you," she put down her sandwich and said, coolly, "Can I help you, Mr. Durant?"

"Yeah. Somebody's dumping medical waste and other stuff all over the southwest side. Barrels started showing up Friday night. Here's a list of the sites." He came in, handed her a sheet of notebook paper covered with writing and diagrams, then he walked out.

"Hey, wait a minute."

He turned back and those eyes glowed like brimstone.

Whatever Lacy had planned to say vanished under the force of his direct stare. "Thanks for the tip."

He nodded and left.

Lacy's first call was to the mayor's office. Rhonda said he was in a meeting but would alert him ASAP. Lacy's next call went to the Michigan State Police. She explained the situation then faxed them a copy of Lenny's list. A few minutes later a trooper called back and told her squad cars and the Hazardous Materials Unit, known as HazMat, were on their way. He asked that she meet them there. Lacy hung up and went to find Ida.

By eight that evening the area around the barrels had been cordoned off with yellow tape, and the HazMat crews in their plastic suits, air regulators, and gloves were loading the barrels into their trucks. The barrels had been discovered behind a small grocery framed on both sides by vacant lots. Lacy looked up and down the street. Even in the dark it was easy to see that this was one of the city's poorest neighborhoods. Most of Detroit's Spanish families lived here next to poor Whites, Blacks, and Chaldeans.

All the police activities had drawn a curious crowd of local residents. Lacy wondered if anyone had seen anything. She walked over to the tape and asked, "Did anybody see who dumped the barrels?"

No one had. "Okay, my name's Lacy Green. I work for the city in the Environmental Office. If anybody saw anything, please tell me so we can put these thugs away."

Nothing.

Ida met Lacy's eyes and shrugged.

Lacy hid her frustration. "Then can I get some people to help me form a Neighborhood Watch here to look out for dumping? The city's going to have some new laws soon, and if we can get pictures of the trucks or the people doing this, it'll help with the prosecution."

An older Chaldean man stepped into the arc of the streetlight. "I'll help you. That's my store. The policeman said I may have to shut down until they find out whether the stuff in the barrels is poisonous. How am I supposed to take care of my family?"

Lacy sympathized with his dilemma, and took his name and contact information. Five other people volunteered to add their names to her list, and she was encouraged. She spent a few more minutes asking if there was a place in the neighborhood where a communitywide meeting on the dumping problem could be held. A Mexican woman who'd been standing by the tape with a child in her arms suggested the local

Catholic church. Lacy wrote down the name of the priest in charge and promised to give him a call.

She could see the trooper in charge giving her the high sign, so she excused herself and she and Ida went to see what he wanted. She saw Drake standing a few feet away, talking to a group of reporters, but she was intent on the trooper. She'd get with Drake later.

The blue-uniformed state policeman had bitter-sweet news. "Your tipster was pretty accurate. According to my dispatcher, six more sites have been found not far from here. It's gonna be a long night."

And it was. In addition to the medical waste behind the Chaldean grocery, the troopers found barrels beneath an expressway overpass, others behind a school and in the parking lot of a rest home. The HazMat workers weren't sure what was in the barrels, but preliminary tests showed the liquid waste to be toxic. Lacy was furious that the polluters would target the health of children and senior citizens.

When she finally got a chance to talk with Drake, he was as upset. "I'm with Lenny Durant. Let's just shoot them. What kind of sick person leaves toxic waste on a playground?"

As the night got longer, Drake and the troopers suggested she and Ida head home, but they refused and followed the HazMat unit from site to site. By the time they finally did head home, it was 1:00 A.M.

Once there, an exhausted Lacy fell across the bed. All she could think about were the heartless polluters and their toxic surprises. With so many barrels found within that one specific area, did it mean all the stuff was the work of one crew, or were there multiple polluters at work? She didn't know. Everytime she thought about the barrels at the school and the old people's home she got mad all over again.

Myk handled NIA's day-to-day operations from an upstairs room in his house the organization called the War Room. It was jammed with computer monitors, satellite equipment, and everything else needed electronically to oversee NIA and its missions. Drake, Myk, and Myk's personal driver, Walter, were huddled in the room now. Walter was one of the organization's top lieutenants.

Drake handled all of the computer programming, graphics, and charts. At the moment, the three men were gathered around a monitor showing a map of the city. Drake was keying in markers on the streets and businesses where the illegal dumping had taken place. He was trying to determine if there was a pattern, but other than the fact that all the incidents were confined to the southwest side, no other similarities could be seen. He also wanted a copy of the map for his own files for future reference.

He turned to Myk and Walter. "If we can pull some NIA crews from other projects and let them patrol the area, maybe we can catch somebody in the act."

Myk agreed.

Walter said, "I'll see who can be freed up."

Drake input a few more locations and told his brother, "I had a real ugly meeting with Parker yesterday."

"About what?"

"A new magistrate's office we're setting up to prosecute blight code violators." Drake then told him Parker's reasons for opposing the new office.

Myk asked, "So what does the councilman have his dirty fingers in that he's concerned about?"

Drake shrugged. "I wish I knew. Maybe then I could get him off my back permanently. He asked about the recent Dope Busters sighting. Wanted to know why I wasn't more concerned about a gang of vigilantes terrorizing the citizens."

Walter asked, "Did you wash his mouth out with soap? He's the biggest terrorist in the county."

"It was like he was looking to see how I'd react."

"Do you think he knows something?"

"That's how it felt, but? . . ." Drake shrugged, unable to make it any clearer.

"Well," Myk said, "if I were Parker, I'd be more worried seeing vans from the Federal Prosecutor's Office."

"How's it going?"

"Nothing on Wheeler, still. We're assuming he's dead at this point."

Drake turned from the screen. "Since Parker is in the trash business, when are you going to start searching the landfills?"

"Soon as we can convince a judge to issue the order. Right now, the courts keep telling us we don't have enough evidence."

Walter said, "The judge thinks our mole may have disappeared on his own. Las Vegas. The Bahamas.

Turns out Wheeler had a large offshore shell corporation set up. Had almost fifteen mil stashed away."

"Wow! Did his wife know about this?"

"Nope, and she's hopping mad. Apparently, she was working midnights as a waitress to help out with what her husband told her were their financial problems."

"Why'd he drop a dime to the feds on Parker if he was embezzling?" Drake asked.

Myk shrugged. "Maybe Parker was threatening him. I don't know. The feds said he showed up one day and wanted to talk."

Walter said, "Maybe he didn't think they'd be interested in his embezzling if they were too busy trying to fry Parker."

Myk said, "Who knows? The only thing in stone right now is Wheeler has disappeared and one of Parker's trucks was carrying marijuana."

"Knowing what we know about Parker," Drake said, "Wheeler's disappearance looks real suspicious to me."

"That's what we tried to tell the judge."

Drake did a zoom on some of the intersections to get the street names. He wanted these people caught, if he had to catch them himself. He made a mental note to track down Lenny Durant to see if his people had come up with anything new.

Myk, changing the subject, asked, "So, now that the woman you ran off the road is talking to you, have you had dinner with her yet?"

Drake smiled.

Walter laughed. “I’ve seen that look before. He must’ve gotten lucky.”

“Luck, no. Charm and game, yes.”

Myk rolled his eyes. “Bet you didn’t tell her you were still writing back all those crazy women from the magazine article.”

“I did.”

Walter said, “And what’d she say?”

“That she thought the women were crazy too.”

Myk howled.

Drake took the teasing good-naturedly. “Laugh if you want, my dragon brother, but she’s coming to Gran’s party with me.”

“Good for you. Can’t wait to meet her.” Then Myk added, “Bet you didn’t tell her you had a brother cloned from Inspector Gadget, coat and all.”

Drake thought about their half-brother Saint with his coat full of tricks, and he admitted freely, “That, I didn’t tell her.”

Walter said drolly, “I don’t blame you, man. Things like that have to be seen to be believed.”

The War Room echoed with laughter.

Ten

Lacy and her officemates spent the rest of the week dealing with the dumping incident. Calls from residents sent her and the HazMat techs scrambling to check out new sites, and while the techs evaluated, tagged, and hauled the evidence away, Lacy added the information to her reports and fumed over the rising number of incidents.

Drake was in Chicago for a three-day Great Lakes Regional Water Commission meeting, and although he'd called her, her late night forays with HazMat made her so tired, their conversations were short. By Friday evening she was so glad to leave work she wanted to yell "Hallelujah." She was really looking forward to the dinner with Drake on Saturday night.

Saturday afternoon, Drake drove slowly through the distressed southwest neighborhoods where the dumping had taken place. Although he'd gotten updates on the situation from Lacy and Rhonda while he was in Chicago, he wanted to make sure the tape cordoning off the areas was still intact. It wasn't his job, but he was the mayor and he felt a certain responsibility. Guided by the map he'd printed out at Myk's, he checked out the Chaldean store, the elementary school playground, and the parking lot of the tired-looking rest home. The tapes were all intact, and Drake's jaw tightened at the thought of polluters using poor neighborhoods as their toilets, while keeping their own communities clean. According to Lacy's Blight Court report, polluters had all kinds of excuses for justifying dumping their toxic loads in the city's alleys. They blamed high taxes, tariffs, endless red tape, and the sometimes business-strangling laws governing transportation, packaging, and disposal. Some of the dumpers were convinced that the struggling neighborhoods of big cities like Detroit, Chicago, and Philadelphia were sewers anyway, so a few more tons of toxins and polluted waste wouldn't make a difference. That attitude, more than anything else, was why groups like BAD wanted to take these people out by any means necessary. The polluter's disrespect and their assumption that it was okay to dump barrels of syringes and bloody toweling on school grounds and in the parking lots of nursing homes made Drake angry too. The last time he'd been this angry, he'd formed NIA, and the city's drug dealers had been looking over their shoulders ever since. He wanted to give the polluters the same kind of hell, but he had to find them first.

Frustrated by the fact that there was nothing more

he could do about the dumping for now, he drove his cobalt blue Mustang out of the southwest side and headed east. He needed a haircut, and the only place in town where he could be himself was at Clyde's on Baldwin and East Forest. He put in his new favorite CD, *The House of Urban Groove*, and let it soothe the savage beast. Over the sounds of the jamming horns and thumping bass, he cruised his city.

Drake drove around whenever he had the chance; sometimes late at night, other times at dawn. Medical school and the vampire hours of residency and interning seemed to have permanently lessened his need for sleep, so while everybody else in the city not working midnights were home snug in their beds, he would be out driving. He rarely took his bodyguards, Lane and Cruise, with him, something his lady police chief didn't like, but Drake never worried about his safety. Number one, who was going to mug the mayor? And two, anybody foolish or brave enough to try would learn that the mayor, like a good portion of the city's residents, rolled armed.

But Drake especially liked driving around on sunny Saturday afternoons like today. Sometimes he'd stop and talk to folks waiting for the Dexter bus, or stop and say hey to a bunch of brothers hooping in one of the city's parks. He'd also been known to stop and buy a chicken or a rib dinner from a storefront church selling the food to raise money. Invariably his arrival would bring on a stunned silence, and then all hell would break loose as the kitchen ladies fluttered and tried to feed him like a prodigal son. So far, none of these close encounters had ever shown up in the paper, and for him, that was the best part because the interactions were between him and the citizens, and had nothing to do with the newspapers at all.

Drake pulled into the tiny lot behind Clyde's Barbershop and sat there a moment to look around. The old neighborhood was still hanging on. There were a few more boarded-up buildings, but there were also a few formerly boarded-up places that now held new small businesses. Drake was determined to make the neighborhoods part of the city's renewal. Past administrations had focused on reviving downtown. He thought that was okay, but the neighborhoods needed to be revitalized if Detroit was to have any chance of regaining its stride.

His arrival at Clyde's was greeted with applause, signifying, and back-thumping hugs from the regulars. Clyde Miller, the owner, had been cutting Drake's hair since Drake's mother moved the family to the east side when he was nine. Clyde was no longer the player he'd been back then. Over the years, the fast-living hustler life had been replaced by the strict life of diabetes. Clyde's once string-bean frame now resembled a ham hock.

Seeing Drake, he came out from behind his chair. His light brown face peppered by freckles held a wide smile. He gave Drake a big hug. "How you doing, boy. Ain't seen you in so long thought maybe you had put us down."

"Never," Drake promised. "How are you?"

"Not bad. Still trying to get the forty-eight-year-old

wife to let me trade up to two twenty-four-year-olds, but she ain't buying it."

The six customers laughed. Everybody knew Clyde's fiery wife Glenda, and that if there was any trading to be done more than likely it would be Clyde's fifty-two-year-old self being exchanged for two twenty-six-year-olds. Drake shook everybody's hand then took his seat to wait his turn.

In any other shop he could probably have pulled rank and been the next person in the chair, but at Clyde's it had always been First Come, or Wait Your Turn, just like the sign said on the wall. Clyde didn't care if you were President of the United States, or the mayor of Detroit, for that matter.

Duke Givens, the other barber, and Clyde's brother-in-law, asked Drake over the balding brown head of his customer, "How's that pretty mama of yours?"

Drake picked up a sports magazine, one of many spread out on the rickety table in front of the old comfortable couch he was seated on. "She's doing just fine. I talked to her this morning."

"Tell her I said hello."

"Will do."

Duke, a widower, had been trying to hit on Drake's mama for the past ten years, but Mavis Randolph wasn't feeling him. Even though she was sixty-three now, Mavis could still make the men of her generation walk into trees when she passed by. Duke was one of the ones with a permanent knot on his forehead.

While Drake waited his turn to sit under Clyde's clippers, he leafed through the magazines and added his two cents to the myriad conversations in the shop that touched on everything from what the Detroit Tigers needed to do to having a winning baseball season to what was wrong with the fools in Lansing, the state capital, and in Washington. Drake found himself laughing more than a few times as the opinionated Clyde verbally got into it with the "I voted for the President" Duke.

By the time the freshly cut Drake drove away from Clyde's, his spirit had been renewed. He also had more than enough time to go home, take a shower, and hook up with Lacy.

Just thinking about her made him smile. In his mind's eye he could see the sexy little twists and the expressive eyes. The sweetness of her kiss came back too. He couldn't wait to show her off at Gran's party because he knew his grandmother, Eleanor, and the rest of the Vachon family would like her. His mother wanted to meet Lacy too. Although he'd tried to tell Mavis that a dinner date in no way meant wedding, he was certain she was already picking out names for her new grandchildren.

Lacy was dressed. She wasn't one of those women who spent years deciding what to wear. A pair of black linen pants, a dark purple linen twin set, and her short-heeled black mules had done the trick. She looked at herself in her mirror and was pleased by what it reflected. She hadn't always embraced herself, as the psychobabble folks called it. As a teenager, she'd wanted to have her mother's voluptuous curves instead of the skinny B cup body she'd been given. Now at the age of thirty-two she'd long ago made peace with her lack of bosoms, as her grandmother used to say. Her body was her body, and it was serving her well. She turned in the mirror and looked at the fit of her pants. She thought she had a pretty good butt, too.

The buzzer rang. Lacy strode confidently to the intercom. "Who's there?"

"Hey, baby."

"Hey," she said softly. "Come on up."

He knocked on her door a few minutes later, and when she opened it, their eyes met, and then their lips.

"Missed you," he whispered.

Seeing stars, Lacy murmured, "Missed you, too."

Drake could see that the kiss had shaken her a little bit, and he liked that. "You look nice. Purple is the color on the Vachon crest."

Lacy closed the door and wondered if the kiss had affected her hearing. "What crest?"

"Our family crest."

"You're talking about the crests you can by for 29.99 in the magazines?"

He laughed. "No. My family has a *real* crest. It has two dragons with their necks entwined. One purple, the other gold."

"What do the dragons represent?"

"My really great-grandfather, Galen Vachon, and his wife Hester."

Lacy was impressed. "I love that." She'd never

heard of such a thing before. "How far can you trace your people back?"

"France. Seventeen hundreds."

Lacy stared. She studied his handsome face. Then she gave him a look. "You made this up, right?"

He shook his head. "Nope." He raised his hand. "Scout's honor. I was an Eagle Scout, you know."

She smiled. "No, I didn't know. Altar boy too, I'll bet."

"Yep. St. Mattie's on Woodward."

Lacy found him so interesting. "So this dragon great-grandfather came from France?"

"His father did. Galen was born in Louisiana."

"Okay. I'll bite. You can tell me all about this family of yours over dinner."

"I'm not making this up."

"Whatever you say, Mr. Mayor." Lacy grabbed her purse and keys. "I'm so interested that I'm going to let you ride in my new car."

Drake, being a Vachon said, "But—I brought my Mustang."

Lacy just looked at him. "Please. Once you see my mother's birthday present, you're going to take that 'Stang back to the dealer."

Drake drawled, "Them's pretty strong words, ma'am."

She tossed back, "And I got the horses to back 'em up, Your Honor." She beckoned a coy finger. "Come with me."

As she locked up her place and led Drake back

down the hall to the elevator, he watched the swing of her behind in the black pants and knew he'd follow that sweet walk anywhere.

The garage was underground. They walked for a few moments, then Lacy pointed like Vanna White at her new car.

Drake's jaw dropped. "Damn!" He couldn't decide where to look first. "I apologize." Mesmerized, he took a slow walk around her Crossfire while the pleased Lacy looked on. "I saw one of these at the Auto Show back in January. Your mother bought this?"

"Yep. She drives a Porsche Boxster, so she's into speed."

Drake shook his head. He couldn't wait to meet her. "And it's a stick?"

"Only thing I drive. My mother calls it my only walk on the wild side."

"What's that mean?"

"My mother is a true creative person. She takes risks, isn't afraid of anything this side of the Lord, but I was a real timid child. For a while, there, I was afraid of anything that lived outside the house."

Her bittersweet smile hit Drake dead in the heart. "You're certainly not timid now."

"No, but I'm not as flamboyant or as open as mama thinks I could be."

"When did the timid girl turn into the Lacy you are now?"

"Around the year I turned nine, when she forced

me to be a Girl Scout. Hated it, at first. Hated the leader, the other girls, and then we went to camp."

"Thought you didn't like the outdoors," he said, watching her with a smile.

"I thought I didn't either, but once I figured out that the leader wasn't going to send me home no matter how hard I cried, and that if I didn't participate in the activities the other girls in my cabin wouldn't get their badges, and would probably hate me for life, I stopped being such a spoiled pain in the butt and actually started to enjoy myself. Scouts turned me around in so many ways. Shoot, by the time I was thirteen I was going hunting with my daddy. Had my own rifle too."

She took out her keys and hit the clicker to open the coupe's locks.

Drake said, "Can't see you as a spoiled brat."

Lacy got behind the wheel. "Please. I was the only child of Valerie Garner Green. By the time I was seven years old, I'd been to Paris, Rio, and seen the pyramids. You couldn't tell me a thing."

Laughing, he got in on his side. While buckling himself in, he checked out the silver satin interior. "Nice. It's like a cockpit in here."

"It is nice, isn't it? We'll take a quick ride so you feel this smooth ride, then we'll come back and pick up your Mustang."

She turned the key in the ignition and the engine roared to life. The garage door lifted, and Lacy threw the stick into reverse. Looking over at the mayor, she gave him a grin and headed for the exit. Once she was on the street, she told him, "You know, I wasn't sure about this car when I first saw it, but then I said, 'Why not? I have a new job in a new city. I'm having a whole new life. Maybe Mama's right. Maybe it's time to let the old, staid, Escort-driving, scientist Lacy go, and act like her for a change.' " Then she added, "But only to a point. I don't think I'll be dancing on table tops in Morocco like she did when I was thirteen."

"She dances on tables?"

Lacy headed the car up Jefferson Avenue toward the freeway. The evening traffic was fairly light. "Yep, and this particular time it was with some man claiming to be a prince. He wanted her to marry him."

Drake chuckled.

She looked his way for a moment, then went back to the traffic. "It's funny now, but it wasn't back then. I used to travel with her every summer. By the time I was fifteen, she was embarrassing me every time I turned around, or so I thought. I told Daddy about her and that prince the minute we got home."

"What'd he say?"

"Told me, one, nobody liked a tattletale, and two, since I was so embarrassed by Mama, next summer he'd get me a job sorting mail in the post office where he worked." Lacy laughed. "Shut me right up."

Drake joined in. "I'll bet it did."

Lacy stopped at the red light in front of the IHOP owned by Anita Baker and said, "So, yes, I was a spoiled brat. Did your mother and sisters spoil you—you being the only boy?"

"Hell, no."

They both laughed while she pulled away from the light.

"My mother said I was not going to grow up and be cute and useless, as she called it, so I did dishes, ran the vacuum, and did my own laundry once I turned twelve. The only thing I can't do is cook. After I burned up a few of her good pots, she wouldn't let me anywhere near the stove."

When Lacy entered the tunnel leading to the freeway, she said, "Hang onto your seat. This baby can roll."

And she was right. She had the speedometer up to eighty in no time.

Drake said, "You need to slow down, little girl. The papers will have a field day if we get a ticket."

Lacy knew he was right, but she kept the speed steady. They flew for a few minutes more, then she exited the freeway, turned around and headed back the way they'd come. Grinning, she looked over at Drake. "We'll go back and get your car now."

Drake shook his head and said, "Thank you."

Keeping her eyes on the traffic, she asked, "Since you can't cook, what are we eating?"

"If you don't slow down, we'll be eating county food at the jail."

They were approaching downtown again, so Lacy eased back on the gas, took the transmission down to fifth and then down to third as they entered the tunnel to Jefferson. "Better?" she asked him.

"Much," he told her. A second later his phone rang

and Drake cursed softly. Putting the phone to his ear, he said crisply, "Yeah."

Lacy focused her attention on driving.

Drake said sharply, "When? . . . Okay. I'm not far. Be there in a few minutes . . . Okay." He clicked off and told her grimly, "Two officers were shot about twenty minutes ago. One's dead. I need to go see the family."

Lacy nodded tersely and drove back to her place. He directed her to where he'd parked the Mustang.

Getting out, he told her, "I'll call you later if it's not too late. Sorry about dinner."

"Go do what you have to do. We can have dinner anytime."

He kissed her good-bye, got into his car and drove away. As his car disappeared from sight, Lacy sent up a prayer.

Drake genuinely hated this part of his job. Three times in the past seven months he'd made the same, long grim walk down the bustling corridors of Detroit Receiving Hospital to where a grieving police officer's family sat waiting. Unlike other mayoral duties, which grew easier with practice, this hadn't. In fact, each incident seemed harder than the one before. As always, he was accompanied by his lady police chief, Cassandra Robinson. She found the task difficult as well.

Drake asked, "What's her husband's name again?"

The six-foot-two former Marine drill master dressed in her formal blue uniform answered,

"Harold. Harold Carnegie. He and Mary have three kids."

Drake shook his head at the injustice. "How old?"

"Sixteen, twelve, and eight. She'd been on the force ten years."

They found Mr. Carnegie seated outside the E.R. When he looked up at their approach, his eyes were red with grief. Drake stepped forward and offered his hand. "Mr. Carnegie."

The man nodded and stood. "Hello, Mayor Randolph . . . Chief Robinson. Appreciate you coming."

"We wanted to extend our condolences, and to let you how very sorry we all are for your loss," Drake said sincerely.

Carnegie, who appeared to be in his mid-forties, replied simply, "Thanks.

The chief asked, "Is there anything the department can do?"

He shook his head. "No. Her mother's flying in tonight from Memphis to help with the arrangements. Her sergeant said he'd get all the paperwork for her insurance and everything to me as soon as he could."

"Well, let us know if we can help in any way."

He nodded.

Drake saw the tall teenager standing by the wall watching them. The anger in the boy's face seemed to compete with his grief. Drake walked over. "I'm Mayor Randolph. Sorry about your mother, son."

"I don't want your sorrys."

His father said firmly, "Harold Jr., show some respect."

"For what?" the son tossed back angrily. "That crackhead didn't show Mama no respect!" Then he added, "I hate this city."

"Your mother was trying to make a difference."

"Yeah, and look what it got her."

Drake could see the boy holding back his tears. "We're very sorry."

The kid looked Drake in the eye and said, "You done your duty, so go on back downtown."

Harold Sr. turned on his son. "Stop it!"

Chief Robinson told Harold Sr., "It's okay. That's his grief talking. We'll be giving Mary a police escort at the funeral if that's okay with your family."

Focused now on the chief, he told her, "She'd like that."

"Please don't hesitate to call if you need our help."

He nodded.

Drake said, "Again, we're very sorry for your loss, Mr. Carnegie. Very sorry."

Carnegie looked at Drake. "She knew this might happen one day, and she was okay with it, even if we weren't. She loved her job and she loved this city." Then he put his head in his hands and said softly, "How am I going to live without her?"

Chief Robinson placed a consoling hand on his shoulder. "Stay strong. We'll find the shooter, don't worry."

Harold Jr. said furiously, "It won't bring her back, though, will it?"

Drake shook his head, "No, son, it won't."

Drake watched a lone tear slide down the boy's

face, a grim reminder that beneath all that anger was a grieving sixteen-year-old kid looking at burying his mother. "Your dad's going to need you. Be there for him."

The kid locked gazes with Drake. "I know. You just find the person who shot her."

"We will."

The kid rolled his angry eyes. "Yeah, right."

A somber Drake shook Mr. Carnegie's hand once again, then he and the chief left to see the family of Mary Carnegie's partner, Leo Vasquez. Vasquez was still in surgery.

Lena Vasquez was one of the city's attorneys. Her father Ricardo had been a cop, but Drake knew that the family's ties to the police department didn't make their waiting or worrying any easier.

Lena walked up and Drake gave her a strong hug. They'd been friends since high school. "How you doing?"

She wiped at her eyes with a wadded tissue. "I'm hanging. They say the surgery may take another two hours. The bullet is lodged near his heart."

Lena shook the chief's hand and said, "Thanks for coming down."

She then introduced them to the large contingent of family members waiting with her. Drake shook the hands of those he didn't know and gave hugs of hope and consolation to the ones he did, like Lena's mother and her father, Lupe and Ricardo. Detroit Receiving Hospital was one of the nation's premier trauma facilities, and being a physician, Drake knew that Leo was in the best of hands. If there was any chance for survival, the surgeons would make it happen.

He spent a few more minutes talking with Lena and her family, then he and the chief excused themselves and headed to the parking lot. As Cassandra got into her vehicle, she said, grimly, "Sometimes I hate this job."

"I do, too," Drake echoed. "Call me when the word on Leo comes down. I don't care what time it is, and I want to be kept current on the search for the shooter." He couldn't get the angry face of Harold Carnegie Jr. out of his mind.

"Will do."

She drove off, and a saddened Drake walked back to his car.

Reynard Parker looked at the grainy film on his computer, his henchman Fish beside him. Parker was trying to determine if any of the men in black might be the mayor. He'd gotten the tape of one of the old Drug Buster raids from a friend of his at the police department. The police had gotten it from a citizen who'd filmed the raid on a home video camera. Because the footage had been shot at night, details were hard to determine. In reality, the masked men coming out of the house could be any males anywhere, and just because Parker wanted one of the them to be Drake Randolph didn't make it so. One man in particular drew his eye, however. He was built like Randolph, and as he stood with his weapon raised while looking up and down the street, the camera had gotten a clear view. Parker asked his hacker employee sitting at the computer's keyboard, "How tall would you say that one standing by the van is?"

The blond man looked at the individual. "Six-one, six-two, maybe."

Parker knew that Randolph was six-two. "Could that be the mayor?"

The man turned. "The mayor? You think he's in on this?"

"Just answer the question."

The employee shook his head. "I can't say, and unless you know of a software program that can take masks off of video images, we'll never know."

Parker had no idea if anything that sophisticated existed.

Fish said, "Now if somebody wanted to start a rumor that this is the mayor, there's really no way to honestly prove it isn't him, if you think about it. I mean the body types and the height are real close matches."

Parker agreed. So if he were to anonymously send this film to the newspapers with the simple question, "Is this Mayor Randolph?" would they run the picture or ignore it? He knew that papers were in business to sell papers, and a story like this would definitely cause a stir. It would also put Randolph on the defensive, maybe even start enough clamoring to have the Dope Busters investigated for real. He himself, of course, would go on record as being against the vigilantes and for a complete and thorough investigation. Parker wanted to make Drake Randolph's world hell, and this was as good a way to start as any.

Eleven

Drake got the word on Leo Vasquez's condition around midnight. The surgeons were able to remove the bullet, but the next forty-eight hours would be critical as to whether he'd make it or not. Drake knew how strong Lena's husband was in both mind and spirit, and if anyone could survive, Leo would. There'd been no word on the shooter, however. The street investigation and canvassing was ongoing. According to witnesses, two perps had burst into the party store with guns. They'd demanded cash from the clerk, only to be confronted by Leo and Mary, who were in the store buying coffee. When Leo yelled for the perp to drop his gun, the second shooter somehow came up behind Mary, shot her, and put a bullet in Leo's chest. Leo managed to plug the killer in the leg before collapsing. Then Mary's killer and his bleeding friend ran, jumped into an old Buick, and disappeared into the night. The store clerk guessed the whole incident took less than thirty seconds.

Drake shook his head at yet another senseless loss of life. He was home, and the interior of the mansion was dark. He'd drawn the drapes back and was standing in front of the living room's wide window looking out over the black ribbon of the river at the lights of Windsor on the other side. Myk had been pressuring him to make a decision about reelection, but he still hadn't made up his mind. On one hand, he thought that given four more years he could make a difference in the city's quality of life, but on the other hand, the job seemed to be a thankless one, not to mention having to deal with evenings like this one.

At this point in his life he should be coming home to a wife and a couple of kids every night. Having never had a father, he planned on playing a major league role in his hypothetical children's lives, but because of the choices he was making, he hadn't had time to look for that special lady. He'd done med school, then interned, then took a coveted residency position in Boston. Coming back to Detroit, he chose to go into thoracic surgery, which turned out to be a good move, especially after his successful work on a linebacker for the hometown Lions. The linebacker and the team were so impressed by his skill, they began referring other players to him, who told other players, who in turn told other players, and soon Drake was working on football players, hockey legends, and basketball phenoms from across the country. For a kid from the east side of Detroit, his life back then was off the chain, because everywhere athletes went, parties and women followed.

He had tickets to Super Bowls and NBA All-Star weekends; he went to birthday bashes thrown by athletes, complete with pools and half-naked video hos on the arms of the rapper of the week. He'd partied, tasted the caviar, the women, and he looked up one day and was thirty-five and tired of doing surgery by day and the clubs with his boys at night. For some reason the fast lane became mundane. He seemed to need more in his life. So he closed his private practice and donated his skills to the Detroit hospitals, treating the uninsured. A year later Myk convinced him to run for mayor, and the rest, as they said, was history.

And now here he stood, wondering about the future and what it might hold. He knew he owed Myk an answer, but he didn't have one.

He turned away from the view and looked over at the lighted clock on the fireplace mantle. One A.M. Way too late to call Lacy.

"Might as well go on to bed," he told the darkness. Intent upon doing just that, he climbed the stairs to his bedroom but it took a long time for him to close his eyes and sleep.

Sunday morning Drake got dressed and drove the Mustang to meet his mother, sisters, and their families for the eleven o'clock service at St. Matthew's and St. Joseph's Episcopal Church. The building was on the National Register for historic sites, and for Drake it was historic; he'd been baptized there, taken his first communion there, and even kissed his first girl there. Cathy Kelly. The memory made him smile. He was a thirteen-year-old acolyte, and she'd been twelve and in the junior choir. He remembered being in puppy love with her for months, but when her parents moved to Cleveland, he never saw her again.

Drake pulled into the church parking lot just as his mother Mavis stepped out of her fresh-washed, steel-gray Chrysler 300. The paint sparkled in the April sun, and she smiled and waved a gloved hand. Drake understood why the widowers were always walking behind her with their tongues hanging out. His mama was still hot. She was trim and carried herself like the confident sixty-three-year-old dark-skinned beauty that she was. As always, Mavis had on an elaborate but stylish hat. Today's choice was navy blue to match the fine navy blue suit she was wearing.

When he got out of the Mustang, she walked over and gave him a hug and a kiss on the cheek. "So sorry to hear about the policewoman last night. How's Lena's Leo?"

"Still critical."

She shook her head sadly. "I remember their wedding. Ricardo wasn't sure he wanted to give his baby girl away to someone from California."

Drake smiled. "He did give Leo a hard time, didn't he?"

They began to walk

"Did the police catch the shooters?"

Drake shook his head. "Not yet."

They started up the great stone steps that led to the

door of the big church that was originally known as St. Joseph's. It was built in 1927 and had a White congregation. St. Matthew's, originally established in 1845, was an historic Black Episcopal church, and the third oldest Black church in the state. In 1971 urban renewal forced a merger of the two congregations and the church name was changed to St. Matthew's and St. Joseph's.

Inside, the hushed atmosphere of the sanctuary resonated off the stone columns and statuary. It was an English-style Gothic church with gray limestone trim, and the congregation these days was all Black. Drake ushered his mother into their traditional pew, kissed his sisters and the cheeks of his nieces and nephews, shook the hands of his two brothers-in-law, then stood as the organist began the processional.

After church, the Randolph clan gathered at their mother's place, like they did every third Sunday of the month for dinner, good times, and the chance to catch up on each other's lives. The topic of today was, of course, Drake and Lacy.

His big sister Madey asked, "So, when do we get to meet her?"

He bit off a piece of his fried chicken leg and shrugged. "Soon."

Baby sister Sharon, spoon-feeding mashed potatoes to her toddler in the high chair, asked, "You said that last Sunday. We want to see her, Drake. Are you ashamed of us?"

"Maybe she's hard on the eyes," quipped his brother-in-law.

Drake looked at him. "Et tu, Brute?"

Everyone around the table laughed.

Drake tossed back, "No, the lady is fine, but she is the only child of an only child. I don't want this horde scaring her to death."

Angela, Drake's baker sister, said, "I've seen some of her mother's work and it's very good. Is Lacy an artist too?"

"Not that I know of," Drake said honestly. "I'm still getting to know her."

"Well hurry up. You know how nosey we are," his sister Denise announced. "If she's a potential sister-in-law, we need to check her out."

Drake looked over at his mother. He knew this sister-in-law talk stemmed from her. To which Mavis replied innocently, "Don't look at me. I didn't say a word."

Drake rolled his eyes and tried to ignore all the female giggles.

By five that afternoon it was time for everyone to pack up and go home. As his sisters rounded up their children and his brothers-in-law went out to start the cars, Drake watched his mother turn on the dishwasher. His four teenage nieces had pooled their summer job money last summer and purchased the dishwasher for their grandmother. Mavis had appreciated the gift, but she and everyone else knew the teens had made the gesture just so they wouldn't have to hand-wash so many dishes when the holidays rolled around. Drake asked, "Where was Uncle Burt today?"

"In Chicago," Mavis answered. "Some kind of racetrack convention."

"Is he still mad?"

"Yes, but he'll get over it. He could have killed that girl with his crazy driving. I don't let him drive me to the curb."

Drake chuckled. "Oh, I forgot. Duke over at the barbershop says hello."

Mavis shook her head. "Duke. He's persistent if nothing else."

"You're not too old to have a man, Mama."

She gave him a look. "I know that, Drake, but Duke has never been and never will be on the list. Trust me."

"Okay."

When the dishwasher started up, they both left the kitchen. Drake picked up his coat and she walked him to the door. "What are you doing about all these barrels of poison folks are leaving all over town?"

He shook his head with amusement at her fierce love for the city. "We're working on it."

"Good. The sooner you put them in jail, the better off we'll be."

"Yes, ma'am."

She gave him a kiss on the cheek. "Keep yourself safe, and bring that Lacy around so we can meet her, please."

"I will, soon. I promise."

"Promises, promises. You politicians are all alike."

He kissed her on the cheek. "So are you mamas."

She laughed, and he took the familiar sound with him to his car. He waved good-bye and drove away.

* * *

Lacy should have been at home hours ago, but she was still in the office Monday evening finishing up a report. She figured she had at least another hour and half before it was done. The department's ancient computers were taking a lifetime to crunch the numbers she'd put into the program. If the new software was able to do it, she'd be able to head home. But would she get the answer before next week this time? she wondered wearily.

The report was on the outcome of the federal cleanup of lead-laced soil in one of the east-side neighborhoods. The pollution came from Metro Metals, a large smelting plant that had operated in the area for thirty years before closing in 1984. At the height of Metro's operation, the company's smokestacks sent up two pounds of lead per *hour* into the surrounding air. The cleanup had taken eighteen months at a cost of $3.4 million taxpayer dollars. But what amazed, angered, and saddened Lacy all at once was that federal and local authorities knew about the site, but no testing had been done until one of the local papers put the issue on the front page. By then hundreds of children had been exposed to the potent neurotoxins inherent in high levels of lead. Lacy knew there were sites like Metro Metals all over the nation, and most were in the neighborhoods of people who looked like her.

To distract herself from her growing anger, she added more paper to the printer.

Twenty minutes later she heard a knock on the door. Because she was the only person still in the office, she'd locked the outside doors for safety reasons. There were security personnel in the building, but she felt safer with the locks on.

She walked to the glass and saw Drake on the other side. In his hands were white cartons from somebody's takeout. Smiling, she flipped the locks and let him in.

He grinned. "Heard you were working late." He stopped a moment to kiss her so lusciously, her toes curled. "Thought you might want to take a break and eat."

Rocked again by the power of his kiss, Lacy finally opened her eyes and asked, "Who told you I was still here?"

"Saw your lights on when Malcolm brought me back from my meeting downriver about an hour ago."

"You know my window from the street?"

"Sure," he told her without a lick of shame. "That's what we men do. Never know when I might have to fly up here and rescue you or something."

She chuckled. "Or something."

They spent the next few moments silently checking each other out, and Lacy could feel herself becoming warm in places that let her know the woman inside herself was arising. Looking away, she asked him, "What's in the cartons?"

He set the four containers on her desk. Two were shaped traditionally, but the other two were long and thin. "Let's see, we have Coneys. Fries. Chili. And some peach cobbler."

She grinned.

"I did good."

"You did good. I love Coneys."

"Enough for another kiss?"

"Enough for as many kisses as you want."

He raised a pleased eyebrow.

Lacy walked over to him and placed her arms around his neck. He looked down with amused eyes. "If I had known you were turned on by Coneys, I'da brought you some a long time ago. . . ."

She chuckled, then raised up so she could give him his just reward. The moment her lips met his, the playfulness fled. Passion flared, the kiss deepened, and Drake was pulling her so close Lacy felt the heat of his body merge with her own. He slowly moved his hand to the back of her neck and ran his hand over the tempting twists in her hair while she shimmered with the desire rising in her blood. He placed short, lingering kisses on her mouth that made the fire within increase, and she answered him as sweetly as she knew how. Hands that were warm as a summer night began to move languidly over her back and up her sides, then a palm slid over her already hard breast, causing Lacy to moan softly in response.

Drake wanted to spend the next hour removing her clothes so he could pay sensual tribute to each and every dark and lovely inch of her; take her nipples into his mouth and tease them until she blossomed and ran wet; part her thighs and show her all the ways he could make her come; but right now he was content to explore her, learn her, and show her just how much he wanted to please her.

The kisses continued; dazzling, lingering. Lacy was so caught up in the sensations flowing through her that she didn't protest when his hands began undoing the pearl buttons of her white silk blouse. She wanted his hands and lips in the places that were pleading the most: her breasts; the cove between her thighs. The thought shocked her, but she was too busy pulsing and throbbing to chastise herself for more scandalous wishes; too busy trying to catch her breath as he nuzzled his hot lips against the edges of her black lace bra; too busy savoring the way he made her feel. When he unhooked the clasp and she tumbled free, he took one nipple into his mouth and she came with a raspy cry.

Drake smiled and lifted his lips to hers again. Her small breasts were dark as the night, and he rolled the damp bud with an expert touch. He whispered against her mouth, "We have to work on your stamina, baby. . . ."

Lacy couldn't respond because of the orgasm still echoing within, but knew she would work on whatever he wanted. *Lord!* Had she come so quickly because it had been so long, or because of his scandalous expertise? The only thing she was sure of was that Mayor Drake Randolph knew his way around a woman's body, and her body was glad he did.

Drake was pleased that she'd responded so temptingly. Lacy Green was a very passionate woman, and he could hardly wait to explore that passion to the fullest. He kissed her and said boldly, "Let's eat, and I'll make you come again later. . . ."

Lacy dissolved in response to the sultry promise and to the heat blazing in his dark male eyes.

Drake was hard as a steel beam as he watched her slowly fix her bra and redo her buttons. He handed her one of the Coney containers. She took it out, added chili, and took her first bite. The suggestiveness of her action was not lost on him or his manhood. "Maybe I should have gotten something less—phallic?"

She smiled like a siren, then looking him in the eye, slowly took another slow bite of the dog.

"You're playing with fire, Miss Thing." His manhood had flared like the Fourth of July.

She used the tip of her pink tongue to catch a spot of chili on the corner of her mouth, then responded to his words with playful innocence. "I don't know what you're talking about," before taking another slow and deliberate bite of the dog.

"All right," he warned, chuckling softly. "Just for that, I'm going to make you scream next time around."

The sweet threat made Lacy's knees turn to pudding, but with her chin raised she said haughtily, "I've never screamed in my life."

"You will when I'm done with you," he promised, with eyes that stoked her temperature even higher. "Just wait."

Shimmering with anticipation, Lacy finished her

Coney. She'd never played sexy word games with a man before, and certainly not with Wilton. Sex had always been about him, and because she'd been so young, it never occurred to her that there might be other ways of going about it. They'd certainly never teased each other this way. Wilton had been about wham, bam, thank you ma'am, and when he was done, the sex was done, too. He hadn't cared about her needs because he didn't think she had any. These few encounters with Drake seemed to be proving him wrong. Drake's kisses and touches had set off something blooming inside that had her so antsy and hot, she was having trouble keeping still. Could he really make her scream? She'd always thought reactions like that happened only in X-rated movies and romance novels. Now she wasn't so sure, and the scandalous parts of herself that he'd brought to life were anxious to know the truth. She looked his way and found him watching her with a smoky, knowing gaze that set her heart to thumping.

Drake saw her look go chasing off and he smiled malely. Her mixture of innocence and sultriness was so tempting, it was hard for him to keep his seat and eat when what he wanted to do was make her scream. "You ready for your cobbler?" he asked when she finished that naughty Coney dog.

"Let me check on this report first. It's taking forever for the computer to do its thing."

He took a sip of his orange Faygo and walked over and stood behind her chair while she peered at the screen. "What're you working on?"

"Metro Metals."

Lacy saved the results to six disks, then went back out to the dark outer office and clicked on a few lights. The report was fifteen pages long, and she needed at least ten copies. She didn't want to still be printing pages this time tomorrow on her old, slow machine, so she'd used Ida's and Janika's printers in the hope of making the job go faster.

She didn't know he was behind her until the heat of his body gently warmed her back. As the printers churned, his surgeon's hands gently kneaded the tiredness in her shoulders, causing her head to drop in gratitude. He continued his slow dance on the tense muscles, and she purred. "You're very good at this, Your Honor. . . ."

He placed a soft kiss on her jaw. "These hands are insured for 2.5 mil. Want to see why?"

She smiled in the haze resettling over her senses. "You don't have a modest gene in your body, do you?"

"None of the Vachon men do. . . . I told you, we're special."

His hands slid from her shoulders and wordlessly turned her around to face him. When he lowered his mouth to hers, they began again; kissing, nibbling. Fueled by mutual desire, hands began to roam as they both sought to touch and explore. The hot kisses he trailed down her throat made her head fall back, and the faint scents of her skin spurred him on. This time when he freed her breasts, he feasted slowly, fully; making her nipples blossom and answer to his scandalous Vachon finesse. She was glad her hips were braced against the edge of Ida's desk because the solid support kept her from melting to the floor.

Drake recaptured her lips and spent an inordinate amount of time playing, teasing, and inviting. His palm moved up and down her hip, squeezing, circling, then over the round curves of her behind. The warmth of her skin radiated against his palms, making him want to find the source of that heat. Not breaking the kiss, he filled his hands with her ripe hips and pressed his need against her. She answered him with a slow lusty rhythm that tantalized him into joining in.

With him burning hot and hard against her thighs, and his hand roaming erotically over the front of her skirt, Lacy shuddered in response. Her legs parted of their own accord, and he took full and exquisite advantage; touching, exploring, making her croon her pleasure. She'd never had a man do her this way. Never.

Drake thought she was the hottest little thing this side of the international border. He pushed the skirt up and froze with delight at the tantalizing sight of the sexy little black garter belt holding up the equally sexy stockings. When he spotted the black thong hidden between, he didn't think it possible for him to get any more aroused, but he was. In fact, he had to close his eyes and take a deep breath to keep himself from going over the edge.

Lacy leaned up and kissed him softly, meaningfully. "Problems?"

He slid his hands over the bare skin above the stockings and returned her kiss. "No ma'am. Do you dress like this all the time?"

She smiled and leaned back to look into his face. "Why? Don't you like it?"

He teased an expert finger over the center of her soul and she gasped.

He chuckled lowly. "Oh, yes. Very much. Do you like this . . . ?"

His "this" made her legs wobble, then widen so he could play. Her response was a strangled whisper. "Very much."

Drake was using every bit of discipline he'd learned to keep from lying her down on the desk and taking her until the sun rose. Never in his life had he expected to find such a visual treat beneath the conservative skirts of Lacy Green. Standing in front of him with her skirt raised and her legs encased in that sex queen gear made him want to fall to his knees and pay her the ultimate tribute, but he couldn't stop touching her, stroking her, teasing her. He also couldn't turn away from the passion on her face because he was the one causing it. "You ready to scream now . . . ?"

Lacy knew that the answer was yes; she was three-quarters of the way to orgasm now. She knew how scandalous she must look with her bra undone, her skirt up, and her legs wide, but she didn't care as long as he didn't stop.

He slid in a delicious finger and she groaned. Her

eyes closed and her body tightened around the sweet invasion. "Drake . . ."

He bent to take a nipple into his mouth. "What, baby?" His wicked tongue made a slow circle around the bursting bud while the finger sensually impaling her began to move in and then slowly out.

"Lord . . ." she whispered.

Lacy answered the rhythm without shame. He was watching her with glittering eyes, but she didn't care. All she cared about was the heat this man had built between her thighs and holding onto it for as long as she could.

But she was too inexperienced and he was too good. When he slid another finger inside and began to brand her with his own special magic, her body exploded. The world-shaking orgasm broke over her like waves against a sea wall, and she was shuddering and screaming into his suit-covered shoulder to keep from being heard by her mother in Georgia.

Lacy came back to herself seated on his lap in Ida's chair. When she met his eyes, he was smiling. "Now, what were you saying about never screaming?"

She dug him playfully in the ribs. "Nobody likes a braggart, Your Honor."

He chuckled, and she let him cuddle her closer. Lacy realized that being held this way felt so natural and right it was almost scary; scary in the sense that she could start learning to like this.

He told her, "Next time, though, we need a bed. I was this close from taking you on this desk. Not that I wouldn't mind, but the first time should be on a bed."

The visual of making love on a desk warmed her cheeks, but she tossed back anyway, "How do you know there will be a next time?"

His big hand slid up her thigh to the swollen throbbing place still echoing from the sensual explosion, and began to play. She growled softly and her head fell back.

"That's why," he told her in a voice as soft as his touch. "Need another example?"

Lacy's hips began to slowly circle in response to his wicked coaxing. "No . . ."

"Sure?" His free hand went to work on her still damp nipples.

The sensations from the hand above and the wicked one below made her breathe out, "Yes."

Drake kissed her longingly. "Good."

Lacy let herself enjoy the moment for a bit longer, then reluctantly dragged herself away from his spell-casting hands and lips. "I need to check the printers."

He nodded. She stood and righted her clothes while he watched, his handsome faced as pleased as a maharajah. Lacy wondered if the pulsing between her legs was ever going to stop. Shaking her brain to get it back in the game, she went to check on the reports.

The printers were done. She and Drake collated the pages and placed them in labeled folders. The report was ready for tomorrow's presentation.

"Thanks for your help," she said.

He was standing over by the windows, arms folded and with a look in his eye that reminded of what they'd shared. "Any time," he said. "Ready to head out?"

"Let me clean up this stuff we left, first."

The two of them gathered up the remains of their dinner and placed the now empty boxes in the trash. "We never ate the cobbler," she said.

He shrugged. "That's okay, the dessert we had was better anyway."

Once again heat came to her cheeks and she dropped her eyes.

"Am I embarrassing you?" he asked with a soft laugh.

"A little bit, I guess."

He walked over and put his arms around her. He kissed the top of her twisted hair. "Sorry. Part of my nature."

She looked up. "More of the Vachon charm?"

He nodded. "Yeah, I guess you could say that."

"No shame in your game?"

"Not a bit." Then he added, "Not a lot in yours either, Miss Garter Belt."

Lacy dropped her head against his chest. "It's just underwear. If I'd known ahead of time that we were going to . . . you know, I'd have probably put on something different."

"Oh, no. It's too late to be changing up now. I've already seen your act and I can't wait for round two."

"You are outrageous."

"Me? I wasn't the one screaming the building down."

She had to laugh. "Quit picking on me. I'm kinda new at this."

"And I kinda like that."

They studied each other for a long smile-filled moment, then he said, "Let's go. I'll walk you to your car."

Downstairs in the deserted parking lot, Lacy took out her keys and freed the locks. There were lights flooding the space but because it was so late her car was the only one around. She opened the door and tossed her briefcase and purse on the passenger seat. "Thanks again for dinner and *dessert.*"

"Any time. I'd kiss you except there are cameras down here and I don't want us to wind up on the eleven o'clock news."

"Me either." But she wanted one more kiss, one more feel of his arms around her.

"I'll call you later."

"I'd like that."

Their eyes were locked. They both read each other's hunger.

"Good night, Drake."

" 'Night, baby. Drive safe."

She nodded and got in. With a wave, she and the coupe roared off. Drake stood and watched until the taillights disappeared down the ramp.

Twelve

Lacy was in the tub soaking away the day and grinning at the memories of Drake's loving when the phone rang. It was Drake.

"Hey," he said.

She used her toes to raise a fluffy cloud of the scented bubbles. "Hey back. Are you home?"

"Yep. Did I wake you?"

"Nope. I'm soaking in the tub."

"With or without the garter belt?"

She smiled. "None of your business."

They spent the next forty minutes talking, laughing, and flirting back and forth. She had to turn on the hot water a couple times to bring the temperature up but was enjoying herself too much to get out and dry off. They were in the middle of talking about the Piston's chances of winning another NBA title when the call waiting beep sounded in Lacy's ear. "Hold on a minute, Drake. I've got a beep."

"Go ahead."

Lacy clicked over. "Hello."

"This is Lenny Durant."

Lacy went still. "How'd you get my number?"

"Not important. We found fourteen more barrels on the east side tonight and a shitload of tires on Belle Isle."

Lacy let out a very unladylike curse.

"Exactly," Lenny said. "I think we may have a lead, though. If it works out, I'll be in touch." And he was gone.

Lacy clicked back. "Drake? You still there?"

"Yeah. You okay? You sound kinda shaky."

"That was Lenny Durant," she told him, still confused over him having her home number.

"What did he want?"

"To let me know that his people have found more barrels, on the east side this time, and somebody dumped a big load of tires on Belle Isle."

Drake hissed a curse.

"Yeah, but how did he get my home number?"

"You didn't give it to him, I take it."

"No."

"Then that's a good question."

"Well, I'll ask him again when I see him. He said he might have a lead on who's doing the dumping, but he didn't give a name. Just said he'd be in touch."

"Okay. If he calls back, let me know. In the meantime I need to make some calls on the barrels and get hold of HazMat again."

"I'll call them and meet you back downtown in about thirty minutes. This is my job, you know."

"I know, but there's not much you can do besides watch."

"What about canvassing the neighborhood to see if anybody saw anything?"

"Police can handle that for now."

"Drake—"

"Lacy, I appreciate your dedication, but it's okay if you're not riding the first horse into the battle on this one. Believe me, if anything jumps off that needs your immediate attention, I promise I'll call."

"Doesn't matter the time."

"Even if it's four A.M."

"Okay."

"You sound skeptical."

"Because I am."

"Don't be. If I needed you here, believe me, you'd be here."

"All right."

"I'll fill you in when you get to work in the morning."

"Sounds good."

"You get some sleep."

"You too."

"Good night, baby," he said softly.

Her tone matched his. " 'Night, Drake."

When Lacy got to work the next morning, no sooner did she step in the outer door than Ida appeared and said in a rush, "The *Free Press* wants you to call them, so does the Detroit News. Channels 2, 7, 4, and 9 over in Windsor want to do interviews."

Lacy stopped. "What for?"

"The barrels that turned up last night. The papers are calling it an epidemic and want to know what the city plans to do about it."

Ida handed Lacy the morning *Free Press*. Sure enough, there was an article on page one titled: DUMPING SPREE SPREADS. Lacy gave the paper back and started the walk to her office. "Do you know how Lenny Durant got my home number?"

"BAD's Lenny Durant?"

"The one and only." Lacy set her briefcase on her desk. "My home number is unlisted and I never put it on the business cards that I hand out."

"You know, some of his people were arrested a few months back for hacking into the EPA's computers. Maybe they did something like that to get your number."

Lacy didn't know, but she planned to find out when she saw him again.

Ida asked, "Why did he call?"

"To tell me about the new barrels on the east side and the tires somebody dumped on Belle Isle. Has the mayor's office called down so we'll know what to say to the media?"

"Rhonda said to refer all the interview requests to the office."

"That's easy. Anything else on the stove?"

"Yes, this."

Ida handed Lacy a piece of paper. On it was a

grainy picture of a man in a ski mask holding a gun. Beneath the picture were the words, *Is this the Mayor, a Dope Buster?*

"Where'd you get this?"

"It was stapled to the light pole in front of my house this morning. I know it wasn't there last night when I got back from playing cards because Herbert or I would've seen it."

Janika added. "Everybody in the building's talking about it. I guess whoever printed these is putting them up all over the city."

"What's a Dope Buster?"

So Ida explained.

"Really, and whoever put up these flyers thinks Drake is part of these Dope Busters?"

"Evidently."

"He wouldn't be involved with something like this."

Ida said, "Doesn't matter. The real people of Detroit, myself included, wish we had more folks like the Dope Busters. Back when the Busters were rolling every night, people cheered when they took down crack houses in their neighborhoods."

Janika said, "Shoot, one Sunday my pastor had the congregation pray for the Dope Busters. He called them 'God's wrath.' "

"So everybody liked them?" Lacy asked.

Janika tossed back, "Everybody but the dealers and the crackheads. There were some reports about dealers being hauled away, but hey, what's one less dealer? The Busters took down dope houses near schools the police wouldn't touch, and those houses didn't reopen a few days later like they do most times."

Lacy didn't know what to think. "And the police never caught them?"

"Nope."

She looked at the blurry figure on the flyer again. *That couldn't be Drake, could it?* She shook her head and handed the paper back to Ida. "I need to get ready for the Circus." The Circus was the name Ida and a few hundred thousand Detroit citizens called the Detroit City Council. Lacy had to present the info on Metro Metals in one hour. She was not looking forward to seeing Councilman Reynard Parker again.

One hour later she was standing against a wall in the jam-packed boardroom of the City Council waiting for the long agenda to wind its way down to her and her report. She was standing because there was no place to sit. Although the council members had seats around the long executive-size table, the surrounding chairs were filled with citizens waiting to state their cases on various issues, local media representatives, secretaries, aides, police officers, and a slew of other folks in the room for whatever reason. And because of all the bodies, the temperature in the room was warm enough for Lacy to feel a sheen of perspiration on her forehead.

The council was known for its feuding, bickering, and sometimes bizarre interactions between its members. In the past, members had challenged each other to fights, talked about folks' mamas, and generally behaved worse than spoiled children. Today there were no such shenanigans. The agenda items were handled precisely and professionally.

Fifty minutes passed before it became Lacy's turn. She stepped up to the podium, introduced herself, and referred the council members to the packets given to them earlier by one of the council aides. She had just begun to speak when Councilwoman Lola Draper stopped her with a wave of her beringed hand. "This is that site on the east side that was in the paper?"

Lacy studied the middle-age face of the former beauty queen. She knew Draper had a reputation for being difficult. "Yes."

Seated beside Draper was Parker, and he didn't bother to hide his look of contempt. Across the table sat Councilman Winters. The rotund, gray-haired Winters was a former schoolteacher. Back in February, his wife had stormed into a City Council meeting demanding to know about Winters and his "*other woman*." The local media had had a field day. Next to him sat Carolyn Clawson, the oldest member of the council at age seventy-eight. She raised a liver-spotted hand and asked, "Are you the same L. Green who put this together?"

Lacy saw that she was holding a copy of the Blight Court report. "Yes, ma'am."

"Forget Metro Metals, talk to us about this."

A surprised Lacy grabbed hold of her scrambled brain and began to speak.

When she was done, Clawson said, "Councilman Parker has decided this is a waste of money. What do you say to that?"

Lacy ignored Parker's truly angry face and said, "Mr. Parker has expressed his concerns, but I believe anytime we can make the environment cleaner for our children, the small amount of money we invest now will reap thousands more in future benefits. We can have fewer hospital visits for children with asthma, cleaner ground water, cleaner alleys, and fewer abandoned homes. I don't see it as a waste, and this program has worked successfully in Chicago for years."

Parker said, "The landlords of the city already have a big enough burden. They've removed lead paint, put up smoke detectors. Even when the tenants tear them out, the landlord is required to put up new ones. They don't need any new ordinances."

Councilman Pierce, the youngest male on the council, cracked, "No, they just need new tenants." Then he said, "I like this proposal too, and I make a motion that we put this to a vote, here and now."

Lacy forced herself not to show surprise.

The vote was nine to two. The dissenters were Parker and Draper, the Scalia and Thomas of Detroit politics.

Lacy was congratulated by the members who'd voted in favor of her proposal. Draper left the room to take a phone call, but Parker watched Lacy with such evil eyes, she left the room as soon as she could. Only after she entered the elevator did she smile at the victory.

When Ida and Janika got back from lunch, the happy Lacy was in her office seated at her desk.

Ida said, "Brought you something back. How'd it go?"

Lacy took the salad and set it aside. "They want to implement the Blight Court as soon as possible."

Ida looked confused. "I thought you went to talk about Metro Metals?"

"I did." Then Lacy explained what happened and Parker's attempts to derail the proposal.

Ida waved a dismissive hand. "Who cares about Parker? That's fabulous news!"

Lacy grinned. "In about ten days we can start taking down polluters."

"Can we take down Parker too?"

"Only if he's the one dumping the barrels."

"We should be so lucky." Ida smiled and headed back to her desk.

Janika stuck her head around Lacy's door. "His Fineness called around 10:45. I told him you were with the council. He said call him whenever you get the time."

"Thanks."

Janika disappeared and Lacy picked up the phone.

When he came on the line, the first thing he said was, "Heard you blew the council away this morning. I'm getting all kinds of calls from folks singing your praises. Even the media."

"Glad you approve, Your Honor."

"I do." Then his voice changed to a more personal tone. "So, how are you?"

"I'm okay. What about you? Ida showed me the flyer."

He sighed. "I've been dealing with the press on that all morning."

"Do you have any idea where the pictures came from?"

"From what I've been told, the image was taken from a home video that used to be in a file over at police headquarters until a few days ago."

"Was it stolen?"

"Looks that way."

"The newspapers aren't taking this seriously, are they?"

"For now, no, but rumors can sometimes take on a life of their own, so I just have to wait and see. I'd like to get my hands on the people responsible for putting up the flyers, though."

"Well, I knew it was you the moment I saw it."

He went silent.

When he didn't respond, Lacy was instantly contrite. "I'm kidding, Drake, I'm sorry. I shouldn't be playing."

"That's okay. I was so distracted by you last night, I forgot to tell you, I'm leaving for Cleveland today. In fact, I'm on my way to the airport in about an hour. Be back Thursday, so I guess we won't see each other until then."

"Okay." She tried to keep the disappointment out of her voice but failed.

The amusement in his voice was easy to hear when he said, "I can put you in my suitcase. No one would ever know."

She did enjoy his humor. "Maybe next time."

"You sure?"

"Positive."

"Okay, then I'll call you soon as I get back."

"You'd better," she said softly.

" 'Bye, baby."

"Take care."

She set the phone down, then leaned back in her chair and thought about how much she was already missing him.

Drake set the phone down and wondered how a relationship based on untruths could ever work. Lacy had been right about the man on the flyer looking just like him, because it was him. NIA knew the film existed. It had been shown repeatedly on the local television stations during the height of NIA's initial campaign a few years back. However, because of the terrible quality of the video, no one associated with NIA had been concerned about it being kept as evidence in a police file. Now they were, at least on the surface. It was still impossible to prove that he and the man in the film were one and the same, yet it alarmed NIA that someone had seemingly made the connection. The police brass were scrambling, trying to get a line on who might have taken the tape from headquarters. NIA's question was: What did this all mean? Did they have a mole in their secret organization? Were there going to be more revelations? They had no way of knowing, but the search for answers was on.

At Drake's press conference that morning the media had a ball trying to connect the dots. Drake called the photo a hoax and did his best to answer as many of the questions as they put to him. There'd been plenty: from what did he think, to was that really him, to what was the city doing about finding the mysterious black vans and their vigilante occupants? He'd been pleasant, witty, and charming, but underneath the facade had been fury. Whoever printed the flyers had to know how damaging a rumor like this could be to him, and it made him wonder if that had been the intent. Maybe they weren't targeting NIA at all but were after him. Whoever it was had to have had help in order to blanket the city in such a short amount of time. It begged the question if there was another shadowy organization out there somewhere. If so, he couldn't wait for them to be found, and he had no doubt they would be because he wanted to know who they were.

In the meantime, he had to live with the guilt of having lied to Lacy, and hoped this would be the first and last time.

At two that afternoon Lacy's phone rang. Seeing Ida's light, she picked it up. "Yes, Ida?"

"Lenny Durant's on the phone. Wants to talk to you."

"Thanks." Lacy clicked over to the outside line. "This is Lacy Green. How may I help you?"

"It's me. Lenny."

"What can I do for you?"

"How you been?"

"Fine," she responded coolly. "Still wondering how you got my number."

"Got a friend in Personnel."

"I see. Lose my number, Lenny. I don't want you calling me at home."

"Whatever."

"No *whatever*. Don't call me. If you do, I'll turn you in to the cops."

"Okay, okay. I won't call again."

"Good." Lacy wondered what this young man did in real life besides target polluters and illegally access people's phone numbers.

"Got somebody I want you to meet," Lenny said.

"Who?"

"A man who works for the dumpers."

Lacy went still. "What's his name?"

"Can't tell you right now."

"Then take him to the police."

"So they can mess it up? No. When he's ready to talk, I'll let you know."

"Okay, but—"

He hung up.

Frustrated, Lacy replaced the phone. She wished she had a way to track him so she'd know what he was up to. She also hoped he'd been telling the truth, because she wanted this dumping epidemic to end.

She went back to her work, only to have the phone ring again. It was an outside line. She hit the speaker button. "Lacy Green, may I help you?"

"Hello, Ms. Green." The male voice was unfamiliar.

"Yes, speaking."

"We don't like people coming into our town and changing up the way things are done."

"Who is this?"

"Somebody giving you some advice, so you won't get hurt."

Lacy went still.

"Landlords around here don't want you changing the codes. Businesses doesn't want changes. You're making a lot of enemies, Ms. Green. If I were you, I'd be real careful, especially driving that sweet car of yours. Have a nice day."

He hung up.

Lacy's heart was racing and she was shaking. "Ida!"

The police sent over a detective named Mitchell Franks. Nice-looking man, but he hadn't come to be judged on his cute quotient. He asked questions, and Lacy answered as best she could.

"You've never heard the voice before?"

"Never." Lacy could see Ida and Janika looking on with concern.

"And this is about what proposal again?"

"I'm assuming it's the Blight Court," she said, and explained the plan as quickly as she could.

He was taking notes on the pages of a pocket-sized spiral notebook. "People can get real serious about stuff like that, especially if they think its going to, one, affect their economics, and two, if they think it's going to negatively impact whatever illegalities they're involved in. Looks like your proposal may be hitting two nails with one hammer."

He looked up from his writing. "Has anyone been particularly upset about this plan, besides your caller?"

"Councilman Parker. He's been very vocal about how he feels."

"And how does he feel?"

"That it's a waste of money." She told him about the visit Parker had paid her and how furious he'd been.

"Mr. Parker is a pretty big fish. I can't see him being behind this, but I'll talk to him on my way back to headquarters. In the meantime, I'll file my report, and you watch your back. Let me know if you get another call. Maybe we can get a lead on where he's calling from."

Lacy didn't care what the police had to do. She just wanted the person found. "Thank you, Detective Franks."

"My pleasure." He gave her his card. "Make sure you contact us if he calls back."

"I will."

Once he left the office, Ida said, "I can't believe this."

"Neither can I."

Janika added, "I wonder who it is?"

Ida said, "Not telling, but somebody's mad."

Lacy found this all so crazy. She wanted to talk to Drake but he was already gone. She'd just have to wait until he called. Admittedly, it was getting kind of scary.

Ida asked, "Remember you telling me about your daddy asking about your gun license?"

"Yes?"

"Now's the time, baby girl. Now's the time."

Lacy had no desire to carry a .45 in her purse, but maybe her daddy and Ida were right. She didn't know if she had it in her to actually shoot another human being, but if push came to shove, she needed to be able to protect herself. The police couldn't be everywhere. "I'll call the detective and find out what I need to do to bring my license up to date."

Ida nodded. "Good girl."

Janika nodded her approval too.

Lacy finally got back to work, but the threatening voice on the phone kept replaying in her mind. What kind of drama had she stepped into?

At three o'clock she and Ida took their fifteen-minute afternoon break and went outside. Janika's daughter had a doctor's appointment, so she left for the day.

Lacy took in deep breaths of the fresh air and basked in the warm sunshine. She wanted to get in her car and go home, but quitting time was five o'clock, not three-fifteen, so she regretfully followed Ida and the other workers back into the building.

Back inside, she felt much better until she saw Councilman Parker standing by the windows in her office. Before she could ask what he wanted, he turned and barked, "How dare you sic the police on me."

Lacy fought to remain calm. "Good afternoon, councilman. How are you?"

"Don't get cute. You told Franks I threatened you?"

She went to her desk and sat. "No. Franks asked me if I knew anyone upset about the Blight Court and you instantly came to mind."

"I had nothing to do with the call you got today."

"I never said you did."

"You don't want me as an enemy."

Lacy bit her tongue. She already considered him one. "Is there anything else?"

He studied her. "You think you're pretty damn smart, don't you?"

She remained silent.

He looked her up and down. "This can be a violent town sometimes, Ms. Green. Let's hope your meddling doesn't make you a statistic."

And he left.

Lacy dropped her head on her desk and banged it softly. First a threatening phone call and now this. All she wanted to do was help clean up the city!

At the end of the day Ida stuck her head around Lacy's door. "How you doing?"

"Terrible."

"Well, I'm not going home until you do, so get your stuff and let's go. Herbert and I have our ballroom dancing class tonight. If I'm late, he won't tango with me."

Lacy smiled for what seemed the first time that day. Herbert was a former defensive lineman, and the image of the six-foot-seven-inch football player tangoing with his short five-by-five wife was a sweet but comical one. "Okay. I was going to stay late, but I just want to go home."

"If you're worried about being alone tonight, you know you're more than welcome to one of the spare rooms at the house."

"I know." When she first moved to Detroit, Ida had been kind enough to let her stay in one of her upstairs bedrooms while she looked for a place to stay. "I think I'll be okay, at least for now."

Ida said, "If you change your mind, just come on over."

"Thanks."

On the heels of that, the two women left the office and headed to the elevator.

Back home, Lacy parked her car in the garage of her building then went upstairs to the community mailboxes to see if she'd received anything. There were bills, a couple of magazines, and a postcard from her mother. It read: *Amsterdam is smoking. Have a high old time. Hope you like the car. Love, your mama!*

Lacy started to laugh. Her fifty-four-year-old mother was a trip! Shaking her head, she headed down the quiet carpeted hall to the elevator. She spotted Wanda Moore, the building manager, coming toward her. "Hey Wanda. How are you?"

The tall dark-skinned woman had on a green T-shirt that read, *KISS ME. I'M BLACK IRISH.*

Lacy said, "Like the shirt."

Wanda grinned. "Not many folks get it." She then looked up and down the hall before leaning close and asking, "Is the mayor really a Dope Buster?"

Lacy whispered back, "I don't think so."

Wanda looked disappointed. "I was hoping you had the scuz."

Lacy smiled, "No scuz, no 411, no nothing."

"Oh well."

"But I did have a man call and threaten me this afternoon, so could you tell the guards on the gate to be careful about letting strangers into the complex?"

"What happened?"

Lacy explained the call and why the person had threatened her.

Wanda shook her head. "Folks are crazy. Just because you came up with a cleanup plan—that I like, by the way—somebody wants you to step back?"

"Yeah."

"Talk about shooting the messenger. Well, don't worry. I'll let the guards know."

"Thanks."

Wanda walked on, then called back, "If you need anything, just holla."

"Will do," Lacy replied.

After getting off the elevator, Lacy let herself into her apartment and felt the space embrace her like a sanctuary. She'd just dumped her briefcase and keys on the couch when her cell phone rang. She fished it out of her purse and snapped it to her ear. "Yes?"

"Heard you talked to the police."

It was him. Terror raced through her like wildfire.

"Not a good idea, Lacy. This was supposed to be just between you and me. You talk to the law again and I might have to come see you in person."

Thirteen

There wasn't really much Detective Franks and his partners could do except take down Lacy's statement and add it to the one he'd taken earlier at her job. Her cell phone's ID had registered the caller as unknown. When Franks contacted Lacy's phone provider, he was told the call in question had come through on a phone card used at a pay phone on the west side of the city. Franks dispatched a couple of uniforms to the location to canvas the area for clues but he didn't hold much hope that any would be found.

Wanda had come to sit with Lacy. When Ida's cousin Remmie saw all the policemen in the hallway, she'd come over too. Unlike her short and stout cousin, Remmie was a slightly built bird of a woman with flaming red hair and way too much makeup.

Lacy was glad she was there though. Cousin Remmie might not be able to keep a secret, but the arm she had around Lacy's shoulders radiated strength.

Franks finished up his preliminary report, then put his notebook back into his pocket. "Wish we could be of more help."

"You getting here so quickly helped a whole lot." Lacy walked him to door. "Thank you."

"No problem. I'm just sorry that there's no quick way to stop this."

"What do I need to do to get a permit to carry a concealed weapon?" Lacy asked.

On the couch, Remmie pumped a thin fist. "You go, girl."

Wanda smiled.

Franks replied, "Do you know how to use a firearm?"

Lacy told him about hunting with her father. "I haven't picked up a gun in fifteen years, though."

"I know I'm not supposed to say this, but if you were a female in my family or at my church, I'd say getting a piece might be a good idea, especially if you know how to use one." He took out his notebook and wrote something down. He tore off the sheet and handed it to her. "Those are the names of some local firing ranges you can go to and get the rust off your skills." He then told her what she needed to know about the paperwork involved with obtaining a permit. "The permit has a forty-five-day waiting period, but under extenuating circumstances you can get a temporary cert right away. This is one of those extenuating circumstances."

Lacy agreed. "Thanks again."

"You might want to consider having a friend stay with you, or you stay with them until this is done, but we'll catch him. Don't worry."

On that hopeful note, the policemen left and Lacy closed the door. Remmie and Wanda both volunteered to stay the night, but she graciously turned them down. "I should be okay. I won't be answering the door or any calls from anyone coming through as unknown. I just want to chill and fall out."

"You sure?" Remmie asked.

Lacy nodded.

Wanda looked doubtful but didn't argue.

"If I need you, you'll hear me screaming. Don't worry."

The women gave her a hug, then left her alone.

The first thing she did was go through the apartment and throw the locks on all of her windows. Satisfied, she headed to the kitchen. Even though she was too wound up to eat, she was hungry, but in the end she closed the fridge and went to the living room and sat in the yellow chair. The man's words kept playing in her mind over and over again like a song she couldn't get out of her head. In an effort to distract herself, she turned on the TV, but after a few minutes she knew it wasn't working. She picked up the remote and turned it off. There were no two ways about it, the man had scared her to death. How he'd gotten her cell number was a question neither the police nor her phone company could answer. Did he know where she lived? He'd given every indication that he did.

Lord. Rather than go running to hide beneath the bedcovers, Lacy did what every girl does when they're scared and in need of comfort. She picked up her phone and called her mama.

Her mother answered on the third ring, "Hey baby. How are you?"

"Terrible."

Once Lacy finished telling the story, Val was outraged. "I have friends in the Fruit. Arrangements can be made to a have a team there first thing in the morning. Does this man know I will hunt him down if anything happens to my only child!"

Lacy would have laughed had the situation not been so serious. It didn't surprise her that her mother had contacts with the Fruit of Islam. The Fruit was the security wing of the Black Muslims and sometimes offered their protective services to Black celebrities, and common folks as well. The bow-tie-wearing brothers of the Fruit had a reputation for being both fearless and efficient. Lacy hadn't been surprised because her mother seemed to know every Black person of importance, no matter the arena. She had close friends in entertainment, sports, and politics. When Lacy was young, it wasn't uncommon to come home and find the great artist Romare Bearden at the dinner table, or see Jesse Jackson and Julian Bond at one of her mother's famous barbecues. To this day Val swore that the only reason Wilton had married Lacy was to have access to the movers and shakers of Black America.

Val asked, "So do you want me to make the call?"

Lacy didn't know. "Let me see how I feel in the morning. Right now the adrenaline is pumping so tough I can't even think."

"You have a right to be upset, darling."

They spent the next thirty minutes talking about the threat, and soon Val had Lacy laughing over some of the silly things Val had seen or heard while in Europe.

Lacy said, "And I got your card, crazy woman."

Val laughed.

"Are you still in Amsterdam?"

"Yep, and I thought I'd be here until the end of the month, but I think I'm going to head down to Madrid and check out some of the markets. This is strictly an inspiration-gathering trip."

At the end of the call, Val said, "Make sure you call me tomorrow, so I'll know that you're okay and you can give me your decision about the Fruit."

"I will."

"Feeling better after talking to your mama?"

"Much. Thank you."

"It's what mamas are for. Get some sleep, sweetheart. I'm sending you much much love."

"I'm sending you love too. Thanks, Ma."

" 'Bye, sweetie."

As Lacy hung up she did feel much better. Smiling, she went to the kitchen to find something to eat.

Seated at her desk in her office the next morning, Lacy read the preliminary reports from the HazMat scientists on the first set of barrels. The chemicals found inside were handled by only three disposal firms in the state. Two of the companies were up north in Saginaw and Midland. The other was Parker Environmental. She went out to Janika's desk. "I need everything you can find on Councilman Parker and his company, Parker Environmental. His is one of the companies licensed for the disposal of the stuff in the barrels."

"Oh, really. I'll get right on it."

"Oh, and do the same for our friend Lenny Durant."

Lacy went back to her desk, picked up the phone and called the city's legal offices. When she got one of the city's lawyers on the line, she explained the preliminary report to the female legal beagle, then asked what kind of evidence the city would need to nail the dumpers.

"We need *concrete* proof tying the barrels to a specific company. Until we get that, we can't take anyone to court."

"Thanks." Lacy hung up and called the HazMat folks back.

In answer to her question as to how long it would be before they could nail down the source of the barrels, the man on the phone replied, "Six to eight weeks, if at all. Pray that all three companies didn't get their barrels from the same company, otherwise we may never know."

Lacy found that less than encouraging. "Six to eight weeks?"

"Hey. The EPA is understaffed and overworked just like everybody else in the government. They'll get the results to us as soon as they can."

She thanked him and ended the call.

After lunch, Janika brought in the information on Parker and Durant. Lacy looked through the Parker stuff first. She read about the lotto ticket that began his career, the myriad businesses he owned, and the local charities he supported. She scanned a six-year-old newspaper report on the death of Parker's first wife. The police called her drowning on Belle Isle suspicious. According to sources, Parker had been a person of interest in the case, but due to a lack of evidence, no charges were filed. Lacy didn't like that part. The rest of the material was mundane; an article on him being named Man of the Year for his work with felons, another about him touring some of the local schools to speak on recycling. Lacy wondered if that had been his cover for scoping out places to dump his poisons.

She took that back. She wasn't being fair to the man; she couldn't stand him, but there was no proof tying him to the dumping. Rumors weren't going to solve this, facts were.

With that in mind, she picked up what Janika had turned up on Lenny Durant. He was thirty. Graduated from one of the local high schools. Served in the army. Sharpshooter. That got her attention. Given an honorable discharge. Formed BAD three years ago. Members arrested twice for assault—once on a man from Troy found dumping tires, and the other for a fight with police officers at a demonstration outside the Fermi nuclear power plant down in Monroe. Then she came across the incident Ida had mentioned. BAD's computer geeks had hacked their way into the

EPA computers. One of hackers was now serving a three year prison term.

She shook her head and tossed the pages on her desk. She didn't know any more now than when she came to work this morning. The only thing she knew for sure was that someone was using the city as their own private landfill and that someone else, or maybe the same individual, was trying to scare her to death, and doing a pretty good job. She'd called her mother earlier that morning and told her to hold off on contacting Minister Farrakhan's people. She wanted to give the Detroit police a chance to solve the case before calling in the cavalry. If this dragged on, she'd let her mother get involved.

So far, the day had been a quiet one. The only thing that would make it better would be seeing or talking to Drake, but he hadn't called, and she knew he wouldn't be back until tomorrow.

Just before lunch Rhonda Curry called down and asked Lacy if she would come up to the mayor's office for a moment to discuss an aspect of the blight proposal that needed clarification.

"Be right up," Lacy told her.

Because of the threatening phone calls, Ida wouldn't let her even go to the restroom without checking in first, so she told Ida about Rhonda's call before heading up to see what Drake's assistant wanted help with.

When Lacy walked into the mayor's office, Rhonda said, "This way please, Ms. Green."

Lacy followed her into Drake's office, and Rhonda

closed the door. "Mayor Randolph is on the phone. Line one. Take as much time as you need."

Rhonda left, softly closing the door behind her.

A confused but elated Lacy picked up the receiver and punched the blinking red button labeled LINE ONE on the console. "Drake?"

"Lacy. Are you okay?" The concern in his voice was clear.

"I've been better."

"I heard about the calls."

"You did?"

"Yes, from my bodyguard Simon Lane. He heard about it at headquarters and called me."

"Man scared me to death. The police have no idea how he got my cell number or who he is." Wishing he was there with her, she asked, "How are the meetings going?"

"No idea. I'm on my way home."

That surprised her. "But I thought you were supposed to be there until Thursday?"

"I am, but I'm coming home. You're way more important than a discussion on the algae content of Lake Erie."

"Awww."

He chuckled. "I'll be there in under an hour."

"Can we have dinner tonight?"

"Dessert too."

"Mmm," she murmured. "I like the sound of that."

"In fact, I'm making an executive decision. I want you to go home and pack enough clothes for four days. When I get there, we're going to take off. I'll have you back by Sunday afternoon. How's that sound?"

"The old Lacy would have said, 'Can't go, I have work to do.' But the new and improved Lacy said, 'Sounds wonderful.' "

"Good. See you in a minute."

Lacy walked out of Drake's office feeling as if she were floating on air.

Rhonda looked up from her desk and asked with a smile, "You okay?"

"I am now. Thanks, Ms. Curry."

"Call me Rhonda."

"Call me Lacy."

"Will do."

Lacy floated back downstairs

Both Ida and Janika thought Drake's plan was an excellent one and promised to keep the getaway a secret.

Ida said, "Just don't tell Remmie."

Lacy grinned and went to her office so she could grab her purse and keys and leave. Once she was ready, she told Janika and Ida, "I'll see you all on Monday."

"Have a good time," Ida told her.

"Oh, don't worry," Lacy said meaningfully. "If it gets too good, I may not come back." With a laugh and wave she was off.

When Drake ended the call to Lacy, his brother Myk looked over from his seat across the plane's aisle and asked, "Better now?"

"Yeah." Talking to Lacy had calmed him immensely. Hearing from Simon that she'd received threatening calls not once but twice yesterday, he had been ready to walk from Cleveland if he'd had to. Instead, he was on his way home courtesy of Myk and the Chandler Works private jet, *Dragon One*. Myk and his pilot had flown in to pick him up this morning. Because the flight was less than thirty minutes, Drake knew it wouldn't be long before he could see for himself how his lady was doing. When the police tracked down the man responsible, he planned to feed his balls to the crocs at the zoo. According to Simon's detective friend, Franks, Lacy had held up well, considering the circumstances. She'd been frightened but kept her head enough to call for backup in spite of being warned to stay away from the police by the caller.

Myk asked, "She's doing okay, I take it?"

"Yeah. The detectives talked to Parker about the calls. Apparently he was in her office throwing his weight around yesterday too. When are we going to move on him?" Drake asked.

"All indications point to soon, but officially the police will go in looking for clues on Wheeler. We're still holding the truck driver with the pot. So far he's not giving up any info on his boss."

"How long do you think the search'll take?"

Myk took a swallow from the glass of ice water in his hand. "Don't know. All three of his landfills are acres across, and almost as tall. With one dog per site, we may be out there for months and still not find anything."

"What about Wheeler's wife? Still nothing?"

"Nothing. She's still claiming ignorance, and doing a pretty good job of it. Passed a polygraph. She doesn't know anything about the hidden money, or if he's alive or dead."

"After all this, I still vote for dead."

"Me, too.

"So, our friends are looking at Parker as suspect numero uno?"

Myk nodded. "If Wheeler had embezzled that kind of money from me, I'd have fed him into a compactor too."

Drake took a swallow of his own water. "Now now, brother. We're supposed to be the good guys. When are the dogs going in?"

"Bright and early Saturday morning. Let's hope the snow is through."

Drake raised his glass in toast. "Amen to that." Like every other resident of the state, he was ready for winter to be gone for good. "You know Lacy could be the woman I marry."

"Could?"

"Yeah. No guarantee she'll say yes."

Myk sat back in his seat. "You know, there are men who marry meek quiet women and spend the rest of their married lives in peace, but we—meaning you, Saint, and me—find these fireballs who singe off our eyebrows half the time."

Drake laughed. "I like the analogy, especially from a man whose stove had to take out a PPO on him."

Myk, known for not being able to cook an egg, took mock offense and threw a pillow at him. Drake ducked and spilled water all over his shirt and brown suit coat. "Aw man!"

Drake grabbed a napkin and blotted himself while his older brother looked on, laughing. In their younger days this would have turned into a playful, rolling all over the floor wrestling match, but they'd gotten too old to wrestle each other, especially on planes. "I owe you one."

"You deserved it for that crack. Especially since you can't boil water your damn self."

They grinned at each other. They'd always been close in spirit, but since Myk's marriage, the bond seemed to have tightened. Drake attributed it to Sarita and her calming influences on his dragon brother. Her love for Myk had softened the razor-sharp edges, cast a light into his dark den, and made him more attuned to his family. Drake loved his sister-in-law for many reasons, but the most important was how much Myk had changed. "Do you think we'll ever know what really happened to the old man?"

The subject of their rolling stone father had come up between them many times over the years. When they were much younger and spending summers together in Louisiana with Gran—their father's mother—Drake and Myk often talked about where Roland might be and how they'd act if he ever walked back into their lives. Drake planned to be forgiving, but Myk always said the man could go to hell.

Now, in answer to Drake's question, Myk shrugged. "Who knows."

"Do you care?" Drake asked.

Myk studied his brother for a long moment, then answered, "Two years ago I would have said no. Now with the baby coming? Yeah, I'd like to know everything from start to finish. I never wanted to hear it before. I don't even know who my mother was."

Drake knew the circumstances surrounding his own out-of-wedlock birth. His mother, Mavis, revealed the full story to him on his twelfth birthday. "Maybe it's time you asked Gran."

Myk nodded his agreement. "Maybe."

Harboring their own thoughts, the brothers remained silent for the rest of the short flight home.

Lacy checked her overnight bag for the fiftieth time to make sure she hadn't forgotten anything, but everything she needed was inside, just as it had been the other forty-nine times she'd checked. She was nervous and excited. This was a big step for their budding relationship. She just hoped they'd have fun, so she could forget about the craziness of the past few days.

At 1:35 the buzzer went off. "Yes?"

"It's me."

When he knocked after what seemed an eternity, she pulled open the door, and there he stood with his sexy male self dressed in a sweatshirt and jeans. On his feet were brown hikers and in his dark eyes were a smile. "Hey, there."

So happy to see him at last, Lacy tossed back, "Hey yourself. Come on in."

"Ready?" he asked.

"Yep. All packed."

"No, ready for this. . . ."

The kiss he gave her was long, dizzying, and wonderful. When he pulled away, she was light-headed.

Showing his boyish grin, he said to her, "Now, you can get your bag."

As she did, Lacy walked on very shaky legs.

The weather cooperated wonderfully, and they left the apartment complex and then the city under a brilliant blue sky. They were heading to Holland, on the western side of the state. According to the map Drake showed her before they left her place, the drive in his Mustang would take them first to Lansing, the state capital, then to Grand Rapids, the second largest city in Michigan, then to Holland, which was nestled on Lake Michigan.

Lacy loved the scenery. Because it was only mid-April, the farther west and north they drove, the more snow there seemed to be, but it appeared to be melting. The piles that remained around the trunks of trees and on the open fields beside the highway glistened like diamonds in the sunshine.

They reached Holland a little past five-thirty. He looked her way and said, "We'll do the tour tomorrow. Right now, I just want to get to the house and chill out. Been a long ride."

And it had been, but the sky-kissing pines growing along the narrow two lane road now made her feel like they'd entered a fairy-tale forest. She could see houses built upon the dunes rising up from the road, and every now and then she got a peek at the sparkling blue water of the lake behind them. "It's peaceful."

"Yes it is. I'd like to put a place up here too, someday."

"Would you live here year-round?"

He shrugged. "Maybe, or maybe just use it when I want to, like Myk does."

"Is that where we're going? Your brother's place?"

"Yep. And so that you'll know my intentions are honorable, you'll have your own room."

"And if I don't?"

He looked her way. "I'm sure we can make some adjustments."

Their grins met but neither of them said a further word.

A few miles later he turned off the main road and onto a narrow road with a sign beside it that read: PRIVATE. NO TRESPASSING. NO HUNTING. A tall wrought-iron gate was open in welcome, magnificently framing the entrance to the property. Lacy could see nothing but trees. Towering pines with thick trunks blocked the sky overhead. The road climbed a few degrees, and when it opened up, there sat the glass and metal home gleaming in the sun. The structure was rectangular, but it was more complex than that. One part of the house flowed into another smoothly and precisely. There was a large cube on top, and two large cubes extending from each end. It appeared to have been built into the side of the dune, because Lacy couldn't see what lay behind it. Right now, that didn't matter. She was too busy marveling over the house's beautiful modern lines.

"My mother would love this house," she whispered in awe.

"Myk's an architect and he designed the place."

The metal framing the dark-tinted windows was a polished copper that made the glass seem to shimmer. She bet the window washer was paid a pretty penny; there wasn't a speck or a smudge to be seen. "Is your brother Midas?" Lacy couldn't imagine how much the place must have cost.

Drake turned the key to shut off the engine, then drawled, "We think he is, but we're still waiting on official verification."

Lacy shook her head at his humor. "Does he know you talk about him like this?"

"Yep, and knowing him, he's probably back at home talking about me the same way."

"Can't wait to meet him."

"He said the same thing about you."

"Oh really? Been talking about me, have you?"

His eyes were shining. "A bit, yeah. Only good things, though."

The heat was rising in the car and they could both feel it. Lacy reached out and cupped her hand against the curve of his cheek. He turned the palm and placed a kiss in the center of her palm. "Let's go in before we wind up being out here all night."

"Lead the way," she said softly.

The place was freezing when they entered.

Drake raised his head and said aloud. "Heat. Seventy-two degrees, please. Thank you."

Before Lacy could react, a computerized female voice replied, "*Heat. Seventy-two degrees. Estimated time for desired temperature, twenty minutes. Thank you.*"

Lacy was impressed. She'd seen computer-controlled homes on television reports but had never been inside one. She followed Drake from the large foyer to the living room, where the glass walls offered a breathtaking view of the water. "Wow!"

It was as blue as a lake on a map, and stretched as wide and as far as her eyes could see. She walked farther into the beautifully furnished room. She had no idea Michigan had views like this. The sight was awesome. Standing close to the glass, she could see the wide stretch of light brown beach below and the foamy-tipped water breaking against it. "This is Lake Michigan?"

Drake walked over and stood beside her. "Amazing, isn't it?"

"You see the word 'Great Lakes' on the map, but I never knew it meant *great* like in big. It looks big as the ocean."

"On the other side is Chicago and Wisconsin."

"And Michigan has five of these?"

He was enjoying her response. "Four of them touch our borders. They're not all this big, but they're all a good size."

Off in the distance she could see a barge churning by. Closer in, gulls circled in the sun. "I could stand here all day."

"How about we go out for a walk later?"

"I'd like that."

"In the meantime, how about a tour?"

"Thought you'd never ask."

He showed her the library, with its highly polished wood and hundreds of shelved books; the music room, which held the grandest black piano Lacy had ever seen; the two guest bedrooms, each with a small deck overlooking the water; and the large master suite, complete with its own deck, master bath, and sitting room with fireplace. The rooms were fabulous, as were the furnishings. African-inspired art was everywhere. "Your brother has a beautiful home," Lacy said as the tour drifted into the sleek modern kitchen.

"Yes, he does. Are you hungry?"

"Starving."

"Well, let's see what Mrs. Alvarez left us in the fridge."

"Who's she?"

"Myk's housekeeper, and the caretaker when he's not here. If she knows one of us is coming up, she'll spend the week before cooking and stash it all in the fridge. She's from the islands and misses cooking for her big family."

He pulled open the polished black door. Out came a ham, a roast chicken, spaghetti, green beans flavored with onions and ham, potato salad, wild rice, and a pan of wax paper covered yeast rolls ready for the oven. Sitting in the center of the island counter was a Muhammad Ali cookie jar. Inside were a few dozen of Drake's favorite Toll House cookies. He fished one out and took a big bite. Chewing, he looked over and saw another one of his favorites—a German Chocolate Cake poised like a queen on top of an elegant, elevated, silver cake plate. "I think I've died and gone to heaven," he said, munching and smiling.

"I think I've gained ten pounds, and I haven't eaten a thing."

Their smiles met and held. Drake said, "I promised myself I'd be on my best behavior while we're together. How am I doing so far?"

"Excellent, so far."

He walked closer. "Would wanting a kiss move me up or down?"

Her eyes sparkled. "Probably up."

He eased an arm around her waist, and she fit herself closer. His lips brushed against her forehead. He whispered, "That's good to know. . . ."

A heartbeat later his lips met hers, and the sweetness of the surrender made them both groan.

Fourteen

Lacy had been waiting for this first real kiss since leaving her apartment. She explored the strength of his arms and chest through the soft cotton of his sweatshirt, all the while wondering where in the world he'd learned to kiss so well. Each press of his lips to hers stoked the embers still simmering from the last time they'd been together, making them rise and then slowly flame. Because of him, she now understood the word *need* and all its lust-filled implications. The way he kissed her, touched her, seduced her, made her *need* him in a way that was as awesome as it was new. His big palm slowly circling the point of her breast made her lips part and her eyes close. He fit his mouth over hers and slid her sweatshirt up until he found her bra. He filled his hand with the soft weight of the lacy cup, then played his thumb over the bud until she drew in a shaky breath.

"You have a perfect little body," he whispered against her ear. Expert fingers freed her from the black lace, then she was in his hand and trembling. "Perfect little breasts too . . ."

She husked out, " 'Little' being the operative word."

He gave her that pleased male chuckle and said hotly, "More than a mouthful is a waste. . . ."

Fitting actions to words, he took her dark breast into his mouth, and a rippling Lacy cried out, her body arching for more. He dallied masterfully, making her moan pleasurably, while his surgeon's hands slowly explored and skimmed their way over her hips, legs, and thighs, teasing and circling with touches that made her part her legs so he could increase the flame.

Drake raised his mouth to hers and drank deeply from her parted lips. One hand continued to tease the damp, tight buds of her breasts, while the other teased the humid heat sheltered in the vee of her thighs. He boldly slid the waist of her pants down and filled his palms with her tempting behind. The flesh was soft, smooth, and he circled it possessively. He touched her heat, felt her tremble, and kissed her fervently. When he slid a finger inside, she came with a strangled shout, and Drake knew he had to get this woman on a bed.

Lacy rode out the orgasm, carried through the house in his arms. Every few steps he stopped to kiss her, making her arch up and groan from the body-shaking sensations. Then she was placed gently onto a large bed, and through the haze of desire she saw him taking off his shirt and undoing his belt. More shameless than she'd ever been, she sat up and drew her shirt over her head. Then she was slipping out of her pants, socks, and shoes. Wearing nothing but her twisted black lace bra and a matching thong, she smiled.

Drake almost came right then. The slow way she'd silently removed her clothes to reveal her absolutely wicked underwear made him take a deep breath and pray his body would hold out just a bit longer. He knew they had days to enjoy each other, but he wanted this first time to be slow and sweet so the lovemaking would be memorable for them both. With that in mind, he reached down between her slightly parted thighs and teased the sweet dampness bisected by the thong until she growled and sensually raised herself for more. On fire, Drake played with her for a few hot moments longer, then reached into his pocket for a condom.

Lacy watched him undress, then roll the condom over his magnificent desire. Dressed in her scanty underwear, she felt like a courtesan in heat. When he joined her on the bed, she couldn't wait for him to pay her tribute.

Drake ran a worshipping hand down the length of her black satin body, then bent so he could circle his tongue around her tempting dark nipples. No, she didn't need to be a D cup for him to enjoy pleasuring her. Response was the only requirement, and the sexy Lacy Green was doing just fine in that department.

Lacy was still throbbing from the remnants of the first orgasm and wasn't sure how much more of his loving she could take and not explode again. His mouth moving over her skin was hot, and his hands were glorious. The slow, tantalizing rhythm in her hips began again in response to the wanton touches playing between her thighs. When had her thong come off? She didn't know, and she didn't care. Feeling him hard and thick and working his way into the place she wanted him the most became her entire world.

Drake felt her heat closing around him, and his first instinct, the male instinct, was to stroke her for all he was worth. She was so tight and so hot, his body didn't want to hold back, but he did in order to savor this erotic, initial feel for a lifetime. Her response to his slow rhythm was perfectly timed; she met him stroke for stroke and ran her hand over the hair clouding his chest, to tease a sculpted nail over his flat nipples. Drake threw back his head and increased the pace. They were moving faster now. Desire had them both enthralled. Growling, Drake grabbed her hips and deepened his thrusts. A moment later she came with a cry that fired him even more. Then his own release shattered over him and he surrendered with a lusty yell that shook the silence of the house.

Later, as they both lay breathing loud in the aftermath, he leaned over and kissed her softly. His hand teased a nipple and he decided that he wanted to lie here just this way for the rest of his life.

She opened her eyes and smiled. "Now I see why your hands are insured."

He replied softly, "Told you." Then he added, "Between my hands and my extensive knowledge of human anatomy you're going to be a very lucky woman while we're here, Lacy Green."

She kissed him softly and whispered, "You are so full of yourself . . . but I can't wait."

They got up and showered in separate bathrooms. Under the force of the hot water, Lacy washed away the leavings of their love, but knew nothing could erase the throbbing in her nipples or the pulsing between her thighs.

Back in the kitchen, the computer turned on the oven, and once the desired temperature was reached, they put the rolls in and reheated the food prepared by Mrs. Alvarez. When everything was ready, they took their piled plates over to the kitchen table to eat and to enjoy the expansive view of the blue lake through the sparkling windows.

The sun was going down in fiery reds, oranges, and pinks. Lacy couldn't remember ever seeing such a dramatic sunset. It made the one she was accustomed to seeing from her balcony pale in comparison. "I could live here just for the sunsets alone."

"It is pretty nice, isn't it."

It was, and having Drake with her made the moment even nicer. "How long has your brother had this place?" she asked while enjoying Mrs. Alvarez's well-seasoned green beans.

"About ten years. He'd like to buy more land, but with all the development that's been going on, there's very little open land left."

"So where would you put the house you said you wanted to build?"

"Probably just down the way. Myk has offered me and Saint a split of this property."

"Saint's your other brother."

"Yes."

"What's he do?"

"Works for the government," Drake replied casually.

She nodded and went back to her plate.

Drake was glad she'd expressed only a passing interest in his outlaw-coat-wearing half brother. Saint worked for some pretty shadowy entities on a regular basis, and the less nonfamily members knew about his comings and goings, the better. Of course, he had his own secret life too, and wondered what she would think if she knew.

They finished their meal and cleaned up. The dirty dishes were fed to the dishwasher and the uneaten food went back into the refrigerator. Drake put on a pot of coffee. When it was done, they filled their cups, got their coats, and stepped outside onto the living room deck. The light was almost gone, and the brisk breeze filled Lacy with its chilly energy. She sensed Drake step up beside her. He draped an arm across her waist and she smiled over her smoking cup. The peace here was strong enough to touch. She never wanted to leave.

Content, she looked up and found him watching her. In that moment, Lacy thanked the powers above for placing this man in her life. Even if the relationship ended up crashing on the rocks, she'd have the memories of this time here. Meeting a man like Drake Randolph was as rare as it was beautiful. When he slowly lowered his head, she met the kiss with a sweetness that she wanted him to feel.

Drake did, and wanted to immerse himself until he drowned. Her mouth with its kiss-swollen lips tasted of coffee. He set his cup down on the small tile-topped table and pulled her closer so he could feel her warm body against his own. She blindly set her cup aside and her head dropped back in response to the trail of heat moving down her arched throat.

"Let's go back in," he whispered thickly against the shell of her ear. He couldn't believe how soon his arousal had returned. In reality it had never left, he supposed, because he wanted her now as much as he had earlier. "Otherwise you're going to wind up naked out here."

Lacy fed herself on his kiss and wondered what it might be like to make love outdoors. His kisses left her mindless but not to the point that she would willingly risk frostbite or pneumonia.

They kissed their way back inside, and Drake shut the large patio door behind them. He traced a finger over her parted lips, then said to the computer controls, "Lights down. Fireplace. On."

The gas fireplace at the far end of the room came on with a soft whoosh, and the lighting went from functional to intimate. There were more shadows than light, and the leaping flames of the fireplace added their own component to the mood. Drake led her over to the brown leather love seat facing the fire and drew her down onto his lap. Recapturing her lips, he kissed her until they were both breathless, then ran his hand over the front of her floppy turtleneck sweater. The gray fabric was loose enough that it moved under his hand, and feeling her nipples tighten in response, he hardened even more. He lifted the garment and nuzzled the skin above the bra while she moaned contentedly. He pulled the sweater up over her head and greeted the bare skin with kisses and caresses that set her senses aglow. A few minutes later her jeans were pulled down her legs and his eyes burned over the black lace, boy pants covering her sweet little behind. He teased the heat between her thighs and said, "You're killing me, you know that?"

Lacy groaned in response to his touches and her body arched up shamelessly to his hand. "How?" she managed to ask.

"Every time you undress you've got on something that makes my eyes bug out. . . . But I know what to do for you. . . ."

After removing her bra, he took her panties from her, then prepared the damp pulsating place with a surgeon's skilled hand. "Come down on the floor with me, baby. We mess up Myk's couch and he'll kill me."

He grabbed at the thick red throw on the back of the couch and spread it on the carpet before the fire. A boneless Lacy slid down onto it and stretched out. He kissed her mouth while the heat of the fire added its own warm kiss to her bare skin.

"Ready for your anatomy lesson?" he asked softly.

The tone of his voice matched the pressure of his finger circling and mapping her curves and valleys.

He bent and gently bit her nipple. "You have to answer me, Lacy, or you won't pass the class. . . ."

She was panting softly. The erotic play had her slowly twisting and raising herself greedily to his hand. She wanted to pass the class. "I'm ready. . . ." she whispered.

He smiled like his dragon grandfather Galen, the ancestor of the Vachon line. "Good. We'll start with a history lesson . . . ?"

Lacy could feel her essence dampening the inside of her thighs. "Okay."

Drake bent his mouth to her breasts, and as he tasted and sucked and circled, he asked her, "Did you know that science once thought women couldn't have pleasure?" He slid a damp finger over the hard little jewel between her thighs. "Maybe, they didn't try this. . . ."

"Drake," she pleaded from within the hot haze shimmering around her.

He placed a finger against her lips. "No talking allowed during exams, Miss Green."

Lacy was going to come. "Drake," she whispered.

"You're almost ready for the last question, aren't you?"

"Yes."

"Then let's not make you wait."

He teased the core of her soul until her legs were spread in erotic invitation. "Perfect." He licked at the whorl of her navel, then spread her tiny wings so he could worship at the temple.

Lacy's hips came right up off the floor. He placed a gentle hand on her belly to keep her from running away and loved her until she couldn't stand anymore. The orgasm split her in half and she screamed loud and long. She was still coming when he eased his condom draped hardness inside. It was too much; way too much. Before she knew it, she was coming again and he was thrusting as if their lives were in the balance. She rode his rhythm without inhibition, wanting nothing more than the feel of his power. Tightening herself around him, she felt him explode in response. He grabbed her hips, lifted her and stroked himself to paradise.

In the silence that followed, a thoroughly sated Drake cracked softly, "Remind me to eat my spinach the next time I go someplace with you."

Lacy smiled. "You're the one with the insured hands." She then rolled over on her side and faced him. "Thank you, Drake."

He studied her serious face. "What for?"

"For the last few hours. It's been very, shall I say, eye opening."

Drake was confused by her words, but contented himself with tracing her full mouth. "In what way?"

"I never knew it could be this . . . good."

He smiled his understanding. "Well, there's plenty more where that came from."

She shook her head in amusement. "I'm looking forward to it."

"Always at your service, ma'am. Literally."

His meaning embarrassed her so much she fell onto her back and placed her hands over her face.

He laughed. "I embarrass you again."

Lacy said from behind her hands, "I've never had anybody do . . . that before."

He looked her way with surprise. "Really?"

She took down her hands. "Really."

"That's one of my favorite pastimes."

"Drake!" she shouted, scandalized.

"Well it is. Let me show—"

Lacy backed away, laughing. "Oh no, you don't."

His eyes glowed with sensual mischief. He loved playing with her. "Didn't you like it?"

"I did, maybe too much."

His grin met hers. "Then my job here is done."

Lacy grabbed up her clothes. "I'm going to get in the shower."

He nodded. "Me too. Can I join you?"

"Only if you're going to behave."

"Behave like whom, what?"

Lacy said, "We'll figure it out when we get there. Race you!" And she took off.

He jumped up and took off after her. "No fair. You take all my strength and then you want to race."

He ran her down and scooped her up while she screamed with laughter. He stood there for a moment, just holding her and looking down at the sparkle in her eyes. Drake knew that at that moment, he would give up NIA if he had to in order to have her.

Lacy saw the emotion in his face and asked softly, "What's wrong?"

"Nothing. Just enjoying being with you, that's all."

"I'm having a good time too."

He kissed her softly, then carried her upstairs to the shower.

By the time they washed, made love—another new experience for Lacy—and washed again, over an hour had passed.

The remainder of the evening was spent in the basement theater room watching DVDs on the big screen mounted on the wall. The large room was decorated like an old movie palace, complete with heavy velvet drapes, a couple of soft leather couches, comfy red movie seats, a large stand-up air popper, and a well-stocked bar. The large DVD and VHS library held titles that covered everything from the original *Cotton Comes to Harlem*, starring Godfrey Cambridge, to the modern day Lord of the Rings trilogy.

By the time the credits for *For Love of Ivy*, starring Sidney Poitier, began to roll, Lacy's eyes were so bleary and she was so tired, she said to Drake, who was cuddled on the sofa beside her, "I need to go to bed, Your Honor."

He pulled her close and kissed her forehead. "Me too. Can I walk you home?"

Lacy looked up at his smiling and handsome face. "Yes, you may. In fact, you can even come in and spend the night."

"Now that's what a brother likes to hear."

Taking her by the hand, he led back through the

house and upstairs to the bedrooms. The king-size bed was more than large enough for two, so they got in, snuggled under the covers, and Drake said to the computer, "Lights out."

The female voice said softly, "Thank you. Good night."

Lacy laughed in the dark.

Drake pulled her close. "What's so funny?"

She made herself comfortable against his strong chest and thighs and reveled in the feel of his arms around her. "All this high tech takes getting used to. The computer isn't taping what's going on in the house, is it?"

"Lord, I hope not."

She laughed again.

He kissed the top of her head. "I need to go to sleep. I am one whipped mayor. I was the one in Cleveland earlier today, remember."

"Yeah, but it's not like you walked. You flew, remember."

He tickled the base of her spine. "Are you saying I don't have a reason to be tired? I drove here too."

She giggled and arched away from his fingers. "Excuses, excuses. I wanted another lesson."

He laughed. "Go to sleep, woman. You've had two lesson already tonight."

"Thought you were supposed to be Dr. Lovemaster."

"Who?" He laughed.

She turned and faced him in the dark. "Dr. Lovemaster."

"I'll show you Dr. Lovemaster."

Before she could blink, he lifted her, and she came to rest laughing and stretched out on top of his hard chest and legs. "Is this Lesson Three?"

His hands were moving the thin fabric of her black lace nightgown sensually over her hips and languidly up and down the backs of her thighs. "Yes. It's called 'Riding.' "

She kissed him softly and passionately. "Riding what?"

"This . . ."

Lacy stilled, then said with surprise. "Really?"

Drake couldn't help it, his laugh filled the room. Lacy Green was one of a kind, and he was having the time of his life. "Yes, really. Are you ready?" he asked before slipping a hand beneath her gown and teasing the honey-filled place he wanted to claim as his own forever.

Lacy purred, "Yes."

So Drake, aka Dr. Lovemaster, gave her a lesson she never ever would forget, and after she screamed out the answers for the final exam, they both drifted off to sleep.

The next morning, they hopped into the car, swung by a fast food place for coffee and a bag of breakfast, then took off up the road to see Holland State Park. Lacy loved the view of the water that lined the narrow road they were on. There were small buildings on the shore, and boats of all shapes, sizes, and colors tied up at the slips and at the docks. It was so early in the day, Lacy saw no other cars. It was so early, in fact, the ranger booth at the entrance was unmanned. But the gates were wide open, so Drake drove on through. He followed the cement road past parking lots and a sign that said CAMPGROUNDS, but she had her attention set on the large blue expanse of water that stretched across the horizon. She couldn't get over the spectacular view. Who knew Michigan was this beautiful?

He parked the car on the edge of the parking lot overlooking the water. Soft jazz was playing on the CD, and Lacy couldn't imagine a more perfect scene. To their left was a long concrete pier that extended out into the water. A couple of fishermen bundled against the still brisk April weather stood on the edge tending their lines. Gulls of all sizes lazily circled the marble blue surface, looking for food and enjoying the bright morning sunshine. "This is wonderful," Lacy said, taking in the peaceful vista. "How long have you been coming up here?"

"Since I was real young. I had an uncle who worked in Holland, and he would drive us out here for picnics."

"Can we get out?"

He grinned. "Sure. It's probably pretty windy, so grab your gloves and your hat."

Lacy put on her gear, buttoned up her pea coat, and stepped outside. The wind hit her like the force of nature that it was. Laughing and howling, she turned her back to its force. The wind was laced with grains of sand that hit her face like tiny stinging bees. But the wind and the view and the peacefulness were exhilarating. She raised her face to the elements, closed her eyes, and like a little kid, enjoyed nature's assault.

Drake watched her reactions and knew this woman could really be the one. Instead of complaining about the cold or the wind, she was embracing it. He'd driven women to this spot who'd refused to get out of the car, but Lacy grabbed his hand and they set out across the winter-hard sand for the pier.

After leaving Holland Sate Park they turned onto Port Sheldon Road. According to the map in her lap, Port Sheldon snaked up the coast to Grand Haven, where another state park waited. Along the way they talked, laughed, and asked each other questions.

"Favorite sport?" Drake asked.

"Football. Yours?"

"Basketball. Are you having a good time?"

"I'm having a great time," she said from the passenger seat. "I've never done anything like this before."

"No?"

"No. I've had dinner dates and movie dates but never a see-the-lake date. You're setting the bar pretty high."

"Good."

Grand Haven had another spectacular view. They were now twenty miles north of their starting place at Holland. Lacy looked out at the water from where they were parked and asked, "This is the same lake?" The water once again covered the horizon.

"Yep."

Out on the water she could see men and women in wet suits standing on what looked like surfboards with a sail. Once the surfers were able to catch the air currents, they skimmed across the blue surface as if it were made of glass.

They left Grand Haven, stopped at a chicken place to get some take-out lunch, then headed northwest for their last stop, the big state park in North Muskegon. And what a spectacular place it was. The entrance was lined with tall pines on both sides, and the road rose higher the farther they drove. When the road crested, the water sparkling like diamonds in the sun was all they could see. It took Lacy's breath away. "Lordy."

Drake understood. "No matter how many times I come up here, the first look at the water always blows me away."

Lacy had to agree, and feasted her eyes on the sight. He turned left and took them toward the ranger station. It was mid-afternoon, and the booth was manned by a short squat brunette in a brown uniform. She took the money Drake offered and gave him a blue sticker for his window. She gave them a polite nod and Drake drove on.

He found a place to park in a lot on the shoreline, then they took out their lunch. There were no other cars in sight, and it gave Lacy the feeling that she and Drake were the only two people in the world.

After lunch he had a surprise. Reaching down beside his seat, he popped the lever for the trunk. "When was the last time you flew a kite?"

"It's been years."

"I have a couple in the trunk. Wanta try them out?"

Lacy's grin spread across her face. "You have thought of everything, haven't you?"

"I try." He leaned in and kissed her softly. He finally pulled away and they got out to get the kites. The wind was less forceful now than it had been down south in Holland, but the breeze was still stiff enough to make it a perfect day for flying. The kites were cheap and easy to assemble. Lacy had Sponge Bob, and Drake had Spider-Man.

Lacy had flown a ton of kites during her Girl Scout days. Flying kites was like riding bicycles: Once you get it down, you never forget. Holding the guide string attached to Sponge Bob in one hand, she let him fly on a short leash while she walked around the small dune she'd climbed to test the direction of the wind. Drake, on the other hand, was down on the deserted brown beach running like a kid in a kite-flying commercial, but Spider-Man refused to take off. A smiling Lacy shook her head, then called out, "It's never going to go up like that."

Above her head, Sponge Bob was pulling at his leash. He'd caught the wind and was ready to fly to the sun. Lacy slowly let out a few feet of string, and Bob climbed. The more string she gave him, the higher he went. Soon, all the string had been let out and Bob was a speck in the sky, twisting and playing on the currents.

Drake watched her prowess with his mouth open.

Lacy saw the look on his face. Feeling Bob tugging, she walked in the direction that he wanted to go and called down to Drake, "You have to stand still first, otherwise Spidey can't catch the current. Come on up here, the wind's better."

Drake climbed to meet her, and a few moments later Spidey joined Sponge Bob in the sky.

Lacy had such a good time, on the ride back to the house in Holland she knew she was grinning like the village idiot, but she couldn't help herself. The day had been wonderful. She didn't know any men who kept kites in their trunks, especially none who didn't seem to care that she could beat him flying them. She supposed that quality came from Drake having grown up with older sisters, but whatever the reason, his easygoing manner made him endearing.

Drake had enjoyed the day as well. "So, do you want to do this again?"

Lacy met his eyes. "As often as we can. I love it here."

"Then we'll put it into the rotation."

By the time they made it back to Myk's house, they were both exhausted and starving; it was something about being in the open air that had stoked their appetites. As soon as they hit the door, they heated dinner, then sat back and ate in a companionable silence.

Later, after the sun went down and they'd both showered and changed into comfy clothes, they were cuddled together on the couch in front of the fireplace. The lights had been dimmed by the computer. A nice CD was playing through the speakers, and once again Lacy was content. "Can we stay here forever?" she asked.

He squeezed her gently. "Sure."

"If only we could. You have to go back to running the city, and I have to go back to a crazy man and find out if my friend Councilman Parker is our serial dumper."

Drake went still. "What?"

She nodded. "Yeah." Then she told him about the information she'd gotten from the HazMat. "Only three companies in the state handle the disposal of those specific chemicals, and Parker Environmental is one of them."

"Now that is real interesting."

NIA wanted Parker for murder, and Drake couldn't help but wonder if her investigation would impact their own. He couldn't tell her to back off without giving her a vital reason, because she would definitely demand one. Down the road the Parker issue might turn into a bone of contention between them, but for now he wanted to sit here with her by his side and wonder if she'd like to make love again.

To test the waters, he turned and asked her with his kiss. She responded with a heated yes, and they began the dance.

On Sunday afternoon when Drake pulled into her complex and waved at the guard on the gate, Lacy felt sad. Their interlude had been perfect in every way, and now she had Monday to look forward to.

He cut the engine. "Why so glum?"

"I don't want to come home," she said in a little girl's voice.

He chuckled and traced her cheek. "I certainly

didn't want to bring you home. We'll go back soon, I promise."

"I'm holding you to that."

They shared a long kiss, then got out of the car to go inside her building.

Once inside her apartment, Drake said, "How do you feel about having a bodyguard?"

She shrugged. "Mama wanted to call the Fruit."

Drake stared. "Of Islam?"

"Yep. She says she has a connection."

"Remind me to never make her mad."

Lacy smiled. "She'd never be mad at you. She thinks you're cute."

He eased an arm around her waist and gently pulled her to him. "And what does her daughter think?"

"She thinks the mayor's head is big enough. Another compliment and it may explode."

He kissed her to pay her back. When they came up for air, he held her against his heart and said, "I have a friend named Walter McGhee who is real good at keeping people safe. I'd like him come over and hang out with you for the next few days."

Lacy looked up. "That would be okay. Lord knows I don't want to be one of Parker's statistics."

"What's that mean?"

She explained.

Drake looked down at her face. "He said that to you?"

"Yep."

Drake's jaw tightened. "Did you tell Detective Franks?"

"I did, but he said it wasn't something they could arrest Parker for."

"Doesn't matter. It's on the record. Why don't you come home with me?"

"As much as I'd love that, no. I want to be in my own space for a while."

Drake wanted to argue but knew he wouldn't prevail, so he let it go for now. "If anything jumps off, you call me first thing. Okay?"

"Will do."

He stared down into her eyes and couldn't imagine anyone wanting to harm her, but somebody did, and the knowledge angered him. "I'm going to head home. I'll call you later."

"Sounds good."

They walked to the door. Drake wanted to tell her to lock the doors, don't talk to strangers, and all the other clichés of safety, but decided to kiss her senseless instead. After many many kisses good-bye, he left and Lacy locked herself in.

Fifteen

Sunday night, Parker and Fish were discussing strategies in the trailer that served as the landfill's office. Parker was going over the production printouts for the last thirty days. "According to these totals," he said, "in a few more weeks the dumping will start paying off." Not having to fork over the usual fees and tariffs, the company was saving enough money to maybe straighten out the financial mess Wheeler had made.

Fish pointed out the obvious: "But we don't have a few more weeks."

"I know," Parker replied tersely. According to a tip he'd received from one of his sources, the feds were going to bring in dogs to search his three landfills for Wheeler's body. With that in mind, he knew he couldn't afford to have even a sniff of impropriety around his operations, so everything had ground to a halt. No dumping, no drugs coming across the border, and no smuggling of any kind. Until the feds either found something or grew frustrated enough to quit and leave him alone, he couldn't move a damn thing, and that was going to cost him money too. "At least we can continue to stash some of the garbage in the new subdivisions."

He had worked out a novel way to get rid of a large portion of the tons of garbage the trucks picked up each day—by using the open land of the three new subdivisions his real estate company was building. The construction crews dug down about eight foot, dumped the garbage in, and covered it with topsoil. Once the houses were built on the site, no one would be the wiser. He not only saved money on the disposal of the trash, but by using the trash as fill, he could cut back on the amount of topsoil he needed to truck in for the building sites. It was a win-win situation.

But the feds' imminent arrival was a problem.

Fish said confidently, "I say let 'em look. They won't find anything."

"They found that woman in Utah."

"Yeah, but we made sure Wheeler was in little bitty pieces before we fed him into the compactor. If they find anything, they won't be able to tell him from last week's pizza."

"You'd better be right."

"I am. They can bring in all the dogs they want."

Parker had no idea when the feds would show up, but according to the tipster, it would probably be in the next few days. He had already talked to his lawyer about the possibility. She advised him to sit tight until the search warrant was served, but Parker was finding that hard to do. Because of that bastard Wheeler, his empire was on the verge of collapsing and now the feds were sniffing around looking for his body. If push came to shove, he had his passport and $600,000 stashed in his office drawer ready to go. Having an office less than a ten minute drive away from the airport was a plus too. His wife would have to fend for herself.

Fish asked, "So, the flyers didn't get the reaction you thought they would, did they?"

Parker's jaw tightened. "Is this your I told you so?"

Fish gave him his shark smile. "You're going to need more than a blurry picture to bring down Mr. Mayor, especially if he's in with those Dope Buster people. Nobody has been able to catch even a sniff of where they disappear to after the raids, so finding them ain't gonna be easy. Plus the good citizens love them. Hell, I applauded when they took down the crack house on my block."

Parker cursed.

"You know what your problem is?"

"No, but I'm sure you're going to tell me."

"You need patience. Impatience may have gotten you to where you are now, but it's a new world. You can't throw your weight around and expect people to do what you want anymore. That's old school. These days folks get offended and call the ACLU."

Parker sighed. "What's your point?"

"My point is: Chill. After the feds leave and this mess with Wheeler is over, then we concentrate on Randolph."

"The election's next year. There isn't time to *chill.*"

"Sure there is. Between your contacts downtown and mine underground, we might get lucky and find the truth. At least I might. You'd be surprised at the big names you run into at booty clubs. Once they get a few drinks in them and start getting hot for those women on the poles, they're liable to tell you anything."

Fish's large pupils met Parkers. "Somebody somewhere knows about the men in those vans. Soon as we find the key, we own the mayor. We can make him sing 'Dixie' on the steps of Hart Plaza if we want."

"We?"

"Yes, we. We're a team now, Councilman Parker. Didn't I tell you that?"

"No," Parker said stonily. "What makes you think I need a partner, or even want one?"

Fish smiled. He slid his briefcase toward him and lifted the lid. Reaching inside,. he pulled out the big black switchblade he'd had for so many years he'd given it a name: *Bloody Mary*. The weapon was asleep in its sheath, but with a flick of Fish's wrist, the deadly eight-inch blade revealed itself in all its gleaming glory. Fish smiled as he ran a finger down the edge. "Mary and I have done a lot of work on your behalf, councilman. Haven't we, baby?" he said, talking softly to the blade, stroking it like a lover. He looked up at Parker. "Mary thinks we deserve a partnership, and so do I."

Parker tried hard to look away from Fish's fingers on the knife, but couldn't. He was as mesmerized as a cobra dancing to a charmer's song. "How much do you want?"

Fish shrugged. "Forty, forty-five percent."

Parker exploded. "Forget it. I'm not giving you that much. We'll both go broke."

"Sure you will, and no, we won't." Fish closed Mary and placed her back in his case and closed it. "Once all the dust settles, we'll talk again." He pushed his chair back and stood. "I hear your little tree hugger isn't liking the phone calls she's been getting. Apparently she was so messed up, she and Randolph ran away for a long weekend."

"What?" Parker had no idea Green was now Randolph's woman.

"Folks all over the city garage were talking about it. If you didn't have the people skills of Jabba the Hut, you wouldn't have to hear these things secondhand."

Parker snarled inwardly. He had no idea who or what a Jabba the Hut was but he knew an insult when he heard one. "Are you leaving?"

Fish nodded and said, "Yep, but don't worry. Mary and I will be back."

As he left the trailer, Parker followed him with wintry eyes. He should've had Fish killed a long time ago. Now, it might be too late.

Lacy returned to work on Monday feeling fresh and rejuvenated after the long and memorable weekend with Drake. She gave the eager Ida and Janika the

G-rated version of the trip then happily went into her office.

The first hour of the day was spent making phone calls to some of the east side block club presidents to remind them of the upcoming Environmental Watch meeting to be held on their side of town at Kettering High School later in the week. In response, she got a few answering machines, a few wrong numbers, and two people who cursed her out for waking them up then hung up on her. Lacy grimaced and decided to work on something else.

That something else turned out to be the arrival of Lenny Durant and a man Lacy didn't know. Lenny introduced the big block-shaped man with beady eyes and glasses as David Bales.

Lacy gestured them to the empty chairs in her office. "Please, have a seat."

They sat, and she waited to hear why they'd come.

Lenny started it off. "Bales was part of the crew that dumped the stuff on the southwest side."

Lacy couldn't hide her surprise. "Who do you work for?"

"Parker Environmental."

Her eyes widened. Was this the concrete evidence she'd been after? "Do you have any proof?"

"Yeah," Bales told her. "Pictures and video."

Excited, Lacy wanted to shout Hallelujah. "May I see them?"

"Don't have them on me. Wanted to check you out first. Lenny says you're the real deal, but I wanted to see for myself."

Lacy looked at Lenny, who wordlessly acknowledged her thanks. She asked Bales, "What do I need to do to look at what you have?"

"I'll give it to Lenny and he can pass it to you."

"Okay, but may I ask why you're coming forward?"

Lacy saw his jaw tighten before he answered, "My kids go to that school."

She stared. "Where the barrels were found on the playground?"

"Yeah. Me and the crew I was working with left them there." He met her eyes. "Parker wanted me to poison my own children!"

It was obvious Bales was outraged. "When I told him I wouldn't do it, he gave me the choice of doing the job or be fired, so I did a couple more nights last week, just to get the evidence I needed to bust his ass." Bales was immediately contrite. "Didn't mean to cuss. Sorry."

"It's okay," Lacy assured him. "Do you still work for Mr. Parker?"

"He thinks I do, but I'm not going back. Finding a new job will probably be hard, but I can't work for him knowing what I know."

Lacy had nothing but sympathy for him and the choices he'd been forced to make. "When would you be willing to turn over your evidence?"

He shrugged. "Whenever you want, I guess."

"Would you be willing to testify in court against Parker?"

"Yeah. I want to be there when they drag him off to jail. I have the stuff at my house. I'll give it to Lenny and he can bring it back to you."

"Sounds good. Thank you, Mr. Bales."

"No, thank you," he replied. "Lenny said turning the pics over to you was the way to go. Parker's a big man in this town. If I give the evidence to the police, I might not see it again."

Lacy understood. "Then I'll wait for Lenny and we'll go from there."

Bales nodded and stood. She came out from behind her desk and shook his hand. "Thank you very much for what you're doing."

"No problem. I can't wait to nail his fat behind to the wall."

She turned to Lenny. "Thanks."

He shook her outstretched hand. "I'll be in touch."

And they left.

Lacy pumped her fist like Tiger Woods and whispered, "Yes!"

To celebrate, she hit the power button on the small CD unit sitting on top of one of the bookcases, then dug out the CD she wanted to hear. Slipping the disk in, she walked back to her desk as the first sweet notes of Marvin Gaye's "What's Goin' On" began to play. Lacy sang along, knowing Marvin would be pleased with what just took place.

Parker was late for the council's closed door session and was hurrying into the building. When the elevator door opened, he was startled to see one of his employees, David Bales, standing inside waiting to step out. Bales looked equally surprised, and for just a split second Parker swore he saw fear in the man's eyes as well. The other people stepped out. Parker let them pass then asked Bales, "What are you doing downtown? Shouldn't you be working?"

"Had some business to take care of. Rats."

Parker held the edge of the elevator so the door wouldn't close. He then checked out the man standing with Bales. The face was vaguely familiar, but he couldn't place him at the moment. "So Bales, are you on board now?"

"Yes, sir."

"Good." He and Bales had gotten into a heated argument over leaving barrels at the school his kids attended. Bales had threatened to quit, but had apparently changed his mind because he was still working as far as Parker knew. "See you at the site."

"See you."

Bales walked off with his companion, and Parker got on the elevator. The identity of the companion bugged him, but Parker let it go for now.

Lacy's office phone rang, but she hesitated before picking it up. In the back of her mind were the threatening calls she'd been receiving, and she was admittedly paranoid.

Ida called out, "I'll get it, Lace. Hang on." Janika and Ida were doing their best to catch the phones so she wouldn't have to, and she was grateful to them for it.

Ida came in a few moments later. "It was His Fineness. He'd like you to come upstairs for a moment."

"Good, I can tell him the news about the soon-to-be-ex city councilman. Everybody else will have to wait until we get the evidence. Okay?"

"Understood, now go up and see what he wants."

Rhonda showed Lacy into Drake's office. Lacy smiled at Drake, then noticed a man sitting quietly in one of the chairs.

Drake said, "Hey."

"Hey."

"Want you to meet Walter McGhee. Gee, this is Lacy Green."

The man stood, and Lacy walked over and shook his hand. Walter was as tall as Drake and dark-skinned. He looked fit enough to be a wide receiver or a defensive back. Lacy thought he was kind of cute too. "Nice meeting you," she said.

"Same here."

Lacy sat down on one of the plush leather chairs, and Drake said, "I'd like for Walter to be your shadow for a while."

"That's fine. How much of a shadow?"

Walter answered, "Where you go, I go."

"That much, huh?"

He smiled, showing even white teeth. "That much."

"I suppose it doesn't make sense to have you around if you're not with me."

"Exactly."

"Okay."

"I'll have my own gear, sleeping bag, toiletries. I'll take you to work and bring you home. I'll bunk wherever you have room."

"So you'll be moving in?"

Walter looked to Drake, who told Lacy, "It's the best way, babe."

Lacy wasn't sure how she felt about having a strange man in her apartment, even if he was recommended by Drake, but when she weighed that against the reality of the stalker being out there somewhere, the decision became an easy one. "Do you like French bread?"

The three talked logistics for a few moments longer, then Walter got up and waited outside Drake's office to give Lacy and the mayor some privacy.

Only then did Lacy tell him about Bales and Lenny Durant.

Drake was pleased by the news. "If he has even one good picture, Parker may have to kiss his license good-bye. A lot of times polluters are simply fined, but for a dumping of this magnitude, be nice if he got prison."

Lacy agreed. "What are you doing after work? You still owe me a dinner at the mansion, you know."

"I do, but it can't be tonight. I've meetings until midnight. How about we plan for later in the week?"

"That would be fine."

"Are you okay with Walter staying with you?"

"Don't have much of a choice, do I?"

"He's a good friend. You two will get along just fine." Then he told her, "I wish I didn't have these glass walls."

"Why?"

"So I could sit you in my lap and steal a few kisses."

"Mmm," Lacy purred. "I'd like that. Might even show you my little purple garter belt too."

Drake's manhood tightened. Speculating on what other sexy delights she might have on under her conservative blue suit and pearls was so distracting, he knew that if he didn't get her out of his office he wasn't going to get any work done for the rest of the day. With a grin on his face, he told her, "You need to go back to your office, Miss Hot Pants, before I find a dark corner and take you up on that offer."

Playfully, Lacy looked around the room and pointed to the corner holding a large standing U.S. flag. "How about that one?"

"Out!"

She laughed. "All right. I can take a hint. 'Bye Drake."

" 'Bye, baby. If it's not too late when I get done tonight, I'll give you a call."

She mimicked a kiss and left him to his work, but it took the mayor a long while to stop thinking about little purple garter belts and concentrate on what he was supposed to be doing.

The surprise run-in with Bales stayed with Parker all day. He kept seeing that flash of fear in Bales's eyes. True, Bales recovered quickly, but not quickly enough for him not to wonder what it meant. And who was the other man? Parker's sense that he knew him from somewhere was strong enough to make him stop by the guard station at the end of the day and ask to see the sign-in log.

The female guard handed it over. The log was a security measure. Every nonemployee entering the building for whatever reason had to sign in and sign out. Parker went back through the names until he found Bales. Right above it was the name L. Durant. It registered with Parker like a light turned on in a pitch-black room. Parker had seen Durant in the papers. He then looked across from their names to the column where they'd written their destinations. *L. Green.* Parker's heart began to race. What had they been doing in her office? He could see Durant visiting her; the man was a tree hugger too. But Bales? Alarms went off inside. Surely Bales wouldn't be stupid enough to drop a dime on the operations of Parker Environmental? He drew in a few deep breaths and handed the clipboard back to the guard. "Thanks."

Walking swiftly to the garage to get his car, Parker pulled out his phone and called Fish. They needed to meet to talk about this. Fish came on the line. They set up a time, and Parker got into his vehicle. As he stuck the key into the ignition, he noticed that he was sweating and that inside of his clothes he was soaking wet.

At that night's NIA meeting, Drake told the others on the board what he'd learned from Lacy.

Myk asked, "What's she planning to do?"

Drake shrugged. "Not sure, but she can't do anything until she hears back from Durant."

Myk said, "I wish we knew what this Bales has as evidence."

One of the female board members said, "I hate to

say this, but it needs to be said. We can fry Parker longer if we get him on the federal charges." She looked over at Drake sympathetically. "Mr. Mayor, I know this is your city, but those barrels are small potatoes next to murder and bringing drugs over the border."

Drake met her eyes. Even though he didn't want to admit it, he had to look at the big picture, and he knew she was right. "Okay. I'll have her back off Parker for now. She is not going to like it, but it's all we have."

Someone asked, "Is the driver of the Parker rig that was busted bringing in the pot from Canada still in the county jail?"

Myk answered, "Yes. He's still not talking, but then he hasn't made bail yet either. You'd think Parker would have taken care of him by now."

"Maybe the driver will get mad enough to sing."

The meeting continued, but all Drake could think about was Lacy and how he was going to explain.

The next morning Lacy was just hanging up her coat when Janika stuck her head in the door. "Ms. Curry's on line one for you."

"Thanks." Lacy picked up the receiver. "Lacy Green."

" 'Morning, Ms. Green. This is Rhonda Curry."

" 'Morning," Lacy said cheerily.

"The mayor would like to see you as soon as possible."

Lacy paused and wondered why he hadn't just

picked up the phone. She'd waited for him to call last night, but he hadn't. "Do you know what this is concerning?"

"No," Rhonda said, "I'm afraid I don't."

"Okay. Be right up."

Lacy let Ida know where she was going, then left the office to grab the elevator.

Upstairs, the outer office was packed with people lined up to see the mayor. When Lacy entered, Rhonda, wearing a stunning black suit, beckoned her over. "This way."

Lacy could see folks watching her as she followed Rhonda to the hallway that led to Drake's office. He was on the phone, but gestured her to a seat. Rhonda exited and closed the door softly.

From the conversation he was having, Lacy assumed another city water main had broken. The city's ancient infrastructure was being held together with bobby pins and prayer. The millions of dollars needed for genuine repairs just weren't in the city's budget. He finally said good-bye to the person on the other end.

" 'Morning," Lacy said.

" 'Morning. I need to talk to you about something."

Lacy studied him. He looked very serious, and it made her wary. "What's up?"

"Parker Environmental. I need you to pull up on the case for a while."

Even more wary now, she asked, "Why?"

"There are some other forces at work, and I don't want anyone's toes stepped on."

"In English, please."

Drake could see the skepticism in her eyes. "Let's just say you aren't the only dog in this hunt."

"Is this political?"

"In some ways, yes."

"You know I got fired from my last job because the polluters had more clout than I did. Is that what this is about?"

"No, baby. Definitely not."

"Okay, but we're going to let Parker or whoever is doing the dumping just go on about their business?"

Drake's jaw tightened. "For now, it's the only option."

"I don't like this."

"I know. All I can say is, Parker is the subject of an official investigation."

"Federal?"

He didn't respond.

"So what am I supposed to do when Lenny brings me the pictures and videos from Bales?"

"Hold on to them until I say it's okay."

Lacy sighed.

"Sorry."

She shrugged. "Hey." She asked then, "What if I decide to do my job anyway?"

"Then you won't have a job."

"You'd fire me?"

"As much as I enjoy your company, in a heartbeat."

Lacy's lips tightened and she stood.

"Baby, look—"

Lacy shook her head. "It's okay. You obviously

have your reasons for doing this, and I'm going to trust you enough to follow your directive. I don't have to like it, though."

"That's fair."

"So is the city going to send me on a paid vacation somewhere since you don't want me to work?"

Drake didn't care for the sarcasm, even if he did deserve it. "No. You have the Blight Court to put together. Work on that."

"You're the boss. Anything else?"

He shook his head.

"Thank you." And she walked out.

By the time she'd walked back into the Environmental Office, she was sure steam was rising off of her twists, because Ida took one look at her and said, "Girl, you look hot. What did he say?"

"For us to pull up on the barrels investigation."

"What? Why?"

"All he said was that there were other dogs in the hunt."

"Like who?"

"You got me. He wouldn't tell me."

Ida looked as confused as Lacy had been upstairs in Drake's office. "Well, we know he's a good man," she said. "Just go with the flow and see what happens."

"And while we're waiting for this *good* man to fess up, the dumpings will keep *flowing* into the city of Detroit."

Angry, Lacy continued her walk to her office. Once inside, she slammed the door.

For the rest of the week she fumed and worked on

setting up the Blight Court. Her days were spent coordinating moves with the various agencies involved, like the courts, law enforcement, and the state's environmental departments. The staff worked on the revised warning letters that would be sent out to violators and whispered about Lacy and the mayor not speaking. Although she didn't realize it, everyone in the building knew hers and Drake's business, and down in the mailroom some of the clerks were even taking bets on when the Big Chill, as folks were calling the stalemate, would end.

Sixteen

Parker was in his office trying to play the chess game that had become his life. He was losing. According the federal agent who'd stopped by yesterday, the dogs would be coming in tomorrow morning. His lawyer said nothing in the search warrant implicated him personally in a crime, only that the government was operating on what they'd told the judge was a solid tip. Parker knew better. The agent had asked him all kinds of questions about Wheeler. Did Wheeler have a woman on the side? Did he have gambling debts? Did he know that Wheeler had a sizable amount of cash stashed in the Seychelles Islands? Parker knew Wheeler had been embezzling, but the number the fed quoted as being in Wheeler's account just about knocked him to his knees. When Parker asked how and when he could get the funds returned, he was told the process couldn't begin until the accountant or his corpse was found. Once again Parker couldn't wait to run across Wheeler in hell.

The other big problem involved Bales. He was nowhere to be found. The old lady who lived next door to him told Fish that Bales told her he had a new job waiting for him down South and that he'd sent his family on ahead last week. As close as Fish and Parker could determine, Bales had disappeared right after Parker saw him downtown. He hadn't even picked up his last check. Parker was furious. Bales's disappearance left him vulnerable because he had no idea what Bales might have said in Green's office.

Now, finding Durant had become imperative. More than likely, any evidence left behind would be in his hands or Green's, and Parker wanted whatever it was. Fish was scouring the streets. Parker took heart in one thing: If Durant was still in town, Fish would find him. Parker also wanted to grill Lacy Green, but he couldn't just snatch her up. She had to be handled creatively, so he decided he would put the screws to her in a different kind of way.

Lacy was concerned that she hadn't heard from Lenny Durant. Just a little while ago she'd called the number he'd written down the night they met, but his mother said she hadn't seen him in days. Lacy wondered where he was. After he left her office with Bales, she'd assumed he'd contact her that same day or, at the latest, the next day, but he hadn't showed. Not that it mattered now. Since Drake pulled the plug on her investigation, she couldn't do anything with Bales's evidence even if she had it in her possession.

Drake. Thinking about him made her sigh. A week had gone by since that conversation in his office. In spite of the way they parted, she missed him. Missed him a lot. She and Walter spent their evenings honing Lacy's skills on the firing range, playing the occasional board game, and watching lots of NBA basketball, but the more Lacy and Drake were apart, the more she wanted him near.

Ida stuck her head around the door. "Security just called. Your car alarm's going off."

"Oh, shoot."

She grabbed her keys and ran to the elevator. For some reason, the elevator took a long time to get to her floor. When it finally arrived, she saw why. It was filled with laughing, giggling middle school kids. Lacy supposed they were in the building for a field trip.

She finally reached the garage and was taken aback by all the activity and people. She saw police and the security men and women from the garage. Lacy could also hear the loud pulsating blare of a car alarm. Whatever was going on, she'd have to find out later. She hurried off in the direction of the alarm.

To her confusion, there were policemen at that end of the parking structure too. Again she wondered why. Had a car been stolen, someone shot, what? When she saw Drake and Walter, her steps slowed. Drake looked especially grim.

"Hey," she said. "What's going on?"

"I need your keys."

"I can turn off the alarm, Drake. Are all these folks down here because of my alarm?"

"That and something else. Give me the keys."

She turned to Walter, who said, "You don't want to see—"

Lacy pushed past them, intending to get some answers, but when she saw the car, she stopped, and so did her heart. The keys slipped from her fingers. The beautiful coupe her mama had given her was covered in what looked like buckets of blood and gore. The ghastly sight roiled her stomach so violently, she turned away and involuntarily retched until she had nothing left.

She remembered somebody handing her a bottle of water so she could rinse her mouth, and then Drake was seated beside her. He placed his arm around her shoulders and held her as she watched the tow truck drag the blood-covered coupe away.

Only later, after he and Walter walked her back to her office to get her belongings so she could go home, did they tell her about the note.

Drake said, "The police took it to test for prints."

"What did it say?"

"Where's Lenny Durant?"

Lacy held his grim eyes. "This has turned into a nightmare."

Everyone in the office agreed.

Lenny Durant drove through the early morning streets looking for a place to hide. Word was, a fish-eyed, light-skinned man with a pocked face had been asking after him all over town. Lenny was pretty sure Parker was behind the search, especially after discovering that Bales and his whole family had left town. Bales had talked much stuff on the ride back from Lacy Green's office about what he would do to Parker if he harmed his family. He'd even handed over the evidence, as he'd promised, but in the end, Lenny realized, he must have decided he didn't want to take on Goliath after all and moved his family out of harm's way. Lenny didn't really blame him. Parker had a pretty serious rep.

By today Fish Eyes and his boss would also be aware that Bales had bailed, so that probably put him in the bull's-eye. Parker had seen them together that day downtown, and undoubtedly Parker wanted to talk about what he and Bales had been up to. Lenny didn't want to have that talk. At least not until he had a chance to think over his options. The press was an option, as was turning everything over to Lacy Green, as they'd initially planned, and letting the city have him. But Lenny thought Parker deserved a more just punishment; something more pointed and painful for his sins.

And Parker's crimes were sins. Lenny looked at the rampant blight now ruling the streets of his hometown Highland Park, a small city inside of Detroit. There were streets so blocked with trash he had to go around the block to get to his destination. He and the members of BAD had spent a week last year hauling tires, couch frames, broken windows, glass, and mattresses from one such location. Most of the people on the block had pitched in to help, but others sat on their porches and watched the cleanup as if it were the latest reality show.

But because there were so many other trash-filled areas in need of the same kind of intense attention, that particular cleanup had been nothing more than a pimple on a giant, and folks like Parker just added to the pus. Polluters had left their mark all over the area, in the deaths of children from tainted soil that tested fourteen times higher in toxic substances than allowed by standards set up by the government. Slum landlords and their slow reactions to lead paint removal notices were to him directly responsible for the poisoning of children nationwide. In kids younger than six, lead poisoning impaired the development of their brains. How were inner city residents going to rise if their children were looking at lifelong behavior issues and learning disabilities?

It was a subject that angered Lenny because of his own lead poisoning diagnosis. As part of a routine screening, the army doctors had tested his blood and some tissue samples. His levels were off the charts. The doctors said the high lead concentrations might be responsible for the headaches he'd experienced all his life and for his sometimes violent mood swings; mood swings that got him sent to the brig more than a few times for fighting and for clashes with officers. In the end, the army asked him to leave, but they took his health issues into consideration and gave him an honorable discharge. The lead in his body would eventually put him in an early grave, he was told, and that was just one more reason he wanted Parker and parasites like him dead.

But now he had to find a place to hole up until the heat died down, and so he could think. He and Melissa had made three copies of Bales's pictures and video. He had one set on him. He'd left one in a sealed envelope in his mother's safety deposit box at the bank. And Melissa had the other. The video had been shot at night, and it showed workers in HazMat suits loading barrels on trucks. Another portion showed men leaving unmarked barrels beneath overpasses. There was even footage showing the barrels being left behind at the elementary school.

Lenny drove the Gremlin onto a street that looked as desolate and derelict as a bombed-out area of Mogadishu. The human night rats who supplemented their lives by stripping buildings of everything they could sell had gone through the area like locusts through an African grain field. The few homes still standing were virtual skeletons; even the siding and bricks were gone. Lenny stopped in front of one that had most of its front walls still intact. He drove up onto the curb, steered the car around the back and inside. *Let Fish Eyes think he'd left town too.*

Lacy returned to work a few days after the incident with her car. She was determined to get on with her life. It was obvious that the stalker intended for her to cower in her apartment wringing her hands and sobbing, "Oh woe is me," but she was tougher than that, even if she had been having nightmares about the blood-covered car.

According to a call from Detective Franks, there were no usable prints found on her car and the blood had been human. A blood bank was broken into a few days before the coupe was trashed, and Franks was positive the two incidents were related.

When Lacy relayed the news to Ida and Janika, Ida's face took on a look of distaste. "Human blood?" she asked.

"Yeah."

"That's awful."

Lacy thought so too.

Janika asked, "Still nothing on Lenny Durant?"

"Nope, or David Bales either."

After Ida and Janika went back to their desks, Lacy admitted to herself that she hadn't heard much from Drake either. Although he'd been there for her on that awful day in the parking garage, the two of them had yet to reconcile properly.

Ida reappeared in her doorway. "Rhonda Curry is on line one."

"Thanks." She picked up the phone. "Lacy Green."

" 'Morning, baby."

Lacy went still. "Good morning."

"I told Ida tell you it was Rhonda because I wasn't sure you'd take a call from me."

Lacy was so glad to hear his voice. "How are you?" she asked.

"Not too good."

"What's wrong?"

"I miss you. I'm worried about you, but mostly I miss you."

Lacy could feel tears stinging her eyes. "I miss you, too."

"Can we get together and talk?"

"I'd like that."

"Okay. How about I swing by your place this evening."

"That would be great."

"I'll see you then."

Lacy hung up, wiped at her eyes, and smiled for what felt like the first time in weeks.

She was back to driving a rental car. After talking with her mother about what happened with the coupe, they agreed that selling it was the only option. Lacy had no desire to drive the car again, even if the dealership was able to clean it up, which they weren't sure they could, so Val made arrangements to sell it back to the dealer. Lacy put the proceeds down on a new one. Silver. She'd be able to pick it up in a few days.

After work, she and Walter had dinner, and were settling in for the night's playoff game when the buzzer sounded. The two looked at each other. Lacy wanted the visitor to be Drake but kept her anticipation under wraps, in case it turned out not to be. When Walter went to the intercom and she heard Drake's voice, she smiled.

While they waited for him to come up, Walter told her, "I'm going to take off for a few hours so you two can have some privacy."

"That isn't necessary, Walter."

He smiled. "His Honor says it is."

Lacy dropped her eyes. Drake's knock sounded on the door. In response, Walter picked up his jacket and the keys to the rental car. He opened the door and told Lacy, "Drake's going to drop you off at work in the morning. I've got a dentist appointment, so I'll hook up with you at noon."

He walked out and Drake walked in.

Drake closed the door behind him and stood there for a moment. Since her angry departure from his office, seemingly eons ago, his entire world had gone gray. Then, when her car was vandalized, his heart had broken watching her reaction to the gore the stalker had left for her to find. He'd wanted to scoop her up and take her to a place where she'd never be hurt that way again. Now, being here with her and maybe getting this straight so their relationship could continue to grow, Drake felt the sun reentering his life. "Hey."

She nodded. "Hey."

"Still mad?"

"No."

"Then can I hold you. . . . ?"

Lacy went into his outstretched arms and let herself be enfolded against his heart.

It was the place she most wanted to be. She'd missed him so much.

Relief washed over Drake like rain, and he held even tighter. "I'm sorry for the way I handled that meeting," he whispered passionately. "Pulling you off the case wasn't an easy decision, but I had no choice. I'm sorry I hurt you."

The impact of his sincerity made tears slide down Lacy's cheeks.

He reached down and raised her chin. The tears in her eyes made them shine. "Not being with you has been killing me."

She gave him a small smile. "Hasn't been fun for me either. You know what I missed the most, though?"

"What?"

"Your kisses . . ."

Drake raised an eyebrow. "Oh really?" He took a moment to trace the lips that had been haunting his dreams. "Then let's fix that right now."

He lowered his mouth to hers, and when they met, all the dammed-up feelings and emotions rose like a wild wind and swept them away. Kisses fueled by longing, solace, and acceptance melded with ones of welcome and joy.

When they finally came up for air, Drake wanted to spend the rest of his life holding her against his heart in just this way. And Lacy's thoughts mirrored his. She didn't want to leave his arms ever.

Drake confessed something that he couldn't suppress any longer. "I'm in love with you, woman. Big-time."

She was in love with him too, had been since their long weekend in Holland. "Ditto."

He stared down. "Really?"

"Yes."

He smiled. "When did you know?"

"Holland. You?"

"Truthfully? From the first day we met. I still remember how mad you were."

"True dat."

He chuckled. "Guess we can call ourselves an official couple now, huh?"

She nodded. "I think so."

He hugged her tight. "Damn, that feels good."

She grinned and held him tight too. "Yes, it does."

So Lacy became, according to the newspapers, the First Girlfriend.

Friday morning at work, Lacy's phone rang. Ida came in. "There's a woman named Melissa on the line. She sounds like something's wrong."

"Melissa who?"

"She says she met you at the Northwest Activities Center. She was there with Lenny."

"Oh. Okay."

Lacy picked up. "Lacy Green. How may I help you?"

"Miss Green?" The female voice sounded frantic and scared.

"Yes, this is Lacy. What's wrong?"

"This is Melissa Curtis. Lenny's friend. You gotta come over here and get this tape."

"What tape?"

"I don't have time to explain on the phone." Instead, she gave Lacy an address on the west side. "Please hurry, Miss Green. I don't think we have a lot of time."

"Melissa?" Lacy said. "Melissa!" But she'd hung up.

Lacy set the phone down and hollered for Ida.

Because Lacy didn't know the city well enough, Ida drove. A traffic accident on the Lodge made the trip much longer than it should have been, and by the time they found the street and then the large brick apartment building that matched the address, an hour had passed. Lacy walked briskly up the walk while Ida remained in the Caddy. The neighborhood was not a good one, and Ida didn't want to have to shoot anyone dumb enough to try and jack her.

Lacy pulled the door open and was almost knocked down by a man coming out. He reached out to keep her from falling. " 'Scuse me, ma'am," he whispered, then proceeded briskly down he steps. He had his coat collar turned up, so she didn't get a good look at his face but his big fish eyes were hard to miss.

Inside, she quickly walked past the mailboxes and headed to the elevator. A handwritten OUT OF ORDER sign was stuck to the doors with a piece of silver duct tape. Melissa had given her an apartment number on the third floor, so she looked around for the stairs, found them, then headed up. Her cell phone rang. Since getting a new number, Lacy was no longer paranoid about answering it.

Ida was on the other end. "Are you okay?"

"So far. Did you see that man almost knock me down?"

"The one with the big pop eyes?"

Lacy reached the third floor. "Yeah. Okay, here's apartment 32. Hold on."

She knocked, and it slowly swung open in response.

Lacy stopped. Adrenaline began to pump. She knocked on the door frame and called out, "Melissa. It's Lacy."

She looked at the other four apartment doors on the floor, thinking Melissa might be visiting a neighbor, but the doors were all closed. There was no way to tell how many were occupied, if at all. Pushing Melissa's door open wider, she walked in. A TV was blaring from somewhere inside. "Melissa?"

The narrow kitchen with its dirty dishes and pots of dried food on the stove led to a small living room with two windows facing the street. The place was in shambles, books and VHS tapes strewn everywhere. Furniture was turned over and there was broken glass on the floor. That's when Lacy saw her. A wide-eyed, dead Melissa was lying on the green shag carpet in a widening pool of blood. Her throat had been slashed. Lacy's stomach churned and she ran out of the apartment to the hallway. As her heart pounded, she fought the bile rising in her throat and drew in a few steadying breaths. Trembling, she raised the phone. "Ida, she's dead. I'm calling 911."

The police and an ambulance arrived with sirens and flashing lights about ten minutes after the call. Detective Franks met Lacy in the hallway and took her outside to his car while his colleagues stayed behind to set up the crime scene. Lacy was shook up, and the detective let her take her time telling them the story. "She wanted me to come by and pick up a tape."

Detective Franks said, "What kind of tape?"

"I don't know."

He was writing on his small notepad. "Care to guess?"

Lacy met his eyes, then told him about the visit she'd gotten from Lenny Durant and Bales. "It could be related to that, but I don't know."

"This is Lenny Durant of BAD?"

"Yes, and the name on the note left on my car."

"I remember that. Do you know where he is?"

"No." Lacy couldn't get the image of the murdered Melissa out of her mind. The chills that coursed up her arms made her hug herself. Ida, who was seated next to her, answered the detective's questions, but she had no more information to add about the mysterious tape.

"Did you see anyone while you were entering? Did you pass anybody on the stairs?'

Lacy told him about the man with the big eyes. "He almost knocked me down coming out, but he was polite and kept going."

"Would you recognize him if you saw him again?"

Lacy shrugged. "Maybe."

He then asked Ida. "Did you see the man too?"

"I did. After he left the building, he went toward the corner, but I didn't pay much attention to him after that."

"Think you might recognize him again?"

"I'm like Lacy. He had his coat collar pulled up so I didn't get a real good look at his face. Saw the eyes when he liked to knock her down, though."

"Okay. I need you to come to the precinct and look through our perp albums. Be a real help if we could do it right now."

Both women agreed, so a few minutes later Ida and Lacy trailed the detective back to his office.

It took them over an hour to find him. "Bingo," Lacy called out grimly. "Is this him, Ida?"

Ida leaned over her shoulder. "Sure looks like him."

The picture showed a light-skinned, pock-faced man with eyes like a fish. His name was Benjamin Madison, aka Fish.

The detective asked them both, "You're sure now?"

They nodded.

He smiled. "Good. Thanks. We have some papers for you to sign and then you can be on your way. We'll keep you posted."

Ida and Lacy drove back to the office.

From the window in his trailer office City Councilman Reynard Parker watched the cadaver dog and his handler making their way over the mountain-high landfill. The search had been going on for over two weeks. Parker's anger over having them in his business was tempered by the pleasure that they hadn't found anything, and if Fish was right, they never would, but there were other worries on his plate too.

According to the newspapers, witnesses had seen a man leaving Melissa Curtis's building the morning of her murder. Fish assumed it was the woman he'd run into at the door, but the papers hadn't given up any more details. Fish had killed Curtis because she refused to give up Durant's location. In an effort to find an answer, he'd rifled her apartment and found a VHS on the kitchen counter marked *Parker*. He also found her cell phone, both of which he brought back. The tape had a short, night-shot video of barrels being loaded. The next bit of footage had almost given Parker a heart attack. All of the dumping had been filmed. A hand suddenly came into the picture, lifted the plastic plate the crews used to cover the license plates of the trucks involved and showed the plate numbers to the camera.

Parker had angrily shut if off. He didn't need to see any more. The tape had enough evidence for the state regulatory commission to suspend his license and maybe send him to jail. Finding Durant had become critical. He was too smart to have had only one copy of the evidence. If Fish could find Durant, then Parker would know what he was facing. Right now he was in the dark. It was impossible to know what Melissa Curtis had intended to do with the tape, but the last phone call she'd made from her cell had been to Lacy Green. How the two women were tied together was a mystery too, but since Fish was the one who would be up for murder, it was his job to clean up this mess and make sure the witnesses weren't around to testify.

Parker was just about to leave the office and head downtown to take care of his council duties when he saw a big black car rumbling its way across the uneven ground toward the trailer he used as his office. Everything about the car screamed police, so he simply stood and waited. Before Wheeler's death, his life had been smooth as glass. Now he felt like he was headed for a cliff.

* * *

Lacy put in a call to Detective Franks. "Anything new on the investigation?"

"Not really. You said she called you that morning, right?"

"Yes, she did."

"We can't find her cell phone, and her bedroom had been tossed. Makes us think the killer was looking for something."

"Did your people find the tape?"

"We found hundreds of them in her bedroom. Her mother said Ms. Curtis was also a computer geek, but there was nothing on any of the tapes worth her losing her life over."

"What about Madison?"

"Nothing yet. We ran down his old parole officer and he gave us a lead on where he might be working. Some detectives went to check the tip out this morning, but his employer swore he hasn't seen Madison in at least a week. You wanta guess who his boss is?"

"Who?'

"City Councilman Reynard Parker. Madison works for Parker Environmental."

Lacy felt the hair on her neck rise. "This is getting uglier and uglier, isn't it?"

"You got that right."

Lacy found it hard to think, but asked, "Is Madison the man who's been calling me?"

"Nothing points to that right now. Too bad law enforcement doesn't store voice samples of felons the way it does fingerprints and face photos."

Lacy thought that would have been an immense help.

"We're tearing up the city looking for Madison, though. We faxed his picture to the airlines and the bus and trains stations in case he tries to skip town."

"That's good to know."

"Don't worry, Ms. Green. It won't be long before we catch him."

Lacy hoped he was right.

Lenny was waiting for dark. He'd gotten the call about Melissa's death and knew she'd been killed because of her ties to him. Melissa had come to the environmental movement by way of her older brother, Hugh. He'd served during Desert Storm and returned to the States sick as a dog from something the doctors couldn't figure out. Melissa was a high school student at the time, and she was convinced her brother's sickness came from his time overseas. The army denied any such association, and told thousands of other families with sick and dying vets the same thing. When Hugh died a few years later, fighting environmental hazards became Melissa's whole world. And now she was dead.

Lenny felt bad about that. Real bad. Angry too, because they didn't have to kill her. Was life that meaningless to them? How could profits from trash hauling, of all things, outweigh a woman's right to be on the planet? Her death answered all those questions, however. Once it got dark, he was going to cruise around until he got his hands on his weapon of choice, and then he was going hunting, just like in the old days when he and his old man used to hunt rats at night. Only these rats were going to be the two-legged kind.

He had tried to work through the system by gathering evidence for the folks downtown to use, going to meetings and stuff, and Melissa's death had been the result. Now he was going to do this his way.

Seventeen

Lacy was preparing to leave the office when the phone rang. Now that the police had a tap on her outside line, she felt secure answering it again. "Lacy Green. May I help you?"

" 'Afternoon, Ms. Green."

It was him!

"Did you like my last present?" he asked with a low laugh. "Your car looked so stunning in red. Tell Lenny I need to see him or you may have to join Melissa."

He hung up.

Lacy's hand was shaking so badly it took her two times to fit the phone back into the cradle. *Lord, her stalker and Melissa's murderer were the same man!* Pulling herself together she made two calls : first to Detective Franks and then to Drake.

After Franks and his partner left, Lacy looked across her office to where the tight-jawed Drake stood. The police traced the call to another pay phone. Uniformed officers were combing the area around the phone, but just like the earlier foray, Franks didn't have much hope of finding any clues. Drake had stood by silently during the interview, but Lacy could feel his anger. "Hey," she asked him softly, "you okay?"

"No, and I won't be until they find him."

"Me either."

"Walter and I are not letting you out of our sight." Walter was now down in the garage making sure no damage had been done to her new car.

"That's fine. I'm not some stupid woman in a movie. I *want* somebody standing between me and him. The more the better."

Drake smiled for the first time since her disturbing call. "Good. I'd really rather have you at my place, but I know you won't say yes to that."

"You're starting to know me well, Your Honor."

"We'll put someone on Ida too."

As if on cue, she walked in. "Ida don't need protecting. Herbert and I will be fine. You just take care of my girl, Mayor Randolph."

Herbert was Ida's husband and if anyone did manage to get by him, there were three, six-foot-four-inch sons, all over 280, waiting to step in and take up his slack. Lacy wasn't worried about the pistol-packing grandma Ida at all. If anything, Benny Madison was the one who'd better beware of Ida and her men. Mess around, get his butt kicked and then get killed.

"Just came in to say I'm gone. See you tomorrow."

Ida's exit was Drake's cue to ask, "You want to get something to eat?"

"Only if I can take it back to my place. Not in the mood for a crowded restaurant."

Drake understood.

Lacy walked over and put her arms around his waist and her head on his chest. He wrapped his arms around her in return, and the feel of him squeezing her tight made the awful last few hours much better. "Madison scares me to death."

"I know." The man had threatened Lacy's life, and Drake wanted to exchange the white hat he usually wore for one as black as his mood. He wanted Madison dead. Period. He'd give the police a few more days to bring him in, then he and NIA would start a hunt of their own. "What do you want to eat?"

"Pizza's good."

"Then pizza it'll be."

They called to have a pizza delivered to Lacy's place. Drake also called Walter, who was downstairs in the garage, to let him know he would be walking Lacy down to the car so Walter needn't come back up to the office for her.

Drake wound up riding home with them because he couldn't handle not having Lacy in sight. At the apartment, she opened the locks and let them in.

"Walter, we really need to find you something better to sleep on than that sleeping bag," she said. "It has to be uncomfortable."

"It is, but it's okay. His Honor isn't paying me to sleep."

Drake laughed. "I'm not paying you at all."

Lacy looked between the men. "You two must be real good friends."

Walter nodded. "Me and his big brother taught him everything he knows."

Drake rolled his eyes. "The man lies *a lot,* Lacy, just remember that."

The buzzer blared, and Lacy went to the intercom. Walter gave her a look, then stepped in front of her. "You don't answer the door, the phone, or any other form of communication from now on. That's my job." He hit the buzzer and called, "Yeah."

It was the pizza man.

While he made his way up, Walter said to her, "In the bedroom. If it's not a real delivery, we don't want to be worried about where you are."

She looked at Drake, and he pointed. She put her hand on her hip to show him what she thought of being ordered around, even if it was for her own safety, but she went.

The pizza delivery person turned out to be the real thing, and a few minutes later they were seated on the floor enjoying the hot pie. Drake had taken off his suit coat, and for the first time Lacy saw the holster and gun strapped under his arm. Walter had removed his leather coat to show he was armed as well. Hers was in her purse.

Drake asked, "You still going to the gun range?"

Lacy nodded. "Yep. Walter has been a great help too."

Walter asked, "Do you think you could use your weapon if push came to shove?"

"Yes. Although the first time I shot a duck, I threw up, and didn't shoot anything but targets and skeet after that." She looked at the men. "This is different. The duck wasn't trying to take my life. Madison is."

Drake was satisfied that she'd be able to take someone down if she had to, and that made him feel much better.

Later that evening they gathered around Lacy's TV to watch the game. The NBA playoffs were under way, and the hometown Pistons were on their way back to the Eastern Conference championship if they could eliminate Philly tonight. At halftime Detroit was up by three. Lacy, Drake, and Walter were discussing what might happen in the third quarter when the sound of the door buzzer interrupted them.

Walter hopped up to answer it. "Yeah."

"Let us in," the voice boomed over the intercom.

He laughed. "Come on up."

Remembering her instructions from earlier, Lacy got up to go into the bedroom, but Drake stopped her. "It's okay, it's only my brother Myk."

Lacy smiled. She was finally going to meet the owner of the house in Holland and the man who, according to Walter, helped Walter teach Drake everything he knew.

A knock sounded, and Walter let in first a tall dark-skinned man, who was followed by three other people. One was a tall light skinned man wearing dark glasses and a long dirty trench coat, and two women; one of whom was short and pregnant and wearing a Piston's throwback jersey over a red T-shirt, the other woman was taller, rounder, and in her jewelry, designer suit, heels, and fine leather coat looked like a movie star on vacation.

Drake was over hugging everyone, especially the man in the coat, who cracked, "Hey, don't bend the coat."

Drake laughed. "When did you get into town?"

"About an hour ago. Myk and Sarita picked us up at the airport. We're heading back east after Gran's party."

Drake said, "Lacy, I want you to meet my brothers, Myk and Saint, and their wives, Sarita and Narice."

"Hello," Lacy said. This was a real surprise.

The brothers gave her polite hellos, and their smiling wives did the same.

Lacy sensed they were all checking her out, but since she was doing the same thing, she didn't mind. "Come join us. We were just watching the game."

Sarita threw up a hand and said, "Hallelujah, a woman who likes sports. Good job, Your Honor."

Lacy smiled hearing that Sarita called Drake by his title, too, and that she approved of Lacy.

Sarita then plopped down on the couch, her attention now glued to the halftime analysts.

Narice smiled, took a seat on the couch next to her sister-in-law, then removed her leather coat. "You know, Philly's going to win the second half."

Sarita didn't even look at her. "Narice, I love you, but you really need to stop drinking."

Everybody laughed, even Narice, then they all settled in to watch the second half.

The Pistons won, and Narice's Sixers were forced to try again next year. With the game over, everyone got their coats and gathered by the door to say their good-byes. Lacy had a great time and was thankful that Narice and Sarita hadn't been stuck up or hard to like.

Sarita gave her a strong hug, then said, "Don't worry. With these Vachon men in your life, Madison will have to go through fire to get to you."

For some reason, Lacy wasn't surprised that Sarita knew what was going on. Then Narice added coolly, "And if he gets past them, Sarita and I will be waiting."

The four men looked at each other and shook their heads in amusement.

Walter said, "Where do you all find these women?"

Everyone laughed.

After the visitors left, Drake and Walter went back to the TV to watch the Lakers against the Clippers. Lacy went to bed. She had work in the morning.

When Lacy got up the next morning, the sun was shining and rays of sunshine played against the bare wood floors of her bedroom. She was dressed and ready to go and had been tipping around in order not to awaken Walter, whom she assumed was still sleeping. She stood there in the silence for a moment and tried to gather herself for the day ahead. When somebody calls and threatens your life you really don't want to leave the house, and she was no exception. Madison murdered Melissa Curtis, and the idea that he was now after her, scared her to death. What she really wanted to do was crawl back into bed, pull the covers over her head, and stay there until they caught him, locked him up, and threw away the key. But she decided to go to work; staying home with nothing to do but worry would only make the bogeyman bigger. At least at her job she'd be busy and her mind would be occupied by something other than imagining Madison around every corner. Her decision had nothing to do with bravery or *I'm badder than him*, or anything like that; it just made sense.

Her bag over her arm, Lacy stepped out of the room and saw Drake asleep in her yellow chair. He had the sleeping bag thrown over himself for warmth. The picture he made pulled at her heartstrings. As if he'd sensed her watching, his eyes opened and he smiled at her sleepily. "Hey, baby."

"Hey yourself," she called back softly. "What're you still doing here? Where's Walter?"

"His stepson was in an accident early this morning and he went meet to his wife Shirley at the hospital."

"Is the son okay?"

"Yeah, car was wrecked but Jerome checked out okay. Some bumps and bruises." He sat up, then said, "You sure look good first thing in the morning."

Heat touched Lacy's cheeks and she dropped her

eyes before meeting his smile. "I'm sorry you had to sleep on the chair. You must feel like a pretzel."

"I do, but I knew the job was dangerous when I took it."

Lacy wondered if there was a woman alive able to resist him or that boyish smile. He had become such a blessing in her life. "Was Walter coming back to take me to work?"

He unfolded himself from the chair. "No, he'll be back this afternoon. I'll ride with you to work. Just let me brush my teeth and throw some water on my face."

Lacy could see that his suit and white shirt had taken quite a beating. They were as wrinkled as pretzels, too.

He looked down at himself. "I'll shower and change when I get to the office."

He grabbed Walter's backpack and slipped into the bathroom. Ten minutes later they were outside, heading to her new car, and Lacy's paranoia about Madison returned. "Maybe I've seen too many movies, but my car isn't going to blow up now, is it?"

Drake shook off his tiredness. "We probably saw the same movies. Hold on, let me make a call."

He punched in a number, put the phone to his ear and said, "Let me speak to Uncle Gadget."

Lacy stared in confusion, but he simply smiled.

About ten minutes later Saint drove up in a souped-up black Escalade. When he got out wearing that battered coat, he reminded Lacy of an Old West gunfighter. She wondered if he ever took the glasses off. "'Morning, Lacy. Your Honor. What do you need?"

"Just want to make sure her car doesn't go boom."

Saint nodded as if that made sense to him.

Lacy stared on not knowing what to say or think.

Out of his one of his coat pockets, Saint removed a small device about the size of an Ipod. He pointed it toward her new silver Crossfire then took a slow walk around the perimeter. When he was done, he slipped the little sensor back into a pocket. "Think she's okay. Anything else?"

Drake shook his head. "Nope. Thanks."

"See you later." He hopped back into the Escalade and rolled away.

Lacy watched his departure in amazement. "Who did you say your brother works for again?"

"The government."

"Doing what?"

Drake shrugged. "This and that."

"That's what I figured."

She hit the clicker for the locks, and once she and Drake were buckled in, she steered the coupe out of the lot and out onto Jefferson. They were both grinning.

The driver of the Parker Environmental truck caught smuggling drugs over the border back in early April decided he'd had enough of the city jail he'd been languishing in and began singing like a Temptation to the feds. He implicated Parker in everything from drug smuggling to illegal dumping to kickbacks. An hour later a warrant was issued for Parker's arrest and he was picked up and placed in custody. He posted bond and was out an hour later, but had to surrender his passport as part of the arrangement.

Drake and Myk met with the NIA board over lunch in Myk's boardroom. The conversation centered on the Parker investigation. "Why'd the truck driver sing now as opposed to earlier?" Drake asked.

One of the members said, "Parker promised he'd take care of the driver's family but hasn't so far, and since it was looking like Parker was going to hang him out to dry, the driver decided he wasn't going to be the emperor's sacrifice."

Myk said, "Too bad he wasn't that smart when he first got busted, or this might be over by now."

Drake added, "And Melissa Curtis might still be alive."

Myk met Drake's eyes and nodded almost imperceptibly, but it didn't make Drake feel any better about the circumstances leading to the young woman's death, especially now that the killer was after Lacy. He'd grieve for the rest of his life if anything happened to her. When he first organized NIA, one of the things he and Myk discussed was whether they were doing the right thing in the way they operated. The decision to forge ahead had been okay when they were riding roughshod over the rights of drug dealers and their fat cat suburban suppliers. He hadn't even minded snatching gang bangers off the street and forcing them into education and rehabilitation programs, whether the bangers wanted to be there or not, because the programs had been successful. But this thing with Lacy and Melissa Curtis was different. He and the NIA board had played God, and in their wisdom decided that their way was the only way, and as a result a woman had died.

It was now the second week in May, and a week had passed since Benny Madison's last phone call to Lacy's office. The police still hadn't caught him, and Walter McGhee was still joined to Lacy's hip. The newspapers were filled with stories about Parker's upcoming trial, and he'd become the whipping boy for every urban dumping crime that had ever taken place. BAD members were holding large demonstrations at Parker's construction sites to protest his poisoning of urban neighborhoods, and the police had to be called in on the picketers marching in front of Parker's upscale home. The schools began assigning projects on urban pollution to their students, and the hospitals were giving free lead poisoning tests to children under five.

All in all, Lacy saw some positives come out of the circus now swirling around Parker's arrest; the schools were involved, as were the churches. She and Ida thought it might be a good idea to bring their office's version of the Good News to as many congregations as they could get signed up. Today, she and Drake were on their way to St. Matthew's and St. Joseph's, and they were late.

"Your mother is going to think this is my fault," she said from the passenger seat of the Mustang.

"No, she's not."

"Are you going to tell her you got a ticket?"

He looked at her like she was crazy. "No."

A tight-lipped Drake took the ticket from the smiling policewoman, who said, "Slow down, Mr. Mayor. God wants you in the pew, not in a casket." She nodded at Lacy then went back to her unit.

Drake pulled away from the curb and continued the drive to church.

They slid into the Randolph pew while the choir was still singing the processional, and Lacy met the surprised and smiling eyes of the women she assumed were his sisters. His mother—Lacy supposed it was his mother—was decked out in a stunning beige suit and a hat that Lacy could only describe as gorgeous. Seeing Lacy made her eyes widen with delight, and she immediately made the family members move over so she could work her way down to where Drake and Lacy stood on the end. With her hymn book in hand, and while still singing, she grabbed Lacy's hand and gave it a welcome squeeze. Lacy squeezed back. When she looked up at Drake, he was singing and smiling too.

After church, Lacy laid out her information and brochures on one of the tables and waited for people to drift her way while they enjoyed the fellowship of coffee hour. Many of the mostly elderly congregation stopped by to hear what she had to say and look over the literature, but mostly they were there to check her out: one, because they'd never seen her before, and two, she'd come to church with the mayor. They wanted to know her name, where she was from, if she was married, and if she had a home church. Lacy answered the questions as honestly and as politely as she'd been raised to do and smiled the entire time.

Mavis and Drake stood across the room and watched her dealing with their church family, and Mavis said, "Drake, she is a doll, but you need to go and rescue her from nosey old Mrs. Satterwhite. The only thing that old biddy hasn't done is check her teeth."

"I tried a few minutes ago but Lacy said she was okay."

"She's a better Christian than I am, then."

"Me too."

By the time Lacy began packing up her stuff, the only thing she hadn't been asked by a member of the congregation was the color of her underwear—which was black, by the way, black lace, as always. But not one of the questions had been asked in a negative way; folks were just trying to get to know her, and Lacy had no problem with that.

The family usually got together on the third Sunday of the month, but because of Lacy, they met that afternoon instead. Being the only child of two only children, she wasn't accustomed to so many folks together in one house: the noise, the laughter, the signifying, the babies, the food; the swirl of love that was the Randolph family picked her up and left her breathless.

Eventually Lacy found herself out on the back porch, sitting with Drake's sisters Madelyn and Denise. They were enjoying the lemonade and keeping an eye on their baby sister's babies playing with Mavis's new twin puppies.

Lacy asked, "What was Drake like as a kid?"

"Spoiled," Madie said succinctly.

"Rotten," Denise said right behind her, and all three women laughed.

Angie, the baker, stepped out onto the porch. "What are you all laughing about?"

Madelyn said, "How rotten Dray was when he was little."

Angie took up a position by the porch's post. "Boy was rotten as a bunch of bananas left in the sun. We tried to get the garbage men to take him but they kept bringing him back."

Drake stepped out onto the porch. When he saw his sisters sitting with Lacy, he said, "Oh no. What kind of lies are you telling her?"

Denise waved him off. "You go on back in the house. Only grown folks are out here."

Drake said to Lacy, "See? See how they treat me?"

Lacy laughed softly. "I see."

Madelyn said, "Now beat it, brat. We'll let you know when we're done."

Drake dropped his head and stomped back into the house, promising, "I'm telling mama on y'all!"

The women howled.

On the drive home, Lacy was filled with the joy of the day. "I had such a good time."

Drake grinned. "I'm glad. You were a hit."

"No, it was your family. Even if I had been dirty and smelled bad, I think they still would have been kind."

"I don't know," he responded skeptically. "I had a few girlfriends who stepped out onto the back porch with my sisters and never returned. We're still looking for the bodies to this day."

Lacy shook her head. "Then I'm glad they liked me."

"And they did."

Lacy leaned against his strong shoulder, placed her hands around his arm, and with his cologne drifting faintly to her nose, said, "Good."

"What do you want to do with the rest of the day?"

"How about we go back to my place? I'm sure we could come up with something."

He looked over into her mischief-filled eyes and grinned. "What lesson are we on?"

"Four."

"You remember," he said approvingly.

"Lessons with Dr. Lovemaster are hard to forget." She reached over and slowly ran her hand over his thigh. "Speaking of hard . . ."

Drake's eyes widened and he threw her hand off. "Woman! You're going to make me have an accident!"

Lacy laughed.

"You're laughing now. Wait until I get you back to your place. We'll see who's laughing then."

She dissolved into a fit of giggling, and all Drake could do was smile and thank the Lord for his many blessings.

Leon Tasker was a playa, or at least he used to be until his mama said get a job or get out, and since he was a nineteen-year-old high school dropout and didn't know the first thing about living on his own, he found a job subbing as a gate guard at an apartment complex on Jefferson. He hated it. His duties were to stop each car at the entrance, take down the plate number and the apartment number of the person the visitor was going to see, then raise the gate's red arm so the car could pass.

Leon thought that was way too much work for the peanuts he was being paid, so he found it more efficient to plug in his headphones, listen to some rap, raise the gate to anybody who came calling and wave them on in.

Leon had never sent flowers to anyone; not to his mama, gramma, or baby mama, so when the floral delivery truck pulled up, he didn't know that legitimate florists were usually closed on Sunday evenings, nor did he care. The man behind the wheel was light-skinned and wearing shades. He told Leon he couldn't read the address on some flowers going to a Lacy Green and asked if Leon had the correct address. Leon took out his logbook, looked her up, and gave the man the number. After the truck drove through, Leon put his phones back on and went back to his music.

Fish smiled and headed the van to the back of the lot. It was hard to get employees who gave a shit these days. He laughed. He now had her address. He already knew she lived in this complex somewhere because he'd followed her home a few times. He didn't like the fact that he hadn't been able to get close enough to her to introduce her to Mary, but that would come soon enough. Right now he had a package to leave for her. He'd taken his time picking out the items he'd placed inside because he wanted to make sure she liked them.

Still basking in the good time they'd had with Drake's family, he and Lacy drove up to the entrance of her apartment complex. Drake leaned on the horn to get the attention of the kid in the guard hut. He could see the phones in the kids ears which was probably why he wasn't aware that Drake and Lacy were trying to come in. Drake got out, but just as he did, the guard turned, saw Drake and raised the gate. Muttering, Drake got back in under the wheel and drove through.

"So much for security," Drake drawled. If it was this lax, anybody could enter the complex, including Madison. Drake shook off that disturbing thought and looked for someplace to park.

Walter had taken the night off to attend the anniversary events at his wife's church, so Drake was her body guard tonight. Though they hadn't talked about it, they knew they were going to make love. They hadn't been intimate since the weekend in Holland, and the memories of that blissful encounter added to Lacy's burgeoning anticipation.

Once inside, she tossed her purse on the kitchen counter and looked across the room at him, standing there so magnificently in his tailored gray suit, pure white shirt and gray African motif tie. Her mother was going to eat him up when she met him and Lacy wouldn't blame her a bit. Drake Randolph was a sexy, silly, focused, Christian Black man who opened Lacy's heart first to the possibility and then the wonders of love. And Lacy did love him. She loved him like Ruby loved Ossie; like Jada loved Will. If she could sing, she'd sing about mountaintops and feelings deeper than the ocean.

When he opened his arms and whispered, "Come here," she didn't hesitate. He folded her against his heart then rewarded her with the slow sweet kiss she'd been craving all day. As always, his kisses were magic; it didn't take long for desire to bloom or for Lacy's lips to part passionately. His hands began their sensual explorations and she crooned and preened in response. Her nipples beneath her good silk blouse were treated to his special brand of welcome and then her buttons were opened one by one.

The look in his eyes as he freed them was hot; hot as she felt, making her reach out and run her hand possessively over the firm hard length of his arousal.

Drake's eyes closed in response to the warm hand fondling him so erotically. When she slid down the zipper then slipped inside and found him, he groaned with pleasure. Then she whispered, "You're not the only one who passed human anatomy, Mr. Mayor . . ."

Before Drake, Lacy had never touched a man this way, at least not willingly. She instantly wiped out all thoughts of Wilton and concentrated on the matter at *hand*, as it were.

And it *was good*, Drake thought to himself as the sensual trembles ran through him. For a novice she was damn good. She'd learned her lessons well up in Holland, so well in fact, he had to back away or risk the danger of coming right here, right now.

Lacy smiled at him with glittering eyes. She crooked a finger for him to follow her into the bedroom. Drake didn't have to be asked twice.

Drake made love to Lacy that night like a man making love to his wife. He teased her, pleased her and then filled her until she gasped.

Lacy knew she was going to die from all the pleasure, the feel of him so hot and throbbing inside made her hips instinctively rise and fall. His hands were keeping her nipples tight, and his worshipping caresses added to her inner fire. His sultry stroking became her whole world.

Drake didn't want to leave the heated shelter of her body, ever. He wanted to do her just this way until the sun became the moon and fell from the sky. Everything about her drove him to kiss her, taste her, need her. The thoughts added to his desire and each thrust took them higher. They both came quickly the first time, and once they were sated from that initial coupling, Drake took her on a scandalous journey through the world of pleasure that made her blush, croon and scream.

When they were done, the lighted dial on the clock on Lacy's bedside table read 1:00 A.M. and neither of them could move. Drake cracked, "Girl, you could kill a man."

"I was hoping for one more round."

He groaned pleasurably. "You just stay over there."

There wasn't an inch of Lacy's body that hadn't felt his loving. She was sore but felt glorious. "How in the world am I going to get up and go to work? This is all your fault, you know."

The phone rang. Loud. Insistent. Drake sat up and picked it up. "Yeah?" Then he covered the phone with his hand and said to her, "Wanda has a package downstairs for you. Were you expecting something?"

She shook her head. "No."

"Well, she wants to know if she can bring it up?"

Lacy shrugged. "Sure."

He went back to the phone. "Come on up."

Lacy threw on a robe and Drake put on his pants and shirt. When the knock sounded he answered the door.

The big box was silver and had a beautiful blue bow on top. Wanda left with a wave and Drake handed the box to Lacy.

She asked him, "Did you send this, Your Honor? There's no tag, that I can see."

"Nope. Must be from your other man," he teased.

They both went still.

Drake told her firmly. "Don't open it. Let me make a call."

Ten minutes later, Cruise and Lane were at Lacy's door. Accompanying them was another officer named Mack and his bomb sniffing canine, Daisy.

Mack placed the package on the floor and Daisy spent a few moments sniffing the perimeter, then she sat down.

"Good girl," Mack said and rubbed her neck. He

gave her a doggie treat before turning to Drake and the others. "It isn't a bomb."

Lacy felt relieved. "Then I can open it?" she asked Drake.

"I suppose so."

It took her a few moments to peel back the paper to get to the box inside.

Lane said sharply, "Wait a minute, Ms. Green!"

Everyone froze.

He came to stand beside her. "Look at the bottom of the box. Is that blood?"

Drake cursed.

Lacy stepped away and Drake moved to the box. The entire bottom box inside of the shiny paper was wet and red. Drake opened it carefully. The contents were filled with the carcasses of dismembered cats and dogs. Uttering a shocked curse, he turned away. Lacy came to see and felt her stomach churn.

Drake said to her grimly, "Pack a bag. You're out of here until we find this man."

Lacy didn't argue.

Cruise put the box into a large trash bag. "I'll take this to the precinct. I can't imagine there are any clues in here but you never know."

Before leaving the building, they stopped by Wanda's office and told her about the package. She was appalled.

Lacy asked, "Can you check with the guard and see if he remembers who delivered it?"

"I'll check."

While they waited, Lacy looked at Drake. The

anger on his face was plain to see. Lacy was angry too, but she was also scared. Madison had to be the culprit, she just hoped the guard had gotten a license number.

But he hadn't.

Wanda returned and said with disgust, "His ass was sleep! There's no one registered on the log. I promise you, he'll be fired. I'm so sorry."

Tight-lipped Lacy nodded and she and the others left the building.

Lacy spent the night with Drake at the mansion.

Lenny and his boy Gerald got out of the truck and looked around the deserted construction site. Some of the big fancy houses were completed while others were nothing more than stud encased shells. Overhead the night sky was cloudy and that was in their favor; they didn't need the moon shining on their business. Lenny grabbed one of the red gas cans from the back of the truck, and Gerald, the truck's owner, grabbed the other.

"Let's go," Lenny whispered harshly.

They were both dressed in black, their faces hidden beneath ski masks. With the hoods of their sweatshirts pulled up to further mask their identity they moved across the field like shadows. This would be their second stop tonight. Lenny planned to do this last one, then go back into hiding. He'd heard about Parker's indictment, but for Lenny, it wasn't enough punishment. He wanted Parker's whole life to go to hell first, and then he would kill him.

* * *

"If Madison knows where I live, I need to move until he's caught."

It was just before lunch the next day and Ida had come into the office to hand Lacy some papers to sign.

"Come stay with me and Herbert. You know he's sweet on you anyway."

Lacy chuckled inside. Ida had been kind enough to have Lacy over for dinner more than a few times when Lacy first moved to town. Her husband Herbert was a big old teddy bear and an even bigger flirt, but he loved Ida like pancakes loved syrup, so Lacy knew not to take his teasing seriously. "You sure it won't be any trouble."

"We'd love the company, and you won't have to worry about Madison. I'm not bad mouthing the mayor or Walter but that place you're living in is too big to be trying to protect somebody. Single family house like mine is easier to lock down and secure." This was Ida the former Marine talking now.

"That makes sense."

"So can we expect you?"

"Yes."

"When?"

"Tonight?"

"You can ride home with me."

"Okay."

That evening Lacy, Ida and her husband Herbert, and Walter McGhee were watching TV in Ida's living room after a fine spaghetti dinner.

Two news stories made Lacy sit up and take notice.

One had to do with the mayor's speeding ticket on Sunday. The anchors treated the story with amusement, wondering if the mayor would be driving that fast to his wedding to his new lady friend. Lacy rolled her eyes. Ida grinned.

The next story was far more serious. It began with a night shot of a huge fire at a partially finished suburban subdivision. Fire departments had to be brought in to fight the blaze and it took hours to get it under control. According to the reporter a similar fire was reported a few miles away just hours later. The smell of kerosene was strong at both sites and the authorities were guessing arson. What drew Lacy's interest the most was when the reporter said, "Both sites are owned by Reynard Parker, currently under indictment for charges relating to his trucking company. Mr. Parker was unavailable for comment."

"Wow," Lacy whispered.

Ida nodded. "You got that right."

Parker was unavailable for comment because he had nothing to say, except words that couldn't be printed or shown on the news. His preliminary hearing was tomorrow and his lawyer told him to be prepared for a lot of protestors in front of the courthouse. Parker knew he was going to be the scapegoat for all the city's ills and there wasn't a damn thing he could do to make it stop. The governor stopped taking his calls the day the indictment came down, and none of the other politicians whose pockets he'd lined and greased over the years wanted to have anything to do with him now, either. He had one ace up his sleeve however, the only one he had left. Fish. If he gave him up, the prosecutor might be more inclined to do a deal. He planned to tell them that Fish killed Wheeler and the Curtis broad on his own and that he, Peterson, hadn't known anything at all until Fish confessed after the fact. It was crunch time. All bets were off. Friendship and loyalty didn't mean a thing when you're looking at hard time. It was every man for himself now and Parker was looking out for Number One.

Lacy, Walter and Ida walked over to the courthouse to watch the preliminary hearings on the Parker case. It was a beautiful May day. The breeze was warm off the river and the sunshine coated the water like a blanket of shimmering diamonds. They'd opted to walk because the ladies both needed the exercise.

They heard the chanting two blocks away and by the time they reached the corner the words, "Parker! Parker! Traitor To His Race!" were loud and clear. People carrying picket signs were marching up and down the sidewalk in front of the courthouse, but they were just one part of the large crowd. Mounted police were visible, as were TV cameras from the local affiliates. People wearing T-shirts sporting environmental slogans and logos were handing out literature. Lacy saw men and women wearing BAD T-shirts carrying other signs, but they were all chanting: "Parker! Parker! Traitor To His Race!" He had dumped poison in his own neighborhoods and people wanted his head.

Walter opted to wait outside and enjoy the sunshine and the show. Lacy and Ida had to show ID in order to get past the ropes separating the protestors from the court steps. With each passing minute the crowd seemed to grow and the chanting grew stronger. Lacy hoped Parker and his lawyer were already inside, because if they weren't the police could have a situation on their hands.

Lacy was a bit surprised to see how packed the large courtroom was; there wasn't a seat left vacant. She spotted a small gaggle of TV reporters and journalists in the back taking notes while they interviewed someone. Because of the backs of the reporters she couldn't see who it was, but when they parted and the man stepped away, Lacy's almost fell over.

Ida whispered in a concerned voice, "What's wrong?"

"My ex."

Ida snapped around. "That's Wilton Cox. You were married to him?"

"Yeah." She wondered why he was here? Then answered her own question. He was here because the cameras were. Forget the issues. Her ex was always looking for a photo op. Lacy now understood the circus outside. More than likely his people had put that together. The ringmaster was in town.

The proceedings began shortly thereafter and Lacy studied Reynard Parker as he stood beside his White female lawyer. He was well over six feet tall and was almost as wide. He had an average face and looked to be in his mid fifties. He was dressed well though. That was no Sears suit he was wearing. The fit looked tailored and the white shirt and expensive tie added to the illusion of a wealthy and powerful businessman.

Lacy had been avoiding looking Wilton's way. She figured that if he didn't see her she wouldn't have to be polite and speak to him, but when she glanced over, his eyes were waiting and they were filled with surprise and a smile. Lacy inclined her head but that was it. She turned her attention back to the case.

The person representing the EPA was one of their criminal investigation agents and he testified to what was found in the barrels dumped on the southwest side back in April. "Flammable used solvents, Your Honor. Chemicals like toluene, methyl ethyl ketone and xylene. All highly dangerous and toxic to both humans and the environment."

Some people in the audience booed loudly. Shouting other folks took Parker's name in vain.

The judge banged her gavel and called for order. In the end, Parker was bound over for trial. The date was set for September.

Lacy tried her best to leave the courtroom quickly to avoid having to talk to Wilton but with all the people inside it was impossible. When she and Ida finally exited the courtroom he stepped right in front of her.

"Lacy? Is that you? Look at you. You're all grown up."

"Hello, Wilton. This is my friend, Ida Richardson."

"Friend as in buddy, or friend as in significant

other?" he grinned, eyeing Lacy like she was a popsicle on a hot day.

Lacy didn't need a reminder as to why she disliked him so much but the comment brought it home. "What brings you to town?" As if she didn't know.

"The Parker case, of course. It represents the struggles all inner city residents face when polluters target our neighborhoods. My being here will bring national coverage to the city and this problem."

Lacy knew that he lived in a barely integrated suburb outside of Atlanta, and that no one was dumping anything in his neighborhood. "Well, have a pleasant stay. I have to get back to work."

"I was thinking we could have dinner."

Lacy began to walk to the door. She could feel Ida fuming beside her. "I'm thinking we won't."

"Aw Lacy, come on. For old times' sake?"

She stopped and studied him. He was now over forty-five, balding, and no longer slim. The lines of his once-handsome dark face were starting to break down and soften. The suit was a good one. Not as good as Drake's or Mr. Parker's but way better than one worn by a man who really lived in the neighborhoods Wilton claimed to be championing. In spite of all his talk of unity, and the protests he led, Wilton was as fake as a porn star's boobs. There were a whole lot of things she could say to him, but since none of it was nice, she said simply, "Enjoy Detroit, Wilton. Let's go, Ida."

Outside the circus was in full swing. The protestors

were still marching and chanting and it took her and Ida a few minutes to clear the steps. Walter walked up and asked, “How’d it go in there?”

Before Lacy could respond, Ida fumed. “He wanted to know if Lacy and I were lesbians!”

Walter looked confused and he almost laughed but Ida’s fuming seemed to keep him in check. “Who?”

“My ex. Wilton Cox.”

That made Walter stop. “You were married to Wilton Cox? *The* Wilton Cox.”

“Yeah.”

“Why did he think you all were lesbians?”

Lacy said, “Because he’s a jerk. I’ll explain later.”

Walter shook his head, and they started for the office, but when Lacy looked back at the courthouse she saw Wilton standing on the steps watching them.

Eighteen

That evening Drake joined the Richardsons for dinner. Afterward he and Lacy sat out on the back porch. The early spring tulips and daffodils in Ida's large tilled garden were on their last legs, and were being replaced by the daisies and early roses of mid-May. "You know your ex is in town?" he asked.

"Yeah."

"He paid me a visit this afternoon. Said he came to lend his support to the issue of urban dumping."

"Pompous ass." Wilton had been on Lacy's mind most of the day. He represented a time in her life when she was neither strong nor confident.

Drake smiled. "Not one of your favorite people."

She turned to him. "He wanted me to get breast implants after we married. Said I looked like a boy."

Drake leaned over and kissed her, then slid an

arousing finger over her breast. "I like them just the way they are."

Her anger over the old memory faded under the pleasure that instantly arose from his touch. "I do too. Wilton thought he and I should have dinner."

"And you said?"

"No."

"Good. We Vachon men can be jealous."

"Oh, really?"

He kissed her again. "Very."

"Good to know." Lacy could feel herself melting. She loved him so much. Unlike Wilton's fake behind, Drake was as real as her heartbeat.

Drake had his back braced against the porch column, with Lacy snuggled into his side. The peace of the evening was as close to perfect as it could be. He would love to come home to something like this at the end of each of his hectic days, he thought. "When do you want to get married?"

She looked up into his eyes, studied him for a moment, then asked, "Is that a proposal?"

"Yep," he said confidently.

Lacy laughed. "Then you need you to ask me formally and properly before I can answer."

He grinned and met her eyes in the fading light. He stood up, took her hand, moved down to the step below her and got down on one knee. Looking up into her serious face, he said softly, "Lacy Green, I want to spend every waking moment of the rest of my life with you. When you're away I can't breathe, I can't think. I've never ever felt this way about a woman before, so will you do me the honor of being my wife? Till death do us part?"

His words held so much emotion and moved Lacy so much that she couldn't speak. After a moment she nodded and replied in a tone that mirrored his, "I would love to have you as my husband, Drake. Till death do us part."

He grinned and stood. Filled with his love for her, he asked, "May I kiss the bride?"

"As often and as long as you want."

Their kiss permanently sealed the agreement, then Drake led her back into the house so they could tell everyone their news.

That night after he went home, the still floating-on-air Lacy called her mother. Valerie Garner Green was in Heathrow Airport waiting for a flight back to the States. After the initial hellos, Lacy said, "Sit down, Mama. Got something to tell you."

"I'm down. Go ahead."

"I'm getting married."

Val gave such a great shout of joy, she must have startled some people nearby because Lacy heard her say, "My daughter's getting married!"

Lacy laughed and shook her head.

Val and Lacy spent the next forty minutes talking and laughing.

She then gave her mother an update on the Madison case. "No, they still haven't found him," Lacy said, "but I've been assured they will."

The happiness surrounding the wedding news had been dampened a bit by the Madison story and Lacy didn't want the conversation to end on a note of worry. "When can you and Daddy come visit, so you can meet Drake?"

That put the perk back in her mother's voice. "I'll be back home tomorrow, and after that I'm free."

"Okay. Well, soon as you get home and rested up, give me a call and we'll pick a date. I want you and Daddy here as soon as you can get here." And she did. She couldn't wait to share the man she loved with her parents.

"I will definitely do that. Now, it must be pretty late where you are, so go on to bed."

"Yes, Mama."

"And Lacy?"

"Yes?"

"Keep yourself safe, baby. Okay? I don't want to have to come up there and turn that city out."

Lacy chuckled. "I will. I love you."

"Love you more."

They clicked off.

Lacy put the phone down and immediately realized she'd forgotten to tell her mother about Wilton being in town, but decided it didn't matter. Her mother cared even less about him than she did. Smiling, she pulled the quilts up around her ears and closed her eyes. *What a day.*

The next evening, she and Drake were driving around Belle Isle, the 704-acre island park in the center of the Detroit River designed by Frederick Law Olmstead, who'd also designed New York City's Central Park. It was her first time seeing the pastoral location, and she was surprised to learn from Drake that during the days when the French founded the city back in the 1700s, the Isle, as the residents called it, had been called Hog Island and home to legions of wild pigs. "Are there any left?" she asked, watching the river flow by them.

Drake laughed. "If there were, they were put on a barbecue pit a long time ago."

They parked the car in a quiet spot and he turned off the engine. Instantly, the silence overtook them, and Lacy felt a peace she'd been needing for a long while.

He looked her way. "Want to get out?"

"Yes."

Outside, surrounded by nothing but the water lapping gently against the shore and the high-pitched call of a lone gull, they held hands and set off down the sandy water's edge. There was a bench a few feet away, so they headed toward it, then sat. Nothing was said because no words were needed.

Drake finally broke the companionable silence. "Brought you something." He reached into his shirt pocket. "Close your eyes."

She started to protest, but he kissed her on the nose and said softly, "Close your eyes, woman."

A smiling Lacy did as she was told.

"And keep them closed until I say different."

Her eyes closed, she gave him a mock salute. "Yes, sir!"

He took her by the hand, and she felt a gentle pressure as he slid a ring onto the third ring finger. "Now, you can open them."

Lacy opened her eyes, and the sight of the beautiful sapphire ring sparkling against her skin left her speechless.

He grinned. "Well? Say something."

"Oh, Drake. This is beautiful."

"A beautiful ring for a beautiful girl."

She pulled him to her and gave him a long loving kiss that knocked him for a loop.

When he could speak again, he told her, "If you want a traditional diamond—"

"Oh, no. I plan to keep this one. Look at the deep color."

Drake looked at his ring on her finger and said, "You know, my grandmother once told Myk and me the story of when my many greats grandfather Galen married his wife Hester. He gave her a fabulous string of sapphires to match her blue hands."

Lacy stared. "Blue hands?" She studied him skeptically. "I don't know about this family of yours. You've told me some pretty wild stories."

"No," he said, smiling. "Her hands were blue because she was a slave on an indigo plantation, and working the dye turned your hands that color."

"Oh," Lacy said, understanding now. "Okay, so what about the sapphires?"

"I just wish they were still in the family so I could give them to you. Hester was supposedly a dark-skinned honey like you."

Lacy grinned. "That's sweet, Drake. What happened to them?"

"She sold them right after the Civil War to help pay

off Galen's debts. I guess he owned a big-time shipping business in New Orleans, and the war just about wiped him out. Gran said some of the other jewels he gave her were sold to help build schools for the freed slaves."

"Sounds like a very kindhearted woman. She must have loved him very much to sell her jewelry like that."

Drake smiled back. "And he worshipped the ground she walked on. Gran still has some of his letters to her."

He circled his arm around her, and Lacy asked, "I wonder if our many greats grandchildren will talk about our marriage?"

He shrugged. "I don't know. Something to think about, though."

"Yes it is."

"Maybe I should start writing you love letters?"

"I'd like that."

He shook his head. "Nah, I'm too much of an e-mail junkie."

"So am I."

They both laughed. Lacy looked at his ring. "This is beautiful. Thank you."

"Thank you for wearing it so beautifully. I need to get you back to Ida's."

"On your way to the airport?"

"Yep, Malcolm is waiting at the mansion now, probably wondering where the hell I am. I'll call him in a few minutes."

He took her in his arms. "Take care of yourself while I'm gone."

"I will. You take care of yourself, too."

The threat of Madison stood between them, but they didn't address it; they didn't want to. Instead, he kissed her again, this time so passionately that when he reluctantly pulled away, Lacy was left a bit woozy.

He held her against his heart and whispered, "Will that hold you until I get back?"

"Yes."

"Good."

He gave her a wink and they walked back to the car.

When he drove away from Ida's Lacy began missing him immediately.

Across town, Reynard Parker's world had gone to hell, and he had the two burned-out construction sites to prove it. The police had no suspects, and neither did he. He'd made plenty of enemies on his ride to the top, but none that carried kerosene cans. That it might be Fish had crossed his mind. Parker hadn't seen him in days, and his absence was troubling only because Parker couldn't point the finger at him if he wasn't around to take the blame. His attorney had an appointment with the prosecutor next week to try and work out a deal. If Parker had his way, Fish would be going down.

Meanwhile, the dogs were still sniffing around his landfills looking for Wheeler; the IRS and the EPA had subpoenaed all of his financial and business records; and the bitch calling herself his wife served him with divorce papers last night during dinner. It pleased him that she wouldn't get a dime of settlement, however, because finding any money in his accounts after the feds got done was going to be as hard as picking up raindrops.

Fish was pushing a broom in the city employees' parking lot. Wearing the generic blue coveralls that he'd worn in a janitorial job at the airport a few years back, and some dark glasses to hide his signature eyes, he was as faceless as the pavement he was sweeping. He knew that few people paid any attention to workers like him, and in a city the size of Detroit, there were myriad contracts with cleaning companies all over the place. For the past week no one had challenged his right to push the cigarette butts, gum wrappers, and discarded water bottles into his dust pan and deposit them in the trash can he'd taken off the third level to legitimize his persona. He even had the old ID badge he'd used at the airport clipped to the front pocket of his uniform. No one ever came close enough to read what it said. All they saw was a man wearing ID and sweeping, and that's all he wanted them to see.

Pretending to be someone else was one of Fish's ways of getting the information he needed for whatever he was running. He'd robbed senior citizens while pretending to be everything from a sewer worker to a pastor at the church around the corner. Claiming to be a cable man checking the line of a neighboring home had gained him entry into suburban homes so he could case them for future B&Es. The information he'd needed on the Green woman had been the kind of car she drove and where she lived. Being bent over his broom and acting uninterested in the comings and goings of the people walking to their cars had given him that information. After learning what she drove, it had been easy to park across the street from the lot, wait for her to exit, drive by him, and then slide in behind her into the traffic. He'd been careful to stay a few cars back, and because she lived so close to her job, the tailing had quickly paid off.

Lately, though, she'd been leaving work with the fireplug woman with the gold Cadillac and a tall menacing-looking brother in a leather coat, and she hadn't gone home to her apartment. Any ideas Fish had of jumping the women in the lot died once he got a look at the man. He walked and looked like security, and Fish was sure he was armed. He preferred a blade for its grace and efficiency, but knew that a knife was useless in a shootout.

But time was running out. Each tick of the clock brought him closer to a fate he didn't want. If the police had no witnesses to the Curtis murder, they'd have a harder time proving he'd done it. Lacy Green's death would raise suspicions, of course, but by then he wouldn't be around and the investigation would become just another cold case. Today he planned to follow the gold Caddy when it left the lot and see where it led. If Green was sleeping someplace else, he'd find a way to get her, because it was time for him to get out of Dodge.

After work Ida, Lacy and Walter were heading to Ida's home when Ida said, "Ladies and gents, I think we're being followed."

Lacy leaned down and looked into the mirror mounted on her side of the car.

Walter, in the backseat, said, "You sure? I don't want to turn around and maybe scare 'em off."

"Pretty sure. He's hanging back, but he's been with us ever since we left downtown. Now, maybe it's just some dude going home too, but every time I change lanes, he does too."

"What's he driving?"

"Beat-up green van. Commercial type."

"Okay, get off at the next exit and let's see what he does."

Ida got over into the far right lane. "Here he comes," she said with her eyes raised to the mirror. "He's behind a Focus and an old Firebird."

They climbed the exit, and the van got in behind a couple of cars and followed them off the freeway. Ida turned right onto Van Dyke, passed Kettering High School, and the tail did the same. "Shall I take him on a slow trip to China?"

"Yeah. Do you know where the closest precinct is?"

She nodded.

"Make your way over there. Then let's see if he'll follow us into the lot."

Lacy could feel the tension in the air. One minute they'd been laughing about the new Tyler Perry play coming to town, and now they were silent.

Fish wasn't sure if the people in the Caddy had busted him, but the way the lady was driving made him think they had. She didn't seem to have a real destination in mind, just randomly turning corners here and there. Frustrated, he knew he had to decide if he should keep following her and risk actually being busted, or drop off the chase and come up with another way to find her house. After another few of her maddening turns, he chose the latter.

"He's gone," Ida said, her serious eyes focused on her rearview mirror.

"Good," Walter replied, "but keep an eye out. Don't want him turning up again and we not know it."

They all agreed.

That evening after dinner, Walter, who had been sleeping upstairs in one of the spare bedrooms for the past few days, moved his gear down to the living room. Neither Lacy, Ida or Herbert gave him a hard time, because after the encounter with the van, they were all feeling a little paranoid. Having him downstairs on the front line might make a difference in everyone's safety.

In bed now, Lacy's worries about the van were set aside by thoughts of Drake. She wondered how he was doing and if he was enjoying Japan. She looked down at the sapphire on her finger. There was just enough light from the streetlamp outside to make the stone twinkle like a star. She closed her eyes and sent him a mental message to let him know how much she loved him and that she was safe. Every fiber of her being *knew* that she and Drake were going to have a good life together, have children together, and make love in a thousand places in a thousand scandalous ways. Madison could go to hell.

* * *

The man on the phone, using his most articulate voice, explained his dilemma to the nice woman at the suburban Secretary of State's office on the other end of the line. "I found someone's license in the street this morning on the way to work. Do you guys have any way of finding out who it belongs to? It has a valid sticker. The person probably doesn't even know it's gone."

"You should take it to the nearest precinct, sir."

He replied calmly, "But I have the plate right here in my hand. If I take it to the precinct, there's no telling how long it may sit. This is Detroit, ma'am," he said with that hint of sarcasm in his voice that non-Detroiters used when dissing the city or its services. To keep her on the line, he said humbly, "I know you're probably worried about identity theft and all that, but I don't need the person's phone number, just the address so I can leave it on the porch or in the mailbox." Then he paused and added, "I'm a Christian. A lot of other people just ran the thing over. I almost did too, but I thought about what if it had been my plate? What would I want somebody to do with it? Sort of like, what would Jesus do?"

For a long moment there was silence on the other end, then the woman finally said, "Okay, sir. Give me the number."

The man with the fish eyes grinned like a shark, picked up a small piece of paper and calmly recited the numbers of Ida's license plate.

* * *

That night, the Richardson household was treated to a surprise. Drake! Lacy ran to him, and he held her as if he'd been gone for months.

"What are you doing back?" Lacy asked excitedly.

"When we got to London, one of the execs got a call that our Japanese host had been hospitalized with a heart problem and the meetings were cancelled, so we turned around and came home."

She was so glad to see him.

"And since nobody downtown knows I'm back, I had Malcolm drop me off. I thought I'd join the party and sleep here, Ida, if that's okay with you and Herbert?"

Ida asked, "Am I going to have to put Herbert outside Lacy's room to keep you from sneaking in after everybody goes to sleep?"

Drake grinned. "No, ma'am."

Walter said, "I don't know, Mrs. Richardson. I wouldn't trust him. You know how politicians lie."

Drake said, "Would you shut up? I'm trying to work my deal here!"

Everyone laughed.

Then Drake said to Ida, "I promise to be a good mayor and not sneak into my fiancée's bedroom."

Ida said with mock warning, "Okay now. I still have the belt I used to use on my boys. Don't make me have to bring it out." Then she smiled and said sincerely, "Of course you're welcome to stay."

Every morning around six-thirty Herbert went out to the driveway to start his wife's car. His baby liked her car warm when she got inside. Even though it was May on the calendar, there were still days when the early morning air was cool enough to need heat, and today was one of them. Still in his pajamas and slippers, Herbert started the engine. Once it purred to life, he got out, used the spare clicker to lock the door so no fool jacker could drive off with it, and turned back to go inside. But as he turned he felt the nose of a gun press sharply into his back and he froze.

"'Mornin'," the man behind him said. "Up the steps."

Though Herbert was a big man, he wasn't a stupid one, so he played along, for now.

When Walter saw Herbert being escorted in the door by a gunmen, he immediately went for his weapon, only to hear, "Throw it over here or I'll shoot him!"

Ida, still in her housecoat, came out of the kitchen and whispered in a sick voice, "Oh, Jesus."

Walter, faced with no options, did as he was told, but for damn sure didn't like it. Lacy, standing beside Ida, met the cold fish eyes of the man of her nightmares, but for some reason she wasn't as scared for herself as she was for Herbert. Drake was upstairs getting dressed.

"Now," Madison barked, "Ms. Green, you're coming with me. And don't anybody else move."

But Herbert was an Oprah fan—watched her Monday to Friday—and he'd seen the show on what to do in a situation like this one. So when Lacy moved to step forward, Herbert immediately went limp. The move caught Madison by surprise. A split second later two shots rang out, both of them hitting Madison in the chest. His eyes widened even farther and he peered down at the blood. Lacy was surprised too.

Ida stood beside her with brimstone in her eyes. She'd fired through the pocket of her chenille housecoat, leaving a ragged black-edged hole. Ida lowered her aim, but it was the second shot, the one Drake, on the stairs, had put in Madison's heart, that crumpled him to his knees and then to the floor.

The police and EMS were there eight minutes later. One team of emergency technicians rushed the near death Madison to Detroit Receiving Hospital, while the other stayed to check out Herbert, who kept insisting he was fine. Ida, who was still fussing, cussing and calling Madison out of his name for having the nerve to threaten her Herbert, soon calmed down enough to be interviewed by the police. Drake was holding a very grateful Lacy, who was glad it was finally over.

After everyone gave the police their statements, the police left to file their reports, the neighbors went back into their homes, and the Richardson home was quiet again.

Lacy gave Ida the strongest hug she could. "Thank you so much."

Ida hugged her back. "It's all over now, girlfriend. All over."

Lacy was thankful. Whether Madison lived or died, he was no longer a threat to her or anyone else. She and Drake *would* have that life.

As she and Drake looked on, Walter said, "That was some real good shooting, Mrs. Richardson."

Herbert had his arm around his wife and crowed, "You got that right. Baby, you saved my life."

"Yep, and I want a cruise as my reward."

He grinned down at her and said, "Call 'em up."

While the excited Ida ran to get her cruise line brochures, Lacy left Drake for a moment so she could call Janika. She told her she might be coming to the office later.

Ida said, "But I'm taking the next few days off. Got to counteract the stress of saving Herbert's life."

An amused Lacy promised to sign the vacation request just as soon as she got downtown.

That night, Lacy and Drake stood in her apartment all alone; no Walter, no Madison, no nobody, and it was a glorious feeling. Madison was dead, according to the call she'd gotten from Detective Franks. He said Madison had lived long enough to give the police information that would impact the ongoing Parker trial, and she was glad to hear that as well. Ida would not be charged because she'd shot Madison in self-defense, and so had Drake.

Now, Lacy tossed some bath salts into her large claw-foot tub, turned on the water, and called out, "This tub may not be big enough for two, but if I sit on your lap we should be okay."

Drake appeared in the door like magic. A nude and well-loved Lacy looked over at him and said, "Thought that would bring you running."

Drake grinned and said, "You got any spinach?"

Lacy laughed, then beckoned him to the tub.

Drake didn't have to be asked twice.

Nineteen

Thursday, May 19, was Lacy's birthday, and she began the one-woman celebration by enjoying a call from her mother and by taking the day and Friday as vacation days. Seated on her apartment's hardwood floors, which were dappled by the warm beams of the sun, she sipped coffee and read the morning paper. The first article of interest had to do with Reynard Parker. His attorney was asking for a change of venue. The circus atmosphere orchestrated by Wilton's people and the genuine anger of the city's residents over Parker's alleged toxic dumping crimes were making it hard for her client to receive a fair trail, or so she said. Lacy raised her thumb and forefinger and played the attorney the world's tiniest violin for her whining, then turned the paper to the sports.

Her phone rang. It was the building manager, Wanda Moore. "Ms. Lacy?"

"'Morning, Wanda. What's up?""

"You have some packages down here."

Lacy was surprised to hear that, since she didn't remember ordering anything. "Be down in a minute." She threw some sweats on over her pajamas and grabbed her keys.

The packages turned out to be a bit more than that. Wanda's office was filled with roses. There were vases everywhere; on her desk, the floor, her chairs. There were three on top of the file cabinets and another two on the windowsills. You couldn't take a step without brushing by a vase, and all Lacy could do was stare around with her hands over her mouth.

Wanda grinned and asked, "Are all the mayor's brothers married?"

Lacy laughed, then her amazement returned. "Girl, will you look at all this?"

"I'm looking and I'm thinking, His Fineness is a helluva man."

There were white roses and red roses, and yellows and blues; oranges and bicolors that were peach and gold. Some were tall and others were miniatures, but each and every bloom put a sheen of joyful tears in Lacy's eyes.

Wanda watched her with tears of her own. "Now you got me bawling. Here's the note."

Lacy took it, but instead of reading the note, put it her pocket, then walked around the room and picked some of the roses out of the vases. Once she had a dozen, she presented them to the confused Wanda.

"What are these for?"

"For firing Leon, the so-called security guard."

Wanda hollered, and once she stopped laughing, said, "Any time. Now, let's see if we can find a U-Haul to get all this up to your place."

It took three trips before all of the roses were in their new home. Lacy couldn't stop smiling at the beauty. The colors made her apartment look like a florist's shop, and with the soft breeze floating in through her seventeen open windows, it smelled like one as well.

Only then did she reach into her pocket and take out Drake's note. It read simply:

Happy birthday.
Love, D.

She placed the note against her heart and sighed the contented sigh of a woman in love with a *good* man.

Seated in his office, Drake's thoughts were on Lacy. He hoped she'd gotten the flowers by now. He'd gone overboard, yes, but he attributed that to hanging around with his Midas of a brother Mykal, known for buying up all the flowers on the east side for Sarita. Drake also attributed his largesse to how much he loved her. Lacy was the one for him; he'd said it before and he'd keep saying it until they put him in his grave. He couldn't wait to have a bunch of little dark-skinned baby girls that all looked like their mama and grandmas. Mavis had been ecstatic over the wedding news, as had his sisters. She was already looking at dates to reserve the church.

* * *

When Lacy's buzzer blared, she went to the box. "Yes?"

"Open up, baby. It's Dr. Lovemaster."

She laughed and hit the button.

When she opened the door to his knock, he immediately picked her up, swung her around joyously, then kissed her soundly. "Happy birthday, soon-to-be Mrs. Lacy Randolph."

"Thank you."

They stood holding each other for few sweet moments longer, letting their love mingle and meld, and savoring the feel of being together again. She finally closed the door, and with an arm around each other's waists, they walked into the apartment. Drake looked around and smiled. "I didn't realize I'd ordered so many!"

"Yeah, you did. And I love each and every one of them."

He took a moment to check them all out. "Were you surprised?"

"Totally. I told you my birth date that one time. I didn't think you'd remember."

"It's my Vachon romance gene. I keep trying to tell you, but you don't want to listen."

Lacy was so happy she thought she might burst.

On Monday morning Lacy and Ida walked over to the courthouse to see what was going to happen with Reynard Parker's lawyer's request to have the trial moved. The papers were full of the story, and there were additional articles on the new murder charges filed by the prosecutor. The cadaver dogs found bits and pieces of human remains in one of Parker's landfills. The preliminary findings indicated the remains belonged to a man named Wheeler, Parker's former accountant. According to Drake, Madison had given the police the information on where Wheeler might be just before he died.

Over the weekend, the radio talk shows had reverberated with irate callers convinced that Parker's ties to the governor were going to get him off, but Lacy didn't buy it. She hadn't seen anything in the papers or the TV about the governor intervening, and with the issue of urban dumping such a hot potato, she thought the lady governor too smart to get mired in what was for sure political poison.

The crowds around the court were even larger than they were during the preliminary hearings. Lacy didn't see Wilton. She'd read in the paper that morning that he'd hopped a plane last night to go lead a protest in Virginia, and she was glad he was gone. His people were still in town, though, chanting, singing, and carrying signs. Most of the people around the court looked local, however, and Lacy knew that once Wilton's folks left town, these were the people who would carry on the fight. As she climbed the steps, she saw a woman in a BAD T-shirt. Lacy thought about Melissa Curtis, whose life had now been avenged, and about Lenny Durant. She wondered what had happened to him.

The judge listened to the arguments set forth by

Parker's lawyer and the counterarguments of the attorney representing the Prosecutor's Office. In the end the judge decided to take the defense's position under advisement, and the packed courtroom rose up as one and voiced their protests. It got so rowdy, the bailiffs put their hands on their guns, policemen stationed in the hallways stepped inside the room to let their presence be seen, and the judge banged her gavel for order. Lacy didn't agree with the judge's ruling either, but there was nothing anyone could do but accept it and hope the right thing would be done.

Many of the spectators Lacy and Ida passed on their way to the doors leading outside were grumbling angrily. They were sure the judge was going to rule for the defense, and once the venue was changed to the suburbs, Parker might get little more than a fine and a slap on the wrist for polluting their neighborhoods.

Lacy stepped out into the sunshine. She and Ida were going down the stairs when they heard two loud pops. Gunfire. Everyone hit the ground. People were screaming and others were looking around, terrified, waiting to see if any more bullets were incoming. Then Lacy heard sirens and saw police cars whipping around the corner and go tearing off. She didn't realize how fast she was breathing. A uniformed officer appeared at the top of the steps and all eyes swung his way. Talking through a bullhorn, he told everyone to leave the area. He wasn't taking any questions, though. He just advised everyone to leave.

Lacy and Ida picked themselves up off the wide

stone steps and hurried back to the office so they could turn on the TV and find out what the shooting had been about.

The story was on all channels. Reynard Parker had been shot and killed by two bullets from a high speed rife while walking from the back entrance of the courthouse to his attorney's car. The lady lawyer hadn't been injured, but Parker died instantly. As Lacy watched the report unfolding with the other women in the office, she shook her head.

The shooter who police had yet to identify was in custody, according the reporter, and more on the story was promised for the evening news. She clicked the remote and turned it off.

Neither she nor Drake were the least bit surprised that Parker's killer turned out to be Lenny Durant. They were in the mayor's mansion the next day, watching the shackled environmentalist take the traditional perp walk for the TV cameras. He looked as dirty and unkempt as a homeless man. In his eyes there was a holy fire, and when the reporter stuck the mic in his face, Lenny showed no remorse.

"People like Parker reap what they sow," he snapped. "The children of this city are safer tonight."

Lacy looked over at Drake, who said simply, "Man, what a mess this turned out to be."

She nodded. "Wonder what made Lenny the way he is? Was there someone in his family affected by toxins? Did something happen to him when he was in the Army?"

Drake shrugged. "We'll never know, babe. We do know he's looking at life without parole, since Michigan doesn't have a death penalty."

Lacy was passionate about environmental issues too, but would she pick up a gun and shoot a man for his crimes? She didn't think she could, but all folks were different. It was obvious that Lenny saw himself as justified.

Wanting to get away from the morbid events tied to Parker's shooting, she looked around the well-furnished mayor's mansion and asked, "So do you like living here?"

They were relaxing on the luxurious leather couch in what Drake called his Media Room. He clicked the TV over to the pregame show. "Nope." Tonight was Game 5 of the NBA Finals, between the Pistons and the Western Division champs, the San Antonio Spurs, who were knotted up at two games apiece.

"Why not?" she asked. "It's a beautiful place."

And it was, with its expensive wallpaper, artwork, and highly polished furniture.

"Doesn't have any bottom."

"No feelings?"

"None. Sarita's been after me to make the place my own since the election, but why? I'm going to have to turn the place over to somebody else in the end, so why waste the taxpayers' money?"

"Good point. Why not get your own place? Could you live there as the mayor?"

"I could, but if this place sits empty, that's still

money down the drain because it has to have security. This isn't the South, where you can leave a place standing unused for a long time. Here, winter would bust the pipes, meaning more money. So I just stay and live with it."

"Your home should be a place of refuge. Someplace you don't mind taking your shoes off and walking barefoot."

He looked over at her and grinned.

"So, are you going to run again?"

He shrugged. "Don't know."

"The city needs you, Drake."

"You sound like my mother, but like I told her, I haven't made up my mind either way. Myk's giving me two weeks to decide. He's my campaign chair."

"I see."

Drake asked her seriously, "Do you really want our every move to be on the front page of the paper every morning?"

Lacy shook her head. "Truthfully? No. But if that's what I have to do to support you in what you want to do, I'll smile and be nice for the pictures."

He threw out an arm and drew her to his side. When she was cuddled close just like he liked, he kissed the top of her head. "You'd do that for me?"

"I'd do anything for you except kill somebody or be silent while you romance some other woman."

He ran a fleeting caress over the tip of her nose. "You wouldn't sing 'Stand By Your Man'?"

"No."

Drake chuckled and pulled her onto his lap. "I promise on the heads of our future many greats grandchildren that I would never ever disrespect you that way. And besides, once you get done making love to me, I don't have the strength to romance another woman."

"Say my name!" she commanded, laughing, then placed her head on his chest. She could hear the humor rumbling beneath her ear.

"Woman, you are a mess."

"I know. I think I'm getting more like my mother everyday."

"That's a scary thought."

"Yes it is, but I'm having fun."

Drake squeezed her tight. "So am I. Are you ready to meet my grandmother tomorrow?"

"Yep. We can pick up Mama and Daddy at the airport and head right over, if that's okay."

"Fine with me. Looking forward to meeting the woman known for dancing on tables with fake princes."

Lacy smiled. "And I'm looking forward to meeting the matriarch of the Vachon clan."

"She's not what you might think."

"What do you mean?"

"For a woman celebrating her eightieth-something birthday, she gets around pretty good."

Lacy still wasn't sure what he meant, but guessed she'd find out tomorrow.

And what Lacy found out was that Eleanor Vachon

Chandler was a trip. She arrived at Myk's house, where they having the party, a fashionable one hour late. She entered the living room wearing an expensive black designer dress and gloves, a killer black hat, some sedate yet eye-popping diamond earrings, and draped fashionably across her tall, thin torso was a blue fox mink stole that had to be four feet long. She was dazzling for a woman of any age, but for someone reportedly in her eighties, Lacy was too impressed.

"Charles needs help with the luggage, boys," she said regally. The three grandsons got up and they each gave her a kiss on the cheek before leaving to help whoever Charles was with the luggage.

Mavis walked up and they shared a hug. "Hey, Ellie. It's good to see you again."

"Mavis, you are always so lovely. I bought this hat trying to keep up with you."

Her teasing made Lacy know it was okay to breathe again. She'd had no idea what kind of personality lurked beneath all that fine clothing and jewelry, but seeing her warm up to Drake's mother showed her a lot about what Eleanor Chandler was not, which was stuck up and mean.

She then greeted her granddaughters Sarita and Narice, who both gave her strong, affectionate hugs. Eleanor checked out Sarita's growing stomach. The ultrasound Sarita had last week showed a boy. "How's my great-grandson doing?"

"Lively, but only at night. Keeps me awake big-time. Doctor says it's because when I'm working, all the movement keeps him sleeping, but the minute I get home and put my feet up he's off."

Eleanor smiled. "I remember those days. Remember I didn't like it."

She held out her arms to Narice. "How are you darling? How's the school?"

"Fine, just fine."

"What about that Hatfield and McCoy auntie of yours down in Georgia?"

Lacy had no idea what they were talking about, but Narice replied, "She at least let me repair the roof, but she still won't let me visit her but once a year."

Eleanor shook her head and smiled wistfully. "We old women are a pretty set-in-our-ways bunch. You stay as close as she'll let you. That old bat's going to need her family one day. We all will, if we live long enough."

Her eyes then met Lacy's and she smiled again. "You must be Lacy?"

Lacy nodded.

Eleanor seemed pleased. "Drake described you perfectly to me. It's a pleasure to meet you and welcome to the family, my dear."

Lacy then introduced her parents. Eleanor studied Val, then asked, "*The* Valerie Garner Green?"

"Yes, ma'am."

"Oh my goodness. Lacy, Drake didn't say anything to me about this."

"I'm sure it was just something he forgot."

"No. He didn't tell me on purpose." Her voice was filled with wonder as she held onto Val's hand and asked, "Do you know how many of your pieces I have?"

Lacy and Val grinned.

Eleanor looked to Lacy and said, "And you are by far your mother's and your father's greatest work."

She put her hand to her breast. "I am so glad to meet you all."

Lacy looked to her tall thin daddy and met his grin. There were no other men here his age, but he seemed content as always to bask in the background of the constellation he called his wife.

Charles turned out to be Eleanor's chauffeur. He was a fine chocolate-skinned hunk who couldn't have been older than twenty-five. Lacy thought the Vachon grandsons might be wishing they were twenty-five again, the way they were huffing and puffing while bringing in Eleanor's fourteen pieces of luggage.

At one point during the back and forth trips, Saint put down a particularly heavy bag and asked, "What do you have in here, Gran, your gold?"

"No darling. It's filled with soap to wash that coat of yours."

Narice laughed the loudest and the longest.

Saint drawled, "Good one, Gran." Then went back outside.

That evening after Mavis went home and Lacy's parents were driven back to their hotel by Charles to rest up for tomorrow's full day with Drake's family, the Vachon grandsons and their ladies listened to Gran tell the story Myk had finally decided he wanted to hear.

"My son, your father, Roland, left for Vietnam in

'63. He didn't want to go but he was already in the army and that's where he was sent. They kicked him out in late '64 because while in 'Nam, he'd become a heroin addict."

The brothers stared. Lacy saw Sarita give Myk a questioning look, but his face was made of stone.

"He explained to me one day that getting high was the only way he could deal with where he was and what he was doing. The death, the napalm, the killing of entire villages. It wore him down, I suppose, so he turned to the comfort of the White Horse."

You could hear a pin drop in the room.

Eleanor looked over to her grandsons. "He also came back burning with rage over his situation as a Black man. We Vachons have always been about the race, but he came back talking about genocide and secret government tests and the need for Black men to have as many sons as they could to aid the coming Revolution, as the young people called it back then."

Lacy understood that. Her mother had explained the Revolution concept when she was a teenager. Val said, in the late sixties and early seventies she and everybody else her age were convinced that one day in the near future there would be a seismic revolution in America fueled by the people, which would redistribute the wealth, eliminate pollution and poverty, and wipe the world free of the great isms: imperialism, racism, and nepotism. In looking back, Val said it was nothing more than a crazy pipe dream, but at the time she and her generation believed in the Revolution with all their hearts.

In response to Eleanor's last words, Saint asked bluntly, "So is that why he was running around playing Johnny Appleseed all over the country? He was breeding Black sons for the Revolution?"

Eleanor said, "Maybe. I don't know, Anthony."

It was impossible to see Saint's reaction because of the dark glasses, but his mouth was set in a grim line.

Myk asked, "Since we're playing twenty questions: Who was my mother and what happened to her?"

It was Eleanor's turn to look grim. "She was an addict, and when you were born, you were addicted as well."

Lacy's gasp mingled with Drake's. Sarita looked stricken. Myk's hard face didn't change.

Eleanor said, "I would come and see you every day. You were so tiny, but you were a fighter. Watching you go through withdrawal broke my heart, but you made it, and when the doctors said it was okay, I took you home."

"So who was she?"

"She was your father's high school sweetheart. Pamela Duvais. A good girl back then, just like Roland had been a good boy. They were supposed to marry when he came home from the army, but he came home on that stuff and then she was on it too." She paused for a few moments, as if thinking back, then said softly, "I think that bit of darkness you still have inside of you today Mykal is from all that pain you went through after your birth."

"Why did she leave me at the hospital, and where was Roland?"

"I can't answer either of those questions. My son disappeared about two weeks before she was due. After Pam delivered you, she was discharged, and for the first two or three days after you were born she was right there at the hospital with me. Then she stopped coming. I never saw her again, nor did her family. Her mother's theory was that Pam got hooked again and suffered some tragedy that took her life, but we'll never really know."

Lacy's heart ached in sympathy to the sad story.

Drake raised his hand. "My turn, Gran."

"You know most of your story, though, Drake. Two years after Mykal was born I received a letter from Roland saying you had been born to him and your mother. He sent me Mavis's address here in Detroit, but his letter to me was postmarked from San Francisco."

"So he'd already cut out again."

"Yes."

Drake shook his head.

"I wrote your mother to see if she wanted to give you up, but in words very unbecoming a lady of those days, she told me quite plainly, no."

Drake had never heard that part of the story. "She cussed you?"

"Oh yes. Told me if I wanted to visit, fine, but she was keeping her son."

Drake smiled. Sounded just like his mother.

Eleanor said with a smile, "I knew then that my second grandson was in good hands."

Saint said, "Then I came along."

A deeper sadness crept into Eleanor's eyes. "Yes, darling, then you came along."

Saint saved her the pain of telling the story. "I was born in one of the state's women's prisons to an inmate named Carla St. Martin. Evidently, Roland came back to Michigan long enough to father me, then split again for parts unknown."

It was impossible not to hear the cold bitterness in his voice. "After my birth the state severed Carla's parental rights and placed me in foster care. Carla was doing one-to-five for car theft. Her second offense. I spent the first nine or ten years in one bad place after another until I was placed with Sarita's grandmother and uncles. Then I was happy. Carla overdosed two years after my birth. The end."

No one laughed.

To Lacy it seemed that Drake was the only one of the brothers holding no bitterness, and she wondered if it was because of all the love he'd received from his mother and sisters.

Eleanor said then, "You all have lived without your father, but I've had to live without my son. Good night," she whispered in a soft tear-choked voice. She stood, and Sarita stood too. Sarita put a consoling arm around Eleanor's waist and walked with her out of the room.

Everyone else watched the departure silently.

Later, as Drake drove Lacy home, they were both in

a somber mood. Drake looked her way and asked, "Some story, huh?'

"Yeah. Pretty sad too."

"It is, but in both my brothers' cases, their wives have brought a lot of sunlight into their lives."

"What about you? You don't seem to be as affected."

"Oh, I've go my issues too, but my mother and sisters helped, and so did my uncles. Growing up with no one to call Daddy hurts a lot, especially when you're young and all your friends have fathers."

Lacy understood.

"But I have you now. My own personal sunshine. Just like my brothers have theirs."

She smiled. "And I'll shine as long as you need it."

"Good. Because I'm holding you to that."

Lacy scooted close and wrapped her hands around his arm. "I love you, Drake."

"I love you too, baby. Want to go and neck with the mayor on Belle Isle?"

Lacy sat up with a giggle. "Sure!"

"You're so easy."

She laughed. "Blame it on your romance gene."

Drake looked her way, and the love he had for her made him so full, he couldn't stand it. "How long will you love me?"

She whispered, "Until the stars fall from the sky. Now, let's go to Belle Isle."

He threw back his head and laughed. "You are a mess."

"Say my name!" she whispered, laughing too.

And he headed the car for Belle Isle so he could do just that.

Drake Anthony Chandler came into the world fussing and yelling on Sunday September 18, at 7:35 P.M. The day being a Sunday, Myk had to practically get on his knees and beg Sarita to let him take her to the hospital because Sarita was so engrossed in the day's football games. But much to Myk's and everyone else's relief, the baby was born in the hospital and not in front of the TV during the halftime scores. Both uncles were ecstatic at the news, and Saint and Narice flew in from their farm in Ohio to check young Drake out.

Lacy and Uncle Drake were married a month later, on October 22. The service was held at St Matthew's and St. Joseph's, and Lacy didn't know half the dignitaries and other official people filling the pews. She did know, however, her parents, her sisters- and brothers-in-law; her new nieces and nephews, and Baby Drake. She also knew the man standing beside her at the altar. He was kind, funny, dedicated, and most importantly, the man she intended to have at her side for the rest of her life.

When the priest said to Drake, "You may now kiss the bride," Drake looked down into her eyes and said, softly, "Thank you for marrying me. . . ." Then he kissed her.

And as Lacy kissed him back with all the love in her heart, she just knew she had to be the happiest woman in the world.

Author's Note

After the publication of *The Edge of Midnight* and *The Edge of Dawn*, many readers wanted Drake to have his own book. Because his half brothers, Mykal and Saint, had such over-the-top personalities, it took a while for Drake to open up and let me see the real him. The result was *Black Lace*, and I do hope you enjoyed his and Lacy's story. The issue of urban dumping touches not only big cities like Detroit, but small town America as well. The Blight Court that Lacy was so passionate about is modeled after a recently established initiative in Detroit known as the Department of Administrative Hearings. For more information on the DAH, please visit the city of Detroit website at *www.detroitmis.gov/dah/*.

A thank-you goes out to Lillian Southern, historian for St. Matthew's and St Joseph's Episcopal Church, for the wonderful information she provided on her parish. Because *Black Lace* is a contemporary novel, I was unable to use most of the church's wonderful history, but I know it will come in handy for a future historical project.

Lacy's Crossfire Coupe can be seen at a Chrysler dealership near you or on the Chrysler website.

I've been asked by readers if Roland Vachon Chandler fathered any more sons. Well, I don't know. We'll just have to wait and see.

In the meantime, thanks to all the new readers who have come to the party via Drake and his brothers. Thanks also to the many fans who have been with me since my first Avon title, *Night Song*, in 1994. This is my tenth year in the business. My, how time flies when you're having fun!

See you next time,
B

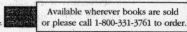